"**A** killer follow-up. . . . Phillip Margolin's *Capitol Murder* is like a cold shower—it grabs our attention and gets our adrenaline running."

New York Journal of Books

"**M**argolin delivers another slam-bang political thriller. . . . A nonstop read."

Library Journal

"**A** roller coaster of a book."

Suspense Magazine

SUPREME JUSTICE

"**A** good old fashioned political thriller. . . . An exciting and enjoyable mystery."

Huffington Post

"**[A**n] intriguing glimpse into the inner workings of the court. As always with Margolin, a roller coaster plot propels the action along, with plenty of twists and turns to keep things interesting."

Portland Oregonian

"**E**ntertaining. . . . Thriller fans who like to see the villains receive their just rewards and the good guys come to no harm will find this a comforting read."

Publishers Weekly

By Phillip Margolin

LOST LAKE
SLEEPING BEAUTY
THE ASSOCIATE
THE UNDERTAKER'S WIDOW
THE BURNING MAN
AFTER DARK
GONE, BUT NOT FORGOTTEN
THE LAST INNOCENT MAN
HEARTSTONE

DANA CUTLER NOVELS

Washington Trilogy

EXECUTIVE PRIVILEGE
SUPREME JUSTICE
CAPITOL MURDER

•

SLEIGHT OF HAND

AMANDA JAFFE NOVELS

WILD JUSTICE
TIES THAT BIND
PROOF POSITIVE
FUGITIVE

VANISHING ACTS (with Ami Margolin Rome)

PHILLIP MARGOLIN

SLEIGHT OF HAND

HARPER

An Imprint of HarperCollinsPublishers

HARPER

An Imprint of HarperCollins*Publishers*
10 East 53rd Street
New York, New York 10022-5299

Copyright © 2013 by Phillip M. Margolin
ISBN 978-0-06-206993-1

First Harper premium printing: January 2014
First Harper hardcover printing: April 2013

HarperCollins® and Harper® are registered trademarks of Harper-Collins Publishers.

Printed in the United States of America

Visit Harper paperbacks on the World Wide Web at
www.harpercollins.com

10 9 8 7 6 5 4 3 2 1

This book is dedicated to Frank Eiseman, who believed that teaching chess to elementary school children would help those students succeed in the classroom and in life; to Dick Roy, who made Frank's dream real; to Julie Young, the executive director and heart of Chess for Success; and to all the board members, program directors, coaches, and volunteers who have made Chess for Success one of the most successful and innovative educational programs in the Pacific Northwest.

SLEIGHT
OF HAND

Part I

The Ottoman Scepter

Chapter One

The American Bar Association decided to hold its annual convention at the Theodore Roosevelt Hotel in downtown Washington, D.C. On Wednesday evening, a who's who of the most powerful men and women in the country circulated at a cocktail party hosted by Rankin, Lusk, Carstairs and White. Charles Benedict was a minor leaguer in the power and influence department but even in this elite company he stood out because he was strikingly handsome and charismatic, the person toward whom the eyes of not only women but men were drawn when he entered a room.

Benedict was six feet two inches tall, with a cultivated tan. His salt-and-pepper hair was cut short and his trim, athletic build, ramrod posture, and chiseled features brought to mind the Special Forces heroes in action movies. When Benedict moved, it was easy to imagine a field of force emanating from him, and there was no question that his physical presence contributed to his success as a trial attorney, although more sinister factors sometimes came into play.

Benedict was charming a partner from a Chicago firm when he was distracted by Carrie and Horace Blair, who were carrying on a whispered argument in a corner of the ballroom. It was rare to see the Blairs together, but Rankin, Lusk handled Horace's legal work, and that was an obvious explanation for the presence of the businessman, who was not a member of the bar.

Carrie Blair was wearing a charcoal-black Gucci suit, and her natural honey-blond hair flowed over its shoulders. She had translucent gray-green eyes that could paralyze the most misogynist male, her nose was the type all the dissatisfied society women begged their plastic surgeons to copy, and her skin was tan and smooth. If someone were to ask what Carrie Blair did for a living, many people would guess that she was a television news anchor and none would peg her as the prosecutor in charge of the Narcotics Unit in one of Virginia's most populous counties.

Carrie's millionaire husband looked every bit the southern gentleman, but he was many years older than his wife, and a stranger would not be faulted for assuming that he was Carrie's father. Horace was gripping Carrie's arm. His face, red from anger, contrasted sharply with his snowy white hair. Carrie wrenched her arm from her husband's grasp and walked out of the ballroom just as Charles Benedict's cell phone vibrated.

"I've got to take this," Benedict said, abruptly

ending the conversation with the Chicago attorney. Her expectant smile changed to a frown. She was attractive, rich, and powerful, and was not used to being dismissed like some hired hand. Had she known more about Benedict, she would have understood why he'd ditched her without so much as an apology. The woman was just another potential notch on Benedict's gun, whereas the caller was going to pay an excessive fee for a highly specialized service that Benedict provided.

"Yes," Benedict said when he was alone in a side hall.

"He's at the tavern," the caller said.

Benedict left the hotel and jogged to a parking garage a few blocks away. He'd boosted a dull-green Chevrolet earlier in the evening. After switching the plates, Benedict had stashed the car on the third floor of the garage. The attorney got into the backseat and took off his yellow-and-blue-striped Hermès tie, his gray Armani suit, and his silk shirt. Then he pulled sneakers, a hooded sweatshirt, and a pair of faded jeans out of a duffel bag. As soon as he'd changed clothes, Benedict drove out of the lot toward Virginia.

Norman Krueger's life, which had been on a downward spiral since birth, had recently gotten worse, something that hardly seemed possible. Norman had been born to a drug-addicted prostitute who had no clue as to the identity of Norman's father. His childhood had ricocheted between physical abuse, sexual abuse, and neglect. The lessons in school, when he attended, were incomprehensible to someone with Norman's limited IQ and attention span. Gangs were not the answer, because he was too puny and frightened to be of use where violence was involved, and too stupid to be trusted with any task that might require guile.

Norman got by on a combination of public assistance and low-paying jobs, from which he was frequently fired for incompetence or absenteeism. Recently, much of his pay had gone toward supporting a drug habit. The origins of his addiction were confusing to Norman. They had sneaked up on him like some sort of controlled-substance ninja, but drugs were now the focus of his miserable life.

Norman's girlfriend, Vera Petrov, was as ugly and hapless as Norman, but she was capable of maintaining steady employment. She was also a second cousin of Nikolai Orlansky, a major player in the Russian Mafia, whom she'd prevailed upon to give Norman a job sweeping up in one of his many taverns.

Norman was the type of person no one noticed, the human equivalent of a sagging armchair that has been stored in a dusty corner of a side room. Evil things happened around Norman all the time and no one seemed to care that Norman had witnessed them. But Norman had eyes and ears and a memory, which, weak as it was, still retained the sights and sounds of startling events involving murder and torture, especially when he was the person assigned to clean up the gore.

Never in a million years would Norman have considered informing on his employer. He had seen what happened to those who crossed the Russian. Then he came to the attention of an undercover federal agent who befriended Norman and listened intently to everything Norman said when he was under the influence of drugs and/or alcohol. Many of his tales concerned horrifying exploits in which Nikolai Orlansky was directly involved, the type of activities that could send the Russian to prison for life or even to death row. So Norman's "friend" set him up, and the next thing he knew he was faced with having to choose between years in prison for possession of a controlled substance with intent to distribute or testifying against a man capable of telling off-color jokes while skinning a living, screaming human being.

Norman had been ordered to show up in the morning at an office in a strip mall identified as the corporate headquarters of International Products Limited. There he would be debriefed in preparation for his testimony in front of a federal grand jury. If he did not show up, he was doomed. If he did show up, he was doomed. Confronted with this lose-lose proposition, Norman drove to the nearest tavern.

By the time his wallet was empty, Norman could barely walk. As he staggered to his car, he was so inebriated that he barely noticed the blustery, chill wind that had driven the temperature down into the twenties. Norman planned to drive home from the tavern. The possibility of being arrested for drunken driving or committing vehicular homicide never entered his alcohol-addled brain. However, he did notice that it was awfully dark in the back corner of the lot where he had parked. Wasn't a light shining down on his space earlier in the evening? Since it took too much effort to answer that question, Norman abandoned the task, even though the broken glass crunching underfoot provided a clue to the fate of the streetlight suspended over his vehicle.

Norman fished his car key out of his pocket and bent over, squinting at the keyhole. It was very dark and his hand wouldn't stay still, so the task of putting the key into the lock presented a problem. He was concentrating so hard on opening his door that he was unaware that someone was standing beside him until he saw a blue-jeans pant leg out of the corner of his eye.

"What the fuck!" Norman exclaimed, adrenaline juicing his muscles enough to permit him to jump back into the side of his car.

"Good evening, Mr. Krueger."

"Who are you?" Norman gasped.

The new arrival showed Norman his hands. They were empty. Then they weren't. A business card appeared where none had been before. The man held it out to Krueger.

"How did you do that?" Norman asked, amazed.

"Magic," Charles Benedict answered with a friendly smile.

Norman squinted at the card. Then he looked at the dirty jeans, ratty sweatshirt, and old sneakers.

"You're a lawyer?"

"I am," Benedict said, as he made the card vanish. "I represent Mr. Nikolai Orlansky."

It took all of Norman's willpower to keep from soiling himself.

"A little bird told Mr. Orlansky that you are planning on singing to the feds," Benedict said.

"No, no. That ain't true. You tell Mr. Orlansky he ain't got nothing to worry about here."

Benedict smiled. "Nick will be very happy to hear that. Hey, want to see another magic trick?"

Even though Norman was anxious to leave, he didn't want to be rude, and the first trick had been mystifying.

"Uh, sure," he said.

"Great." Benedict pushed up the sleeves of his sweatshirt and rotated his hands again.

"Nothing in my hands or up my sleeves, right?"

"No," Norman said.

Benedict waved his hands mysteriously and a large hunting knife appeared. Norman's mouth gaped open. Then he grinned.

"You gotta tell me how you do this stuff."

"A magician never reveals his secrets."

Norman looked disappointed.

"My final trick is a doozy," Benedict said. "For my grand finale, I'm going to make you disappear."

Then he buried the knife in Norman's heart.

In the morning, Norman's car was still parked in the far corner of the lot, but true to Charles Benedict's word, there was no trace of Mr. Krueger whatsoever.

Chapter Two

Death can take many forms. There is the bullet between the eyes, poison secretly administered, or a free fall from a forty-story building, but Dana Cutler was convinced that the most horrible way to die was from boredom. At least a bullet in the brain was quick.

The lives of fictional private eyes are filled with danger and excitement, but Dana's life was a succession of stakeouts during which she sipped coffee from a thermos and prayed her subjects wouldn't do something important while she was peeing in a gas-station restroom. The bulk of Dana's cases came from (a) criminal defense attorneys who hoped she would find a miracle witness who could clear an obviously guilty client, (b) husbands or wives who thought their spouse was cheating, or (c), as in her present assignment, an insurance company that wanted to find out if a claimant was faking an injury. These were not scenarios that inspired the plots of high-octane action movies.

Lars Jorgenson was an athletic, broad-shouldered

accountant with a serious addiction to gambling who had just gone through a brutal divorce. Jorgenson's personal and financial lives had been sliding down a slippery slope until his car was totaled at an intersection. Jorgenson said he'd suffered permanent damage to his back that made it impossible to work, and he had a doctor who swore this was so. If the claim held up, Lars would receive a hefty sum, but the doctor was a well-known quack and the insurance company was certain that Jorgenson was faking. Dana had been following Jorgenson around for the past three days and had nothing to show for her efforts. Tonight, Lars had parked in the lot of a sports bar before hobbling inside in apparent discomfort.

Dana was an athletic five ten with short auburn hair and electric green eyes. Men always noticed her. To keep from being spotted by Jorgenson, Dana had donned several disguises. Tonight she was wearing a brown wig and makeup and clothes that made her look dowdy. Even so, several men at the bar watched her as she walked in.

One of the men watched longer than the others. He had a thick black beard, and his long, greasy hair was pulled back into a ponytail that fell down the back of a leather jacket that advertised Harley-Davidson. When the man made a quarter turn on his bar stool so he could eye Dana, his T-shirt rode up, revealing a gut that lapped over the top of stained jeans.

Dana's stomach tightened, she grew light-headed,

and her breathing increased. She slipped her hand into her jacket pocket and her fingers curled around the handle of a .38 Special, one of several weapons she was carrying. The man turned his attention back to his drink, but Dana couldn't relax, and it took her several minutes before she let go of her gun.

Dana knew why she'd had the panic attack. Before she became a private detective, she had worked undercover for the D.C. police. On her last assignment, she was tasked to discover the location of a meth lab run by a biker gang. Dana infiltrated the gang but her cover was blown. The bikers had kept her prisoner in the basement of their lab, where they raped and beat her for days before making a fatal mistake.

One of the rapists had gotten drunk and staggered into the basement for some fun. He had tossed his beer bottle away before pulling down his pants. It had not registered in his drink-addled mind that the bottle had shattered until Dana shoved a jagged piece of glass into his eye.

When the police arrived at the farm they found Dana naked, covered with gore and staring glassy-eyed into space. A blood-soaked ax lay next to two .357 Magnums, and the ax and the handguns lay near the dismembered bodies of the other three bikers. The man at the bar bore a faint resemblance to one of her kidnappers.

Dana had spent a year in a mental hospital, recovering from physical and psychic wounds. When she left, she moved into a small apartment near the

National Cathedral. For months she had stayed in her sanctuary unless necessity drove her out. When her savings reached rock bottom she was forced to face reality. There was no way she could return to the D.C. police, but police work was the only thing she knew. Working as a private investigator was an adequate solution, and she made certain that her cases were routine and did not involve danger. Then, by chance, Dana had been involved in a case that helped bring down Christopher Farrington, the president of the United States. The danger she'd encountered had made her feel alive and the notoriety she had achieved from this high-profile case had brought her plenty of work, but now it was the rare assignment that induced an adrenaline high.

When Dana entered the bar, she'd seen Lars Jorgenson limping to a table, leaning his cane against its side, and grimacing as he slumped into a chair. Dana found an empty booth that gave her a good view of her quarry. The second half of a basketball game was just starting on one of the large-screen TVs. A long hour later, the Wizards succumbed to the Knicks. Jorgenson, in apparent pain, levered himself out of his chair and limped to his car. Dana followed him home. When the lights in Jorgenson's apartment went out at midnight Dana slumped down in the front seat of her car, took a sip of coffee from her thermos, and prayed that a direct hit by a flaming meteor would end her misery.

Chapter Three

Charles Benedict disposed of Krueger's body, the knife, and the old clothes before abandoning the Chevrolet with the key still in the ignition in the area of the capital with the highest crime rate. A smaller crowd was still schmoozing in the ballroom when he returned to the Theodore Roosevelt to mingle at the cocktail party.

After a reasonable amount of time, Benedict took the stairs to the lobby. As he walked by the Bull Moose Bar he spotted Carrie Blair in a booth in a distant corner, nursing a drink. Benedict took a step back. Carrie was alone. She was staring into her glass, and she looked sad. Benedict had always wondered what "The Society Prosecutor" would be like in bed, and he couldn't pass up a chance to find out. Before he entered the bar, the lawyer took a pillbox out of his pocket and palmed a mild sedative that would make Carrie compliant. Slipping the pill into Carrie's drink would pose no problem for someone with the lawyer's skill at sleight of hand.

Carrie was leaning forward and staring into a

double shot of bourbon. Benedict was certain that most of the men in the bar had eyed her more than once. He bet that they were wondering what could possibly make someone so perfect look so depressed. Benedict was fairly certain he knew the reason for the prosecutor's funk.

Almost ten years ago, when Carrie was a young assistant commonwealth attorney, she had tried Horace Blair for driving under the influence. Horace had become smitten with the woman who was prosecuting him and he had pursued her relentlessly. Their marriage was the scandal of the decade in the circles in which Horace traveled. Everyone believed that Carrie had married Blair for his money, and the people in Horace's set made no secret of their disdain. From what Benedict had heard, living the life of a millionaire's wife had gotten old quickly. Society snubbed Carrie, and her old friends felt uncomfortable around her. Carrie was rumored to live in her office more than in the plush rooms of Horace's mansion.

Benedict slid into the booth across from Blair. Carrie was not happy to see him. The prosecutor knew Benedict well enough to see past his *GQ* model looks. In her office, Benedict was thought of as a high-priced hired gun who had flunked his ethics course in law school. No one doubted his ability. He won more than his share of tough cases. But it was the way he won some of them that raised eyebrows. When the client was in the top tax bracket, or a member of Nikolai Orlansky's crew, evidence disappeared from property rooms and witnesses went missing or developed faulty memories. No one ever proved hanky-panky was involved, but a rank smell wafted over many of Benedict's cases.

"Hey, Carrie," Benedict said. "I thought I saw you at the Rankin, Lusk bash. You must know a lot of that crowd. Don't they represent Horace?"

"What do you want, Charlie?" asked Carrie, who was too deep in her cups to worry about being polite.

"You look down in the dumps, so I thought I'd try to cheer you up."

"Thanks, but I'd rather be alone."

"Okay, I get that, but I did have a business proposition for you."

Carrie tilted her head to the side and studied Benedict. "What might that be?"

"One of your puppies, Mary Maguire, is prosecuting Kyle Ross, Devon Ross's son."

"No deals, Charlie. That little fucker tried to seduce a thirteen-year-old girl by giving her cocaine. Then he offered a bribe to a cop. And his father made a veiled threat to Mary. That will all come out at sentencing, and I'm going to ask for the maximum."

"Whoa, slow down. This is just another case. There's no reason to take it personally."

"Well, you can tell your client I do."

"You're forgetting how green Maguire is. I may eat her lunch. Then there won't be a sentencing."

"Mary's young but she's sharp. And you have no defense."

Benedict pulled a pack of playing cards out of his pocket and fanned them out. While Carrie's attention was on the cards, he passed a hand over her glass and slipped a pill into her drink.

"Tell you what," Benedict said. "Let's settle this like civilized people. You pick a card but don't tell me what it is. If I can't guess it, I'll plead my guy guilty. But you dismiss if I do."

Carrie threw her head back and laughed. "You're too much."

Benedict smiled. "I did that to snap you out of your funk. You looked so sad when I spotted you I knew I had to do something to cheer you up. And I wouldn't have made you drop the case, because I'd always guess your card."

"Oh, yeah? Let me see the deck."

Benedict performed a few exotic shuffles, then extended the cards. Carrie selected one and looked at it. Benedict instructed her to put it back in the deck. Carrie slid the card back into the pack, then drank from her glass. Benedict shuffled the cards before making a few passes over the top of the deck. Then he stared into Carrie's eyes. The prosecutor took another drink before setting down her glass.

"Is your card the three of clubs?" Benedict asked.

Carrie smiled maliciously. "No."

Benedict's brow furrowed. He closed his eyes

and placed his fingertips on his temples. When he opened his eyes, he looked uncertain.

"Was it the jack of diamonds?"

"You'd better practice a little harder, Charlie," Carrie said.

"Damn. I thought I had this trick down. What was your card?"

"The seven of hearts."

Benedict sighed. Then he looked confused. "Hey," he said. "There's a card under your glass."

Carrie looked down. Sure enough, a playing card was facedown on the table underneath the glass that held the remnants of her bourbon. She turned it over. Benedict grinned from ear to ear while Carrie stared dumbfounded at the seven of hearts.

"How did you do that?" she asked. Her speech was suddenly slurred.

"A magician never tells how he did a trick. But I'll show you another one."

Carrie closed her eyes and leaned back. She looked pale.

"Are you okay?" Benedict asked.

"I . . ." Carrie started. Then she stopped in mid-sentence.

Benedict walked around the booth and helped Carrie to stand.

"Whoa, you've had the proverbial one too many."

"I'm okay," she said, but she swayed unsteadily on her feet.

"You're in no condition to drive."

Carrie protested feebly. Benedict found her stub for valet parking. He laid a twenty on the table and helped Carrie out of the bar.

Benedict parked Carrie's silver Porsche in front of his condominium and helped her walk up the steps to his front door. The three-story condo was faux Federalist in style. An attached two-car garage, accessible through an alley in the back of a row of similar condos, housed Benedict's Mercedes.

In contrast to the nineteenth-century exterior, the interior of Benedict's home was starkly modern, with hardwood floors, glass-topped tables, and ivory-colored walls decorated with abstract art. Carrie was unsteady on her feet, and Benedict steered her into his spacious living room before easing her onto a sofa.

There were no interior walls on the main floor. The dining area abutted the living room, and an island topped with black slate separated the kitchen from the dining room.

"Why wasn't Horace with you?" Benedict asked as he put up a pot of coffee in the kitchen.

"Horace and I don't see all that much of each other," Carrie said, her speech still slurred.

"So the bloom is off the rose?"

"The fucking rose died years ago," Carrie answered bitterly, her tongue loosened by the drug Benedict had slipped into her drink.

"That's too bad. I remember reading about your romance and thinking how fairy-tale it was."

"Yeah, a Grimm's fairy tale. Very grim. Never marry for money, Charlie."

"You don't have to worry about me marrying. I learned my lesson a long time ago. One bad experience with wedlock and several stiff alimony payments taught me a lesson."

Suddenly Benedict was sitting beside her on the sofa and Carrie couldn't remember seeing him leave the kitchen. She shook her head to try to jump-start her brain, but it was definitely on the fritz.

Benedict slipped his arm around Carrie's shoulders. "What do you do for companionship?" he asked.

"Nothing with Horace, if I can help it. We haven't fucked in ages."

Benedict's fingers stroked Carrie's neck and brushed her earlobe. It felt nice. Then they were kissing and alarm bells went off. Carrie pushed him away with muscles that barely worked.

"I can't," she said.

"Horace will never know," Benedict whispered as he nuzzled her neck.

"You don't understand. I really can't."

Benedict was genuinely puzzled. "Do you mean that you can't make love?"

Carrie laughed but there was no humor in it. "I ain't menopausal yet, Charlie. I just can't fuck you."

"Why not? Horace may not be able to satisfy you, but that won't be a problem once we're in bed."

Carrie laughed again. "I have no doubt you're a stud, Charlie. I've heard the rumors around the courthouse. But getting laid would cost me millions, and I'm sure you're not that good."

"I don't get it."

"It's the prenup. And don't ask me anything about it because it's a secret."

"Don't worry. A gentleman knows what 'no' means," Benedict said gallantly. "And I think the coffee you so desperately need is ready."

Benedict walked over to the coffeepot and poured a cup for Carrie. Then, with his back shielding his hands from her, he laced the coffee with Rohypnol, familiarly known as "roofie," or the date-rape drug. The pharmaceutical was colorless, odorless, and tasteless and it induced drowsiness and impaired motor skills. Best of all, from Benedict's standpoint, amnesia was a side effect, so his victims never remembered what he'd done to them.

Benedict brought Carrie her cup. Then he smiled when she took her first long taste of the strong brew.

Charles Benedict estimated that Carrie Blair would wake from her drugged sleep around 6:30, so he set his alarm for 5:45. He had brewed a fresh pot of coffee for breakfast and was pouring himself a cup when the door to his bedroom slammed open. Benedict looked up in time to see Carrie stumble on the stairs. Her stocking feet had slipped on the smooth hardwood and she grabbed the banister to keep from falling. As soon as she regained her balance, the prosecutor saw her host looking up at her with a bemused smile.

"What did you do to me?" Carrie demanded, her panic barely under control.

"Relax. Your honor is intact. I was a perfect gentleman."

Benedict extended the cup he was holding. "Here, have some coffee. I just made it, and I think you can use it."

Carrie ignored the cup. "What time is it?"

"Six thirty."

"Oh, God. You mean I've been here all night?"

"Yes. You passed out and I put you in my bed. All I removed were your shoes and jacket. Then I slept in my guest room. You know, you're not the first person to lose an evening to booze, but you might want to see someone if it happens again."

Carrie ignored Benedict and looked around the condo.

"Where are my things? I've got to get home," she said.

"Are you sure you don't want breakfast or a shower?" Benedict asked as he walked over to a closet and took out Carrie's shoes and jacket.

"I can't believe this happened," Carrie said, ignoring Benedict's offer. She pulled on her jacket and slipped into her shoes.

Benedict held out her car key. "If you hurry, you

can get home, change, and be in your office at your usual time."

There was a mirror by the front door. Carrie stared at her image and ran her hand through her hair, trying for some semblance of order. Then she walked outside. Benedict followed her. On the street in front of Benedict's condo a man in a tracksuit was jogging at a steady clip.

"Be careful driving," Benedict cautioned. Carrie turned toward him and started to say something. Then she stopped and stared down the street. Before Benedict could ask what she was looking at, Carrie started screaming and ran toward a parked car. The driver gunned the engine and made a U-turn that left dust clouds and rubber. Carrie's screams had attracted the jogger's attention, and he turned and watched as the car sped off.

Carrie stopped running. Benedict saw her stare at the rear of the car, where the license plate was attached. Then she bent over, rested her hands on her knees, and took deep breaths to regain her composure.

"What was that all about?" Benedict asked when he reached her.

Carrie turned toward him. She looked furious. Then she walked to her car and drove away without answering Benedict's question.

Chapter Four

On Thursday, Dana Cutler got out of bed at three in the afternoon, ran five miles, then went through a set of calisthenics. When she finished a third set of fifty push-ups, she collapsed on the floor of the rec room in the basement of the house she shared with Jake Teeny. Jake, a photojournalist, was away on an Arctic expedition sponsored by *National Geographic*. Dana had met Jake six months before she was kidnapped, and he'd stood by her when she was in the hospital, visiting often and fighting hard to keep her spirits up, even when that seemed impossible. When she was released, he took her to lunch, dinner, and an occasional movie, but he had never tried to touch her until she fell in love with him and let him into her life. Dana had always been a loner until she fell in love. When Jake was gone she felt like a part of her was missing. Tonight, after writing a report on the Jorgenson case, she would try to find something on TV to numb her mind. Then she would go to sleep and wake up to another boring, unfulfilling day.

Dana's last meal had been the beer and burger she'd downed at the sports bar during her surveillance of Lars Jorgenson, and she was starving. After a shower, she walked to the kitchen to scavenge the fixings for a sandwich. She had just opened the refrigerator door when her business phone rang.

"Cutler Investigations," Dana said.

"Dana Cutler, please," a woman said. Dana thought she heard a French accent.

"Speaking."

"I would like to retain you."

"To do what?" Dana asked.

"I would prefer that we not discuss the matter over the phone."

Definitely French, Dana concluded.

"Okay, but can you give me some idea of what you want me to do. If it's not the type of case I handle I can refer you to someone who does."

"I really cannot say more. Your retainer will be very satisfactory if you accept the assignment. Meet me and I will pay you three thousand dollars for a consultation even if you do not take the case."

The sum, which was way more than her normal rate, surprised Dana. "Where do you want to meet?" she asked.

"I do not know Washington. Perhaps you can suggest a place to rendezvous?"

"Are you hungry?"

"*Non.*"

"Well, I am. Why don't we meet at Michelangelo's? I know the owner and he'll guarantee us privacy. The food is pretty good, too, if you change your mind about dinner."

Michelangelo's was a family-owned Italian restaurant located in sight of the Capitol dome, in an area that was shifting from decay to gentrification. Abandoned buildings and vacant lots could be found only blocks away from chic boutiques, renovated row houses owned by young professionals, and trendy restaurants. Michelangelo's, which was anything but trendy, had been a constant in the neighborhood for over sixty years. Sam and Donna Mazzara opened it with their life savings after emigrating from Sicily. Donna had passed away seven years ago, but Sam still came to work every day. Their son, Victor, helped run the restaurant now.

Michelangelo's was a few blocks from the offices of *Exposed*, a supermarket tabloid that had surprised establishment newspapers like the *Washington Post* and *New York Times* by winning prizes in journalism as a result of Dana's investigative work. Patrick Gorman, the newspaper's owner, ran a tab at Michelangelo's, and Sam and Victor knew Dana. When she called, they set aside a small private dining room in the back for her to meet with her potential client. The room was paneled in dark wood and the lighting was subdued. Black-and-white photographs of Sicily hung on the walls.

Dana sat at a table covered in a white tablecloth and ordered a small antipasto and spaghetti aglio e olio. The antipasto had just arrived when Victor opened the door to admit a woman who looked as exotic as her accent. She was carrying an attaché case and wore a trench coat. Dark glasses obscured her eyes, raven-black hair fell to her shoulders, she wore no rings on her fingers, and her lips were ruby red. Dana thought she'd fit in perfectly as the femme fatale in a 1940s film based on a Raymond Chandler or Dashiell Hammett novel.

"Miss Cutler?" the woman asked.

Dana stood and offered her hand. The woman's fingers barely touched Dana's before she pulled her hand away.

"I am Margo Laurent."

"Have a seat, Ms. Laurent," Dana said as she motioned toward a chair on the other side of the table. Then she pointed her fork at her antipasto. "Sure you don't want something to eat? The food here is great."

"Thank you, but I am not hungry."

"Suit yourself. I hope you don't mind if I eat while we talk. I was up all night on a case and I'm starving."

"Please."

Dana waited for the woman to take off her coat. When she didn't, Dana said, "So, Ms. Laurent, why do you want to hire me?"

"How much do you know about the Ottoman Empire?"

Dana had speared a piece of mortadella and a slice of provolone, but she paused with her fork halfway to her mouth.

"Turks, right?"

Laurent nodded.

Dana smiled apologetically. "I'm afraid that's the extent of my knowledge. I was never much of a history buff."

"The Ottoman Empire lasted from 1299 to 1923," Laurent said. "In the sixteenth and seventeenth centuries, at the height of its power, it controlled territory in southeastern Europe, southwestern Asia, and North Africa. Constantinople was its capital city and the empire was at the center of interactions between the Eastern and Western worlds for six centuries. At times, the empire's tentacles reached into Persia, Egypt, Baghdad, Hungary, Transylvania, Moldavia, and the outskirts of Vienna. By the end of the reign of Suleiman the Magnificent in 1566 the empire's population totaled fifteen million people."

"Impressive," Dana said before taking another forkful of Italian delicacies. She had no interest in Laurent's history lesson, but three thousand bucks was three thousand bucks, so she pretended to find it fascinating.

"If you do not know about the Ottoman Empire, can I assume you've never heard of Gennadius or Mark of Ephesus?"

"You got me," Dana said before eating a slice of prosciutto.

"In 1444, the court of Byzantium was desperate for Western assistance against the Turks and it agreed to a union with Rome, yielding on almost all of the important theological issues that divided the East and the West. For example, the unionists agreed to accept the concept of purgatory, which they had previously rejected."

"Where is this going, Ms. Laurent?" asked Dana, whose patience was starting to fade.

"Bear with me. You need to understand the backstory before you can understand why I need your help."

Dana shrugged. "It's your dime."

"Mark of Ephesus was concerned about the preservation of the Eastern Orthodox Church. He was the only bishop who refused to sign the union, and he spoke for the average Orthodox churchgoers who gathered around him. George Scholarius was a judge who made several speeches in favor of the union. When he returned to Byzantium, he saw how the lesser clergy and the common people opposed what they saw as the betrayal of their beliefs. He changed his mind and became a strong opponent of the union. When Mark died, on June 23, 1444, George became the leader of the anti-union camp. This brought him into disfavor with the court and he retired to a monastery and took the name Gennadius.

"In 1453, at the age of twenty-one, Sultan Mehmet II conquered Constantinople and cemented the status of the empire as the preeminent power in southeastern Europe. Mehmet wanted to assure the loyalty of the Greek population so they would not appeal to the West for liberation, which could have set off a new round of Crusades. He needed to find the cleric with the most hostility toward the West to help him cement the loyalty of the Greek populace. Gennadius was the natural choice.

"After Mehmet took Constantinople, Gennadius was captured by the Turks and sold as a slave. Mehmet's men found Gennadius in Adrianople and brought him to the sultan on a beautiful horse from the imperial stable adorned with a silver saddle. The sultan received him in his suite while standing. The sultan rarely stood when receiving visitors, so this was a very rare display of respect.

"Mehmet persuaded Gennadius to be the first Patriarch of Constantinople under Islamic rule and personally gave him a gold, bejeweled scepter as the symbol of his authority. This scepter was immensely valuable, but it was only one of thousands of treasures belonging to the Ottoman sultans. No mention was made of it after Mehmet passed the Byzantine emperor's symbol of power to the patriarch."

Dana was suddenly drawn into Laurent's tale and forgot about eating. Typically, her meetings with clients were laced with phrases like "cheating bastard" and "malingerer." Dana couldn't remember any insurance executive mentioning a silver saddle or a jewel-encrusted golden scepter.

"My grandfather, Antoine Girard, was a fascinating man," Laurent said, changing the subject abruptly. "He studied archaeology and history at the Sorbonne and Oxford. He was a soldier of fortune and was involved in a number of famous archaeological digs. In 1922, Howard Carter and Lord Carnarvon found the tomb of Tutankhamen in the Valley of the Kings in Egypt."

"King Tut's tomb?" asked Dana.

"Exactement. Antoine had a very minor role in the expedition, but he was there when the tomb was opened. Then he and Carter argued. My grandfather never revealed the basis of the dispute, but my father thought they might have fought over a woman both men had been seeing in Cairo, because that is where Antoine went after quitting the dig, and that is where he made his startling discovery."

The door opened and Victor came in with Dana's pasta. Laurent fell silent, and Dana, who had lost interest in her food, regretted the intrusion.

"What discovery?" Dana asked as soon as the door closed behind Victor.

"Antoine found the Ottoman scepter. An open-air market place in North Africa or the Middle East is called a souk, and the largest souk in Cairo is the Khan-el-Khalili. Have you been to Egypt, Miss Cutler?"

Dana shook her head. Her only trips outside the U.S. of A. had been chaperoning Jake when he was photographing swimsuit models in Tahiti and a disastrous week with a fellow cop in Acapulco.

"A pity. Cairo is fascinating, and the Khan-el-Khalili is one of its more exotic attractions. It is a winding maze packed tight with people, restaurants, coffeehouses, and shops selling all sorts of wares. On one of his trips to the souk, Antoine ventured into a shop that purported to sell Egyptian antiquities. Most of them were obvious fakes, but Antoine's eye fell on an interesting item on a shelf in the back of the store. It was a jet-black scepter with no jewels, but there were indentations where jewels might have been at one time. More important, it resembled a gold scepter adorned with jewels Antoine had seen in a museum in Constantinople. Antoine suspected that the scepter was a copy, but something about it fascinated him. He bought it, along with several other items so the owner would not suspect his interest. When he got back to his hotel, he made a startling discovery."

"It was the real deal?" Dana guessed.

Laurent nodded. "Underneath several layers of black paint was solid gold. But the scepter's real value had nothing to do with gold. If Antoine had found the scepter that Mehmet gave to Gennadius, it would be priceless. Antoine spent ten years researching the scepter's provenance and eventually came to the conclusion that it was, as you so charmingly put it, 'the real deal.'"

"How do you know all this?"

"During a sojourn in Paris, Antoine married my grandmother, Marie Levêque. Marie was wealthy and had homes in Paris and Bordeaux. They lived together long enough for Antoine to father Pauline Girard, my mother. My family had a collection of letters Antoine wrote to Marie while he was in Turkey. In one of them, he says that he has uncovered documents that convinced him that the scepter was real.

"Shortly after she received the letter, Marie got word from the French embassy in Constantinople that Antoine had been murdered. Shortly after that, burglars ransacked her villa in Bordeaux, and an attempt was made to break into her home in Paris. Fortunately, the scepter was hidden in a safe in the basement of the Paris mansion.

"When Hitler came to power, Marie moved to America, where she had relatives. Eventually, Pauline married my father, Pierre Laurent, another wealthy émigré. Marie was highly intelligent and had many well-placed friends in the government. She anticipated Hitler's invasion and the weakness of the French army and shipped a great deal of art to America before hostilities broke out. One object she included in her cargo was the scepter.

"While she was living in New York her mansion was burglarized on more than one occasion despite her having alarm systems installed and security guards posted. She could never prove it, but she suspected that the scepter was the object of these home invasions. Then, during a vacation in Europe after the war, Marie was kidnapped and murdered. Another burglary occurred soon after, and an inside job was suspected. Marie had told my mother the history of the scepter and where it was hidden. When she went to the place where Marie had hidden it, the scepter was gone.

"When I was growing up, I heard many stories about Antoine's adventures, and the scepter was often mentioned. When I was a teenager, my mother showed me the letters that Antoine had written to Marie. I became fascinated with the scepter and the Ottoman Empire. I majored in history in college and made several attempts to track down the scepter. All of them were unsuccessful.

"Then I read that a Turkish businessman who had been hard hit by the recession was auctioning off his art collection. Among the items in the catalog was a gold scepter. The picture reminded me of my mother's description. I traveled to New York for the auction and confronted the head of the house. I showed him my proof that the scepter was stolen property but it wasn't strong enough and he said the present owner was willing to risk a lawsuit.

"I hired an attorney but he told me that the scepter had been withdrawn from the auction. Soon after I heard rumors of a private sale. I also learned that Otto Pickering, a professor specializing in art of the Ottoman Empire, had authenticated the scepter. And that is where my trail ran cold."

"Did you talk to Pickering?"

"Despite repeated attempts to set up a meeting, he has refused to see me."

"What is it that you want me to do?"

"I am terrified that the scepter will disappear for good if I do not act quickly. Otto Pickering is a recluse. He lives on an island off the coast of Washington State."

Laurent placed the attaché case on the table and opened it. Inside were stacks of cash, a cell phone, and an airline ticket.

"I have purchased a first-class ticket on a flight to Seattle that leaves at midnight, and I have chartered a boat to take you to the island. Can you leave tonight?"

"That's awfully short notice."

"Miss Cutler, if we do not act immediately the scepter may disappear forever. The twenty-five-thousand-dollar retainer in this attaché case should compensate you for any inconvenience you might suffer."

Dana ran through the projects she had on her desk. Most of them would keep. More important, none of them involved Constantinople, French soldiers of fortune, the Khan-el-Khalili in Cairo, and a mysterious golden scepter. It was no contest.

"I'll be on the plane," Dana said.

Laurent's shoulders had been hunched from tension and she'd been holding her breath. Now she exhaled and her shoulders sagged.

"I cannot thank you enough."

"How do you want me to report to you?"

"My number is programmed into the cell phone in the attaché case."

Dana stood up. "I'm going home to pack. I'll give you an update as soon as I talk to Otto Pickering."

Chapter Five

A torrential downpour pummeled the roof of the pilothouse of Emilio Leone's fishing boat. Violent waves smashed into its hull, and Dana Cutler's fingers gripped a handhold tightly as she fought to keep down the light meal she'd eaten for breakfast. Earlier on Friday morning, Dana had driven to a dockside café in a seaside town thirty miles north of Seattle. When she walked into the restaurant, Captain Leone was working on a cup of black coffee. He was bundled up in a pea jacket and knit cap. A thick black beard concealed a lot of his face, and a black patch covered his right eye. Dana thought he would have been perfectly at home on a pirate ship. Leone was not enthusiastic about sailing in a storm, but Margo Laurent's money had changed his mind, if not his surly attitude. The captain spoke only when necessary, and then he communicated in terse sentences or angry grunts.

Another wave crashed across the bow and the boat fell fast and hard into a trough before miraculously rising. Dana had seen the wave coming and had braced for the shock. It was freezing cold in the pilothouse but a heavy jacket and the wool cap that fit snuggly over her ears helped some. She bent forward and squinted through the sheets of rain that dashed against the window. Outside, massive waves crashed against black rocks that jutted like dinosaur teeth out of the unforgiving sea.

The captain saw where she was looking. "That's the island, Isla de Muerta."

"The Island of Death?"

"If a ship busts up on those rocks and a sailor is thrown into these waters, he's done."

Dana shivered as she imagined how it would feel to drown in the freezing, turbulent water.

Rain and heavy clouds obscured Dana's view, but the captain did not seem troubled by the lack of visibility. Seconds after Leone guided the boat through a break in the rocks the mist parted and Dana saw boats straining against their anchors as the wind and waves flung them about like toys. Leone steered the boat into a small harbor and secured it to a gray, weathered dock. Dana slung her duffel bag over her shoulder and got off quickly, grateful to be standing on solid ground.

"I'm staying at the Stanton B&B," she said. "Do you know where that is?"

"Walk a quarter mile down the road," the captain answered, pointing due north. "There's a sign out front."

"How do I get in touch when I need to get back to the mainland?"

"The Stantons got my number," Leone said. Then he turned his back on Dana and trudged up the dock.

Dana followed and found herself on a short main street where the buildings all had a nautical theme. Peeling, sea-blue paint covered most of the stores. Anchors and wooden seagulls were a common decoration. Dana passed a shop that sold bait and other fishing supplies, and a small grocery store. Ahead of her, the captain disappeared into the Safe Harbor Café, which advertised breakfast all day and a halibut special for dinner.

The rain was hard and cold and Dana walked fast, head down, shoulders hunched, speeding by a store that sold new and used books, an art gallery that displayed seascapes, a clothing store filled with foul-weather gear, and an antique store with brass sextants and an anchor chain in its front window. There were a few people in the café and grocery store but Dana didn't see any customers in the other shops. She guessed that the townspeople made their nut during the summer and scraped by the rest of the year.

The B&B was a three-story yellow house with white trim that had been worked hard by the salt air. It was surrounded by a faded white picket fence grimed with moss. The inn had a front porch that wound around the side facing the sea. Dana imagined that the view would be great when the sun was shining. At the moment, she appreciated the shelter from the storm provided by the overhang.

Moments after she rang the doorbell, a short, plump woman with snowy white hair let her in.

"You must be Miss Cutler," she said, smiling broadly.

"How did you know?"

The woman laughed. "There was no trick to it. You're our only guest."

Dana smiled. "I guess the island doesn't get too many tourists this time of year."

"Or any other," the woman answered solemnly. "We're off the beaten track, so to speak. I'm Mabel Stanton. Let me show you to your room so you can get out of those wet clothes."

"I'm here on business," Dana said as they climbed the stairs to the second floor. "I'll need a car. Is there someplace I can rent one?"

"Miss Laurent asked about a car when she rented the room for you. You can use one of our cars. It's all paid for."

"Great. Can you tell me where Otto Pickering lives?"

"Other side of the island, but I don't know if he'll talk to you. The professor keeps to himself and I hear he doesn't like visitors."

"I won't know if he'll talk to me until I ask him. Can you show me how to get to Professor Pickering's house?"

"That's easy enough. It's off the main road but you won't have any trouble finding it. I already drew you a map. Will you be wanting something to eat before you go?"

Dana realized that she was starving. "That would be great."

"I've got beef stew, or I can fix you a sandwich."

"The stew sounds terrific. And a cup of hot coffee would be deeply appreciated."

"I'll have it waiting for you when you come down," Mabel said as she opened a door to a spacious room with a view of the sea.

"There's fresh towels in the bathroom. Here's your key. Anything else you need, tell me when you come downstairs."

Dana tossed her duffel bag on the bed and stripped off her clothes. She'd take a fast, scalding-hot shower, eat a hearty meal, then drive to the far side of Isla de Muerta to visit Otto Pickering. Her plan sounded simple enough.

Chapter Six

Dana could hear rain rattling against the B&B's windows while she devoured her lunch. She hoped that the downpour would let up by the time she drove to Pickering's house but she was out of luck. If anything, the rain seemed more violent.

The main road was two lanes and it circled Isla de Muerta. The trees on the windward side were sparse, stunted, and bent away from the rocky shore. On the other side of the road, lightning strikes cast a flickering light over a dense evergreen forest. According to Mabel's map, Pickering's house was fifteen miles from the inn and two miles past the intersection of the main road and another road that bisected Isla de Muerta. Dana drove slowly and crossed the island's other artery twenty minutes after she started. Two miles farther on, Dana turned onto a narrow dirt track that led inland through thick woods. A heavy canopy shielded Dana's car from a good deal of the rain but it also made the way darker and created an impression that the trees were closing in on her. It took a lot to frighten Dana, but the closeness of the primordial woods made her very uncomfortable.

Without warning, Pickering's house appeared. It was old, large, and ungainly and painted a dull brown to blend in with the forest that surrounded it. The central portion was two stories, and it looked as if additions had been slapped on without any rhyme or reason. Some were one story, others two. There was even a three-story tower on the side with the best view of the sea. None of the property looked kept up; the yard was wild and the house was badly in need of a paint job.

Dana parked and ran under an overhang. There was no bell but a heavy brass lion-head knocker was nailed to the middle of the front door. Dana pulled it back and slammed it forward, hoping that the clang of metal on metal would penetrate the thick oak door and the din created by the storm. She waited a minute, then used the knocker twice more. She was about to try again when she heard a voice yell, "I'm coming, I'm coming." A minute later, the door creaked open and Dana found herself facing an elderly, balding man with liver-spotted skin. He was stooped with age and clad in a white shirt, a blue polka-dot bow tie, a brown tweed jacket with leather patches on the elbows, and loose-fitting green slacks that did not match his jacket. The pants were held up by suspenders.

"No solicitors," Otto Pickering said brusquely.

"I'm not selling anything, Professor."

"Then why are you here?"

Dana held out her card. "I've come on behalf of a client."

Pickering eyed the card suspiciously.

"I would have called," Dana said, "but your number is unlisted, and I couldn't find an e-mail address. This is a matter of some urgency, so I didn't have the luxury of writing."

"You still haven't told me what you want, young lady."

"I'm here because of the scepter that Sultan Mehmet II gave to Gennadius."

Surprise registered on Pickering's face for a moment. Then he regained his composure.

"Can we step inside, please?" Dana said. "I'm drowning out here."

The professor hesitated, and Dana hoped that he wouldn't slam the door in her face. Then Pickering turned his back on Dana and walked down a long hall. She rushed inside and followed him.

The interior of the house was paneled in dark wood, dimly lit, and drafty. The carpets were threadbare, and a dank odor pervaded everything. Dana wouldn't have been surprised to find mold and mushrooms growing on the walls. Pickering led Dana into a large, high-ceilinged room with French windows that gave her a view of the dense forest when lightning flashed. Faded sofas, chipped and scarred coffee and end tables, and sagging armchairs stood on a large Persian carpet. Only a few of the pieces of furniture matched.

A fire roared in a high stone fireplace and provided welcome warmth. A moose head was mounted over the fireplace and Dana had the eerie feeling that it was staring at her. A black bear and a mountain lion eyed her threateningly from two other walls.

A massive desk illuminated by a gooseneck lamp stood in one corner of the large room. Papers were spread across the blotter and books were stacked next to a laptop, one of the few modern contraptions Dana had seen since entering the house. Pickering sat behind the desk and Dana sat in a straight-back chair across from him. Its seat was not cushioned and it was hard and uncomfortable.

"What is all this about a scepter?" Pickering asked cagily. Dana noticed that his liver-spotted fingers fluttered nervously and he avoided looking at her directly.

"You do know about the gold, jewel-encrusted scepter Sultan Mehmet II gave to Gennadius after the fall of Constantinople when Gennadius agreed to be the Patriarch of the Orthodox Church?"

"Young lady, I have degrees in history from Harvard and Oxford and my Ph.D. thesis was on the Ottoman Empire, so you may assume that I am aware of everything there is to know about the reign of the sultans."

"Yes, well, Antoine Girard, my client's grandfather, found the scepter in the early 1920s in the Khan-el-Khalili. The scepter was kept in a safe in a mansion in New York, but it was stolen in a burglary. Recently, my client learned that the scepter was to be auctioned off by a bankrupt Turkish businessman, but the scepter was withdrawn from the auction. My client believes that you appraised and authenticated the scepter. She needs to know who commissioned the appraisal."

Pickering looked upset. He shook his head back and forth.

"Any such work I may have done would be confidential."

"You're not a lawyer, a doctor, or a priest, so you don't have any legal right to keep client information secret."

"And we are in my house and not in a courtroom, so you have no legal right to—"

Glass shattered and a bullet smashed into the wall above Pickering's head. He looked confused. Dana threw herself across the desk and knocked the professor to the floor.

"What are you doing?" Pickering protested.

More bullets tore through the room.

"Someone is shooting at us," Dana said as she drew the gun she wore in a holster secured to her ankle. "Get under the desk and stay there."

Dana stared into the forest but the light from the fireplace reflected off the window glass. She crawled closer to the windows and crouched behind the sofa, straining to hear any sound outside the house. Then she rose up cautiously and stared over the top of the couch and through the shattered panes. She didn't see any movement in the forest.

"Stay here," she ordered. "I'm going after the shooter."

Pickering didn't protest, and Dana darted through one of the French windows onto a patio. Another shot ricocheted off the outside wall and Dana heard someone crashing through the woods. She waited a moment, drew a second gun from the holster secured to the back of her belt, and crept forward, keeping low and moving her eyes back and forth.

A car engine started and Dana dashed toward the sound. By the time she reached the road, two taillights were disappearing around a curve. Dana debated getting her car but rejected the idea. The shooter had too much of a head start. Besides, she'd been hired to get information from Otto Pickering that could lead to the scepter, and she was curious to see the professor's reaction to this attempt to murder him.

Pickering was still cowering under the desk when Dana reentered the living room. She holstered the gun she kept in the small of her back but held on to the snubnose revolver from her ankle holster.

"You're safe now, Professor. The person who tried to kill you drove off before I could get to him."

"Kill me?" Pickering said as he crawled out from under the desk and slumped in his chair.

"I can't think of anyone with a motive to kill *me*," Dana said. "If I died, my client would send someone else in my place. You're the one with information that can lead to the scepter, so I have to think that you were the target."

Pickering put his head in his hands. "This can't be

happening. I'm just a consultant. All I did was give an opinion about the authenticity of an antique."

"For who?"

"No, I can't."

"Listen, Professor, once you tell me who hired you, the cat is out of the bag and no one will have a reason to kill you."

"I don't know what to do," Pickering said. He was sweating and he was pale. Dana hoped he wasn't going to pass out.

"Professor, someone just tried to murder you. There could be a second attempt."

"But you said there wouldn't be if I told you what you want to know," Pickering said. He sounded desperate.

"I think the odds of another attempt will be small if you tell me who asked you to look at the scepter."

Pickering didn't answer right away. He rubbed his temples. Then he sighed.

"Rene Marchand."

"Who?"

"Rene is an antiques dealer. His office is in Seattle. He specializes in rare European antiquities. He's more of a broker. He doesn't have a store."

"Did he own the scepter or was he representing a client?"

"He wouldn't answer any questions about the piece, but I got the impression that he was acting for a client. He only wanted my opinion on its authenticity."

"What was your opinion?"

"I couldn't say for certain that the scepter was the object the sultan gave to Gennadius, but it could have been. There are few written descriptions of the scepter, and the jewels had been removed. It was unquestionably from the appropriate time period, and the amount of gold used led me to believe that it had to have been created for someone of immense wealth like Mehmet II."

"Where did you examine the scepter?"

"In Rene's office. He was quite explicit about that. He didn't let it out of his sight. There were two bodyguards watching me the whole time. It was rather unsettling."

"Can you think of anything Mr. Marchand said that would help me find his client?"

"No, I'm sorry."

"Is there a police station on the island?"

"What? No, the nearest police station is on the mainland."

"Then you'll have to call them."

Pickering's head snapped up. "No, no police."

"I'm sure the killer didn't expect me to come after him. He may have left evidence in the woods that will tell the authorities who tried to kill you."

"I don't want the police involved. If the police investigate, it will just bring me to the attention of . . . of whoever did this."

"Look, Professor, I can't tell you what to do. It's your decision. If you don't want to go to the police

I'll respect your choice. But I think you're making a mistake. At least think about it."

"I just want this to go away."

Dana got the address of Marchand's office and tried again, unsuccessfully, to convince the professor to call the police.

"You have my card," Dana said as she prepared to leave. "It's got my cell number on it. Call me if you think of anything."

Pickering nodded but Dana doubted she would ever hear from the professor. He looked genuinely frightened and anxious to put everything that had happened behind him.

Dana was alert for cars that might be following her when she drove back to the inn through the storm. By the time she was safely inside the B&B it was late afternoon. Dana found Mr. and Mrs. Stanton reading in the parlor. She asked them for Emilio Leone's phone number and called when she was in her room.

"Captain, this is Dana Cutler. I've finished my business here. Is there any chance we can head back to the mainland tonight?"

"Not in this storm. It's hard enough in daylight. I ain't risking my boat in this weather in the dark."

"When do you think we can go?"

"Maybe tomorrow afternoon, but I ain't promising. Depends on the weather."

"I'll be ready when you are. Will you call me when you know?"

"I'll do that," Leone said. Then the phone went dead.

Dana sighed. It probably wouldn't matter whether they left tonight or tomorrow. Odds were Marchand's office would be closed by the time she got back to Seattle. She hoped it would be open on Sunday.

Dana dialed Margo Laurent's cell.

"Ms. Laurent, this is Dana Cutler," she said when her client answered. "I'm calling from Isla de Muerta."

"Did you meet with Pickering?" Laurent asked. Dana could hear the anxiety in her client's voice.

"I did, but something unexpected happened while we were talking. Someone tried to kill the professor."

"What!"

"Someone shot at him. He's okay, but I think you held out on me."

"I didn't. I had no idea you would be in danger. You have to believe me."

"Whether I do or not, the fact remains that someone is willing to kill to keep the scepter. Do you have any idea who that is?"

"No. I told you my grandparents were murdered and about the robbery. But that was years ago. Did you learn anything from the professor?"

"I know who asked him to authenticate the scepter."

"Who is it?"

"Have you ever heard of a Seattle antiques dealer named Rene Marchand?"

"No."

"There's a storm here, so I can't get back to the mainland before Saturday night at the earliest. I'll try to talk to Marchand, but I'm not willing to take a bullet to help you get back the scepter."

"Please. I'll double your fee."

Dana thought about that. "All right, but I'm off the case if there's another incident like the one at Pickering's house."

"Understood."

"I'll call you after I speak to Marchand. Something else, Ms. Laurent. The people we're dealing with are very dangerous, and you're a threat to them. Watch your back."

Chapter Seven

The storm broke Sunday morning and Captain Leone's boat docked shortly after noon. Dana drove to Seattle on high alert because of the murder attempt on Isla de Muerta, but she didn't see anything that made her think she was being followed.

After checking into the Hotel Monaco in downtown Seattle, Dana walked to Yesler Way, a steep street known as Skid Road in the 1850s, when the area was teeming with trees and a chute was used to skid logs to Henry Yesler's sawmill. When Seattle's city center moved north, the area became a dilapidated haven for drunks and derelicts and went from being called Skid Road to Skid Row, a term eventually used all over America to refer to a down-and-out section of a town or city.

Rene Marchand had an office in a six-story building on First at Yesler. On the way there, Dana spotted a seedy hotel advertising cheap rooms but most of the twenty-five-square-block Skid Row district—now more popularly known as Pioneer Square—was filled with hip boutiques, coffee shops, restored buildings, restaurants, and art galleries.

There was an old-fashioned elevator in the lobby of Marchand's office building. Dana slid the accordion gate open, then closed it and took the car to the sixth floor. Halfway down the hall, Dana saw RENE MARCHAND ANTIQUES stenciled in bright gold letters on the glass in the upper part of a door. She tried the knob but the office was closed. After knocking loudly twice Dana returned to her hotel.

Monday morning, Dana dressed in a black suit and white man-tailored blouse so she would look businesslike and headed back to Marchand's office. During her short walk, she checked for a tail or anything unusual, but nothing aroused her suspicions. This time when Dana tried the door it opened into a small waiting room. There was a desk, two chairs, and a small end table on which lay two magazines about antiques. No one was sitting at the reception desk, so Dana rapped her knuckles on a plain wooden door next to it. Moments later, the door opened and a man in his late thirties with a trim mustache and slicked-down thinning brown hair stared at her through the lenses of a pair of wire-rimmed glasses. The man was slender and several inches shorter than Dana, and he was dressed in an open-neck sky-blue shirt, a navy-blue blazer, and gray slacks.

"Yes?" he asked, apparently surprised to have a visitor.

"Are you Rene Marchand?"

"I am, but I generally see customers by appointment only."

"I didn't know that," Dana said with what she hoped was a winning smile. "But I'm here now, so can we talk?"

"About what?"

"The Ottoman Scepter."

Marchand's only reaction was a rapid blink but it was enough to give him away.

"I'm not sure what you're talking about," the antiques dealer said.

"I think you are. Professor Otto Pickering examined the scepter in this very office not long ago."

Marchand hesitated. Then he stepped aside and ushered Dana in. The furniture in Marchand's office looked secondhand, as had the furnishings in the waiting room. Through a begrimed window, Dana could see the train station, the stadiums where the Mariners and Seahawks played, and the Smith Tower, which had been the tallest building west of the Mississippi in 1914. The view was interesting, but it occurred to Dana that the office was run down for someone who supposedly dealt in high-end antiquities.

"Why do you want to know about this scepter?" Marchand asked when they were seated.

Dana handed the antiques dealer her card. "I'm acting on behalf of a client who is very interested in acquiring it."

Marchand leaned back in his chair and examined the card. Then he set it down on a faded green blotter.

"You're aware of the Ottoman Scepter's history?"

Dana nodded.

"Then you know that the gold alone makes the object expensive but its historical value puts it beyond price."

"My client is very motivated to acquire the scepter. And I'm not motivated to engage in a lot of fencing, so let's cut to the chase. Do you have the scepter?"

Marchand crossed his legs and studied Dana long enough to make her uncomfortable. Dana returned Marchand's stare.

"I'd like you to step into the waiting room while I make a call," Marchand said.

Dana left the room and Marchand shut the door behind her. It occurred to Dana that she had not seen a telephone on Marchand's desk, so she assumed he was using a cell.

Dana wandered over to the end table and thumbed through one of the magazines. It was several years old. Dana smiled. Maybe that was appropriate in the office of an antiques dealer.

Ten minutes passed, then the door to Marchand's office opened and he signaled her in.

"For a price, I can put you in touch with someone with whom you can deal," Marchand said.

"How much?"

"Five thousand dollars."

Dana laughed. "I'll give you one thousand. If your contact is legit, I'll come back with the rest. If this is a setup, I'll find you and take back more than the money."

Marchand lost color. "I don't like being threatened."

"Mr. Marchand, I do not make threats. I make promises." Dana took out a wad of bills and peeled off one thousand dollars of Margo Laurent's money. She placed it on the desk and covered it with her hand. "The name and address, please."

Marchand eyed the money. He hesitated, and Dana knew he was deciding if he could push her. Dana's features hardened.

"Do you know where Victoria is?"

"It's near Vancouver, British Columbia."

"Correct. The countess will be there on Wednesday. She'll be staying in her condominium on the harbor." Marchand wrote an address. "Be there at nine a.m., and don't be late. The countess detests people who aren't prompt."

Dana took the paper with the address and Marchand grabbed the money. As she rode to the lobby, Dana thought back on the past few days. There was something about her meeting with Margo Laurent, the trip to the island, and her meeting with Marchand that didn't sit right, but she couldn't put her finger on it.

When Dana stepped outside, a harsh wind was gusting off of Elliott Bay. Ferries were crossing the stormy waters but the weather was keeping pleasure boats away. As Dana headed back to her hotel she saw movement in her peripheral vision. She paused to look in the window of a coffee shop and pretended to study the menu. A large man with close-cropped blond hair and wearing a knee-length black leather coat stepped into a doorway half a block behind her. He was far enough away so she couldn't make out his features in the reflection.

Dana started walking. She stopped at a restaurant and saw the man reflected in the window. He stopped walking when Dana stopped and pretended to look in a store window. Dana went inside and found a seat facing the street. The man walked by on the other side.

Dana ordered coffee and took her time finishing the cup. When she left the restaurant half an hour later her tail was nowhere in sight but she spotted him again two blocks from the hotel. Dana wondered if her secret admirer was the man who had tried to kill Otto Pickering. Dana had not gotten a good look at the shooter, so she had no way to know. Instinctively, she brushed her pocket and felt the reassuring bulge created by the .38 nestled there.

When Dana was in her room, she locked the door and called Margot Laurent to give her an update. The call went to voice mail.

Chapter Eight

On Monday morning, *Commonwealth of Virginia v. Ross* commenced in the most ornate courtroom in the Lee County Courthouse. It had been built in the days when floor-to-ceiling columns of real marble were affordable and workmen knew how to decorate a high ceiling with frescoes of chubby cherubs and Roman gods. Somber oil paintings of judges past stared down at the litigants and spectators from cream-colored walls, and the bench was elaborately carved oak. All in all, it was a fitting place to hold court if you thought you were royalty, which described the mind-set of the Honorable Preston L. Gardner III.

Gardner had been the youngest judge in the state when he was appointed three years earlier. He had piercing blue eyes fixed in a perpetual squint, thin lips always set in a disapproving scowl, and plastered-down, jet-black hair. He reminded Charles Benedict of the obnoxious nerds he had loved to torment in junior high.

Benedict had been in Gardner's court on a number

of occasions and had never seen him dressed in anything but a black, three-piece suit; blue, red, and
yellow striped tie; and his Phi Beta Kappa key. Gardner wore the key because he loved to remind people
that he was brilliant. The first things one noticed entering his chambers were diplomas attesting to the
honors he'd been awarded at Dartmouth and Harvard Law and the certificate proving that he was a
member of Mensa. If the Guinness Book of Records
kept track of oversized egos, Benedict was certain
that Gardner would be listed.

Sitting next to Benedict was Kyle Ross. The defendant was a twenty-year-old junior at the University of Virginia majoring in prelaw. He had curly
blond hair, soft blue eyes, and a deceptively boyish
appearance. Kyle was an insufferable whiner, but
Benedict could put up with any jerk who paid his
outrageous fee.

Seated behind Benedict was Devon Ross, Kyle's
father, and Devon's trophy wife, a peroxide blonde
who was only slightly older than Kyle. With his heavily veined nose, slightly bloated face, and middle-
age spread, Devon Ross was a preview of what Kyle
would look like in twenty years. Devon was a senior
partner in the Richmond law firm Kyle would join
when he graduated from law school. But Kyle would
never be able to go to law school if he was convicted
of possession and distribution of cocaine.

It had taken the whole morning to pick a jury,
and both sides concluded their opening statements

a little after two. As soon as the opening statements had been made, Judge Gardner told the commonwealth to call its first witness.

"You're on top of this, right?" Kyle asked Benedict nervously.

"Relax," Benedict whispered. "You're going to be fine."

"Because that bitch is lying, and so is that cop."

Benedict restrained himself from smashing Ross in the face. The so-called bitch was an innocent thirteen-year-old girl, and two decorated police officers supported her story.

"The commonwealth calls Anita Lesley, Your Honor," Mary Maguire said. Benedict had met with Maguire a few times to talk about the case. She was high-strung and very insecure, which was not surprising for a new hire handling her first major felony.

During pretrial motions the rail-thin redhead had looked stressed out. She had fidgeted at counsel table, moved files around, tapped her left foot incessantly, and shifted on her chair every few seconds. Maguire argued long after it was clear that the judge was not going to rule the way she wanted him to, and her voice grew strident when an adverse witness did not answer a question the way she had anticipated. Even when she prevailed, Maguire had looked more relieved than happy.

The door to the courtroom opened and a shy, conservatively dressed teenager walked down the aisle to the witness stand. She had wheat-colored hair and pale skin. Benedict noticed that Anita Lesley scrupulously avoided looking at his client and that her hand shook when she took the oath.

"Please tell the jury your age," Maguire said.

The girl's answer was inaudible and the judge told her to speak up.

"I'm thirteen."

"What grade are you in?"

"Eighth."

"Do you have an older brother?"

"Yes, Jerry."

"Where does he go to school?"

"The University of Virginia."

"Is he a classmate of the defendant?"

"Yes, ma'am."

"On the evening of April 7 did your brother have a party at your house?"

"Our folks were out of town and he wasn't supposed to, but he had a bunch of his fraternity brothers over."

"Is the defendant a member of your brother's fraternity?"

"Yes."

"Was the party loud?"

"Yeah, they had the music turned way up and people were yelling."

"Did you come in contact with the defendant during the party?"

"Yes."

"Tell the jurors what happened."

"I knew Kyle," Anita said. She was looking at her lap and her voice quivered. Several of the jurors flashed smiles of encouragement. "He'd been at my house before and he'd always been nice. So I didn't think anything about it when he came over and talked to me."

"What did you talk about?"

"Nothing much. We just talked, you know."

"What happened next?"

"Kyle said it was hot and did I want to go outside. So we went outside and he asked me about school and we walked."

"Where did you end up?"

"On the street where his car was."

"Did he ask you to go into his car?"

"He said he had a surprise for me, a present."

"Where was the present?"

"Kyle said it was in the car."

"Did you get in the car?"

"Well, yeah. I was a little nervous. But he wasn't acting strange or anything and I trusted him because he was my brother's friend."

"What happened in the car?"

"He closed the door. Then he put his arm sort of behind me. Not touching but right above my shoulders."

"Did he say anything to you?"

"Yeah, he told me he always thought I was . . . was hot."

"How did that make you feel?"

Anita shrugged. "Embarrassed, I guess."

"What else did he say?"

"How I was more mature than the stuck-up girls at his school, and smarter. Then he asked me if I wanted my present. I was curious so I said yeah."

"What was the present?"

"He leaned over and kissed me."

"How did that make you feel?"

"A little scared, but I wasn't worried."

"Did you make out?"

Anita turned red. "A little."

Once again, the witness's answer was barely audible. Judge Gardner reminded her to speak up in an uncharacteristically sympathetic tone.

"Did the defendant do anything that made you want to stop making out?" the prosecutor continued.

"Yeah, he started touching me in . . . in places. I asked him to stop. He said he knew I wanted to and I said I didn't."

"What happened then?"

"He got this ziplock bag out of his glove compartment and he said it would loosen me up."

"What was in the bag?"

"Objection," Benedict said. "That would require an expert opinion, Your Honor."

"I'll retract the question," Maguire said before the judge could rule.

"Did the defendant tell you what was in the bag?" Maguire asked.

"No. He just said it would make me feel great."

"What did the material in the bag look like?"

"White powder."

Benedict watched as the jurors turned their attention to his client. None of them looked sympathetic.

"Did you try some?"

"No. I got scared. I said I wanted to go back to the party."

"Did the defendant let you?"

"No. He sort of moved on top of me in my seat, the passenger seat, and he started to . . . to feel me up."

Some of the women on the jury looked upset. Two of the men were frowning.

"What did you do?"

"I tried to push him off and I yelled for him to stop."

"What happened then?"

"There was a knock on the window."

"Who knocked?"

"It was a policeman. He was shining a light into the car. He said to open the door."

"What happened then?"

"Kyle freaked out. He tried to crawl over me to get out on my side. I grabbed the lock and pulled it up."

"Why did you do that?"

"I wanted him off of me."

"What happened then?"

"Kyle scrambled out of the car, but he didn't see the other policeman, and that policeman grabbed him."

"What did you do?"

"Nothing. I was scared, so I just sat there."

"What happened next?"

"After they grabbed Kyle, the first policeman asked me if I was okay. I said yeah. That's when he saw the ziplock bag. He said, 'What have we here?' and I said I didn't know and that I hadn't touched it. Then he told me to get out of the car, and he told me to go away from Kyle."

"What happened between the defendant and the officers?"

"I don't know. I just waited. I was scared and I didn't want anything to do with it."

"Did the officers arrest you?"

"No, they put Kyle in the back of a police car. Then they brought me inside and told everyone they'd had complaints about the noise and everyone should go home."

"No further questions," the prosecutor said.

"Nothing, Your Honor," Benedict said.

Kyle pulled at Benedict's sleeve. "Don't let her off. Cross-examine that lying cunt."

"She's got the jurors on her side, Kyle. If I get on her it will just upset them."

"But she's lying. That was her coke. And I never touched her. I can get any girl I want. Why would I waste time on that scrawny bitch?"

"Keep your cool and remember what you have to do. You're going to be okay," Benedict reassured Ross.

"Call your next witness, Miss Maguire," Judge Gardner said.

Stephen Hurley, the arresting officer, took the stand. He testified that he and his partner had driven to the party because of complaints about the noise. They were walking toward the house when they saw Miss Lesley and the defendant struggling in the front seat of a parked car. Hurley explained how he'd found a ziplock bag containing a white powder in the front seat and had arrested the defendant. Hurley told the jury that the ziplock bag had been turned over to the crime lab for testing.

After Benedict told the court that he had no questions for the witness, Maguire called Justin Wing, a pudgy forensic expert who testified frequently for the commonwealth in drug cases. The prosecutor asked the chemist to list his credentials. Then she picked up an object that had been entered in evidence.

"Officer Wing, I'm handing you Commonwealth Exhibit Six. Do you recognize it?"

"Yes. That's the ziplock bag containing a white powder that was given to me by Officer Hurley."

"Did you find any fingerprints on Exhibit Six?"

"I did."

"To whom did they belong?"

"All of the fingerprints I found on Exhibit Six belonged to the defendant, Kyle Ross."

"Now, Officer, did you test some of the powder in Exhibit Six at the crime lab?"

"I did."

"And what did your tests reveal?"

"I concluded that the substance in the ziplock bag was a controlled substance, cocaine."

"Thank you. I have no further questions for the witness."

"Officer Wing," Benedict said as he crossed the room, "may I please see Exhibit Six?"

The witness handed the bag to Benedict. As soon as he had the bag, Benedict turned his back so that the judge, prosecutor, and witness could not see his hands. When Benedict was halfway to the defense counsel table he dipped his chin a fraction of an inch.

Kyle Ross leaped to his feet. "This is a goddamn frame," he screamed.

Every eye in the courtroom turned toward Ross. The judge banged his gavel and called for order but Kyle kept screaming. Benedict handed the ziplock bag to the bailiff and rushed to his client.

"Stop this, Kyle," Benedict said loudly. He grabbed his client and forced him into his seat. Ross resisted for a moment before dropping onto his chair. Benedict sat beside Kyle and placed a reassuring hand on Kyle's shoulder while he whispered to him. A moment later, Benedict stood.

"Your Honor, may we take a short recess so my client can compose himself?"

Gardner looked at the clock. "It's almost time for the afternoon recess, so let's take a fifteen-minute break."

Gardner sent the jury out. Then the judge cast a stern look at the defense table.

"Tell your client about contempt of court, Mr. Benedict. One more outburst and I'll be the one explaining it to him."

"I'll talk to him, Your Honor," Benedict assured the judge as Gardner stormed off the bench. Benedict conferred with Kyle for a few minutes for appearances' sake. Then he headed up the aisle, out of the courtroom, and down the hall toward the men's room. When he was halfway down the hall, a short, unassuming man passed him going the other way. This man worked for Nikolai Orlansky. Benedict and the short man touched palms. When the short man left the courthouse, a ziplock bag was tucked into his inside jacket pocket.

"Mr. Wing," Benedict said when court reconvened, "you've testified that Officer Hurley gave you Exhibit Six and that you tested the white powder in it and concluded that it was cocaine?"

"That's correct."

Benedict turned to the dais. "Your Honor, I've served a subpoena on the crime lab and I have a person waiting in the hall. I'd like to have her come into the courtroom at this time."

Mary Maguire sprang to her feet. "I object. Mr. Benedict didn't put anyone from the crime lab on his witness list."

"I apologize for not being clear. This person is not a witness. She merely transported some equipment from the lab that I want Officer Wing to use."

Judge Gardner frowned. "Bailiff, take the jury out."

When the jury was in the jury room, Gardner turned to Benedict.

"Have this person come in so we can learn what this is about."

Moments later, Carolyn Bosh walked to the front of the courtroom. She was a forensic expert who was well known to Maguire and the judge.

"Officer Bosh," Benedict asked the forensic expert, "at my request have you brought to court everything Officer Wing would need to test the white powder in Exhibit Six to see if it is cocaine?"

"Yes."

"Your Honor, I'd like Officer Wing to examine what Officer Bosh brought to court and give his opinion on whether he can use these chemicals and paraphernalia to test the white powder in Exhibit Six to see if it is really cocaine."

"Objection," Maguire said.

"What are your grounds?" Gardner asked.

"I . . . he already tested it."

"Out of the presence of the jury, Your Honor," Benedict said. "If the prosecutor really believes that there is cocaine in Exhibit Six she should encourage Officer Wing to confirm his conclusion."

Gardner was quiet for a moment. "I'm going

to allow the retest. This is legitimate cross-examination."

As soon as the jury was back, Benedict began to question the witness.

"Officer Wing, I had some items delivered to you from the crime lab. Is this everything you need to retest Exhibit Six to see if this white powder is cocaine?"

"Yes."

"Then why don't you retest the sample and explain to the jury what you're doing."

Wing turned to the jury. "I'm going to perform what is known as the Croak, or Scott, test."

He showed the jurors a small glass vial containing an amber substance marked DEA-II.

"This vial was prepared by the Drug Enforcement Administration and it contains cocaine hydrochloride, or ninety-nine-percent pure cocaine. Before I test the powder in Exhibit Six I'll test this standard to make sure my reagents are working correctly."

Wing uncorked a small test tube partially filled with red liquid and poured a sample of the standard into it. Then Wing corked the test tube and shook it gently.

"I'm now mixing the standard with cobalt thiocyanate and glycerin, my reagents."

"Ah." Wing smiled as the extract turned a vivid blue. "The change from red to bright blue indicates the possible presence of cocaine, but we're not through yet," Wing said.

"When I add hydrochloric acid to the mixture the solution should turn pink."

When it did, Wing added chloroform and shook the mixture gently. A blue color appeared in the chloroform layer. Wing smiled triumphantly.

"The change of color from red to vivid blue to pink, then back to blue in the chloroform layer, tells us that cocaine is present."

"Why don't we see what happens when you test Exhibit Six?" Benedict suggested.

The bailiff handed Wing the ziplock bag. The forensic expert opened it and used a small stainless steel rod with a flattened end to spoon out a tiny mound of powder from the baggie. Then he uncorked another test tube that was partially filled with reagent and poured the powder into it. He recorked the tube and agitated the contents.

"Something wrong?" Benedict asked when Wing looked blankly at the weak blue color of the mixture. Mary Maguire, the judge, and all of the jurors leaned forward.

"Er, um, the color is a little pale, but . . ."

Wing poured in the acid. The mixture fizzed.

"What's going on, Officer Wing?" Benedict asked.

Wing shook his head and stared dumbfounded at the bubbly mess in the test tube. He added the chloroform but no blue appeared.

"This . . . this shouldn't be happening," Wing stuttered.

"What shouldn't?" Benedict asked.

"It's reacting like baking soda," Wing said in disbelief.

"What!" Maguire shouted.

Gardner rapped his gavel. "Are you saying that the powder in Exhibit Six is not cocaine?" he demanded of the witness.

Wing looked as if a piano had just landed on him. "I swear, Judge. This tested positive for cocaine in the lab."

"Where no one could see the test," Benedict told the jurors. "But when there are witnesses present we get baking soda, don't we, Officer Wing?"

Wing opened his mouth, then shut it quickly.

What Benedict didn't say was that he had memorized everything about Exhibit Six and taken a photo of it with his cell phone when he'd viewed it in the property room. Then he had created a duplicate baggie filled with baking soda, which he'd switched for the real exhibit during Kyle's outburst.

"He did this," Maguire shouted, pointing an accusing finger at Charles Benedict.

"Ridiculous," Benedict protested.

Gardner banged his gavel. "George, take the jurors to the jury room," he told his bailiff.

As soon as the jurors were out of the courtroom, the judge glared at the lawyers.

"Both of you, in my chambers, now! And I want to see Officer Wing, too."

Benedict led his client to the judge's chambers.

Mary Maguire followed with Justin Wing in tow. They found Gardner sitting behind his desk. He did not look happy.

"We're going to get to the bottom of this," the judge said.

"I certainly hope so," Benedict said. "I for one would like to know why Mr. Ross was forced to go through the agony and expense of a trial for possession of baking soda."

The prosecutor turned to the judge. "Justin Wing is as honest as the day is long. If he swore that powder was cocaine, it was cocaine."

"Everyone makes mistakes," Benedict said magnanimously. "I have no idea how or why Officer Wing screwed up, but it's obvious that he did."

"Wing didn't screw up. You had something to do with this," Maguire insisted.

"Enough," Gardner said. "Officer Wing, how do you explain this?"

Wing looked thoroughly befuddled. "I can't, Judge. That powder tested for cocaine in the lab. The only way it could test as baking soda is if it was switched."

"And how was that accomplished?" Gardner asked.

"I have no idea," Wing said. "I put it in our vault after I tested it. Then I brought it to court."

"There was no break in the chain of custody?" Gardner asked.

"I guess someone could have gone into the vault

and switched the cocaine. That's the only thing I can think of."

Gardner looked upset. Maguire looked like she wanted to say something but couldn't think of a thing to say. But Benedict could.

"Judge, I believe it would be appropriate to dismiss the charges against Mr. Ross."

"Miss Maguire?" the judge asked the prosecutor.

"I . . . I'll have to talk to Mrs. Blair. I've never had anything like this happen."

Gardner turned to his bailiff. "George, tell Carrie Blair she's wanted in my chambers ASAP."

Judge Gardner read his mail and signed documents while everyone waited for Carrie Blair. Ten minutes later, Blair was ushered into the judge's chambers and Gardner explained why he had summoned her.

"It's obvious that your case has fallen apart," Gardner concluded. "The question is, what do you intend to do about it? Unless you can suggest something that will keep it afloat, I will entertain a motion to dismiss if Mr. Benedict makes it."

"May I confer with Mary and Officer Wing?" Blair asked.

Gardner nodded and Blair led Maguire and the witness into the hall. She glared at Benedict as she passed him. The defense attorney didn't react. Fifteen minutes later, Blair, Maguire, and Wing reentered the judge's chambers.

"In light of what happened with the retest, my

office has no recourse but to dismiss the case," Blair told Gardner. She looked furious.

"May I assume there will be an investigation conducted to try to discover how this fiasco occurred?" Gardner said. He sounded as upset as Blair.

"Yes. I'll get the ball rolling as soon as I get upstairs." Blair looked at Benedict, who smiled blandly. "And I assure you that the investigation will include a talk with Mr. Benedict."

Chapter Nine

Carrie Blair stormed upstairs, with Mary Maguire and Justin Wing following close behind. As soon as they were in her office, Blair slammed the door.

"What the fuck happened, Justin?"

"Honest, Carrie, I have no idea. Hurley gave me the baggie at the lab. It tested positive for cocaine."

"Could you have made a mistake?" Carrie asked.

"There is no way the powder could have tested for cocaine if it was baking soda. You weren't in court. The powder fizzed."

"So what's your explanation?"

"The only one that makes sense is that someone switched the cocaine for baking soda."

"When could that have happened?"

"It had to have been after I tested it at the lab. Either someone got into the vault or it happened in the courtroom, because I put the baggie in the vault and I took it out of the vault and I had it in my possession until I gave it to the bailiff."

"Tell me everything that happened in court with the ziplock bag," Carrie said to Mary Maguire.

The young prosecutor walked Blair through her examination of Officer Wing and the beginning of Benedict's cross. Then she told her supervisor about Kyle Ross's outburst.

"Wait!" Blair said. "Where was the baggie when Kyle started shouting?"

"Charles Benedict had it."

"Go step by step from the time Benedict got possession of the exhibit."

"He . . . he took it. Then Ross jumped up and . . ." Maguire paused. "I was watching Ross so I don't know what Benedict did. I know he handed the baggie back to the bailiff. I saw him do that. He only had it for a few seconds. Then he calmed down his client."

"What happened after Ross calmed down?"

"Benedict asked the judge for a recess so Ross could compose himself."

"And the judge called a recess?"

"Yeah."

"Where was Benedict during the recess?"

"He . . . he talked to his client. Then . . . I stayed in court and I think . . . yeah, he left the courtroom."

"Fuck!"

Blair grabbed her phone and called the head janitor. "This is Carrie Blair. I'm the head of the narcotics section in the commonwealth attorney's office. I think someone flushed cocaine down one of the toilets in the fifth-floor men's room. Where would the coke go if that happened?"

Blair listened for a few minutes. "Shit!" she swore the moment she hung up.

"You think Benedict switched the dope?" Maguire asked.

"I know he did, but we'll never be able to prove it."

"But how? The bailiff had the baggie, and Benedict only had it for a few seconds."

Blair put her head in her hands. She knew exactly what had happened. She'd seen Benedict pull one of his sleight-of-hand tricks in the bar at the Theodore Roosevelt. She was certain another magician could explain the disappearance of the cocaine and how Benedict had substituted the baking powder.

"Justin, can you look in the toilets and pipes in the men's room and tell if the cocaine was flushed down it?"

"I might be able to find traces if no one used the toilets or sinks after it was flushed but there's probably a lot of traffic in that restroom."

"Get a crew up there. I'll have the janitor close the room."

Wing left and Blair called the janitor again.

"What do you want me to do?" Maguire asked.

"Go home. This isn't your fault."

"But I—"

"Stop. You are not to blame yourself, do you hear? I know who's to blame."

Seconds after Mary Maguire and Justin Wing left her office, Carrie's cell phone rang.

"Yeah," she said distractedly.

"It's me, Charlie."

"You son of a bitch . . ."

"Calm down. I know you're mad, but we have to talk."

"There's nothing to talk about unless you want to confess."

"It's about your prenup."

Carrie froze. "I don't know what you're talking about," she said.

"I know all the details but I don't want to discuss this over the phone. Drive to my condo at eleven tonight. Go down the back alley and park in my garage. I'll leave the garage door up."

"I'm not going to your house."

"Then I'll have to show Horace the DVD."

"What DVD?"

"Tonight, eleven o'clock. Don't be late."

Chapter Ten

Less than an hour after the case of *Commonwealth v. Ross* disappeared, Devon Ross deposited a hefty bonus in an offshore account Charles Benedict kept for income resulting from special illusions such as the magic tricks that had led to the mystifying disappearance of things like Kyle's cocaine and the late Norman Krueger. Benedict celebrated at his favorite restaurant with a fine wine, a foie gras appetizer, and a steak that melted like butter the moment it touched his tongue.

The attorney arrived home a little after ten and parked in his garage, leaving space for Carrie Blair's Porsche. Then he got a DVD from the safe in his bedroom and slipped a snubnose .38 revolver into his pocket. Carrie was rumored to have a bad temper and he wanted to be prepared.

Promptly at eleven, Benedict heard a car drive into his garage. He opened the door that led from the garage to the first floor and pressed a button to close the garage door. Carrie Blair stomped up the stairs and pointed an accusing finger at him.

"You used Kyle Ross's outburst to distract everyone's attention. Then you switched the cocaine for baking soda."

"Whoa," Benedict replied calmly as he held up his hands in a mock defensive gesture. "That's too many negative vibes for such a mellow hour of the evening."

"You think you're so clever. You just had to show off with those sleight-of-hand tricks at the Theodore Roosevelt, knowing I'd remember what you'd done when the coke disappeared. Tomorrow I'm going to find a magician who will show me how you pulled the switch, but right now I'm having the plumbing in the fifth-floor men's room examined, and you know what we're going to find?"

"I would assume feces and urine."

"We'll see how funny you are when I have you perp-walked out of your office with as many TV crews as I can get to film every moment."

"I'm sorry you have such a low opinion of me."

"It was always low, but this stunt . . ."

"There wasn't any stunt, and I don't appreciate being accused of dishonesty. Besides, you and I have more important things to discuss than Kyle Ross. Would you like a drink?"

"No. Now get to the point."

"You have a prenuptial agreement that is supposed to be a secret between you and your hubby. You stand to lose a fortune if you tell anyone about the agreement or if you have an affair before it terminates."

"I don't know what you're talking about."

"Carrie, you told me all about the agreement the evening you stayed here."

"What?"

"You were pretty drunk, so you probably don't remember what you said."

"If such an agreement existed I would have nothing to worry about because I haven't cheated on Horace since we were married."

"Actually, you have. Remember when I told you that nothing happened between us the evening you were here?" Benedict cast down his eyes shyly. "I lied."

"You what!"

"I have a—what do they call them on those celebrity news shows?—a sex tape. It shows a naked Carrie Blair in several intimate positions on my bed. It's pretty risqué."

"You drugged me!"

"Of course not. You were horny, we felt a connection." Benedict shrugged. "These things happen between soul mates."

"You bastard," Carrie said as she fought to keep from panicking. "You gave me a date-rape drug."

"That would be illegal."

"That's why I don't remember what happened. They cause amnesia."

Carrie was filled with rage but she forced herself to stay calm.

"Assuming you actually have this DVD," she said, "what do you want for it?"

"Two hundred and fifty thousand dollars should do it."

"Are you crazy?"

Benedict's features hardened. "Don't fuck with me, Carrie. You told me exactly how much money you've salted away during your marriage. And you're going to be a very rich woman when the prenup terminates. A quarter of a million dollars will be chump change then. Get cheap with me and I'll sell Horace the DVD. Then you'll be out in the cold without a penny. Just be thankful that I'm not greedy."

Carrie felt sick. "Let me see it," she said.

"Have a seat," Benedict said, pointing to a couch that faced a forty-six-inch TV. He turned on the set, inserted the DVD, and pressed PLAY. There was no sound track. On the screen, Carrie Blair was being embraced by a man. The man's face was hidden but Carrie's face was easy to make out, as was the fact that she was naked. Carrie's fists knotted. The son of a bitch had set her up; he'd drugged her and raped her and now he wanted her to pay for the privilege.

On the screen, the man kissed Blair and lowered her to the bed. She fell back and the man mounted her.

"It goes on like this for a while," Benedict said. "Then we do it doggie style, and there's a little oral sex thrown in. Shall I pause the entertainment?"

Carrie showed no emotion. Benedict stood up and crossed to the TV. When he turned his back and bent over to eject the DVD, Carrie grabbed a vase and rushed at him. Benedict stood and threw up a hand. The vase crashed against his forearm. Benedict jumped back and fell against the TV. Carrie flew at him and stabbed at his face with a shard. As he spun away, Benedict pulled the .38 out of his pocket. Carrie was so intent on stabbing Benedict that she didn't see the gun. They crashed together and there was an explosion. Carrie's eyes went wide and she stopped her assault. Benedict jumped away from her. Carrie stared at her stomach. Blood was spreading across the inside of her blouse, dying the white fabric red. She stumbled backward and slipped to the floor.

"I'm shot," she gasped. "You shot me in the stomach."

Benedict had killed people but not in his apartment. He stared at the blood and was suddenly afraid. Blood had DNA in it, and DNA would tell the crime lab that Carrie Blair had been bleeding on his floor.

Benedict rushed into the bathroom and grabbed a thick towel. He gave it to Carrie and told her to hold it against the wound. He wanted her to think that he was helping her stop the bleeding, and he was, but not to save her life. He just didn't want any of her blood in his apartment.

"Get me to a hospital," she wheezed as she struggled for air.

Benedict's mind was swirling. If he took Carrie to the hospital there would be an investigation. What would she say? The sex tape would come out. She would accuse him of blackmail, and he'd shot her with his gun.

Did Carrie tell anyone she was coming here? Fear flooded him. By now, everyone at the courthouse would have heard about the disappearing coke and how angry Carrie was at him. He'd told her to tell no one she was visiting him, but did she tell anyone? Twenty million dollars was at stake, so she had probably kept her mouth shut, but Carrie was unpredictable. Her attack was proof of that.

And there was the Porsche in his garage. What if a neighbor saw her drive in? He had to get rid of the Porsche.

Benedict forced himself to calm down. Carrie moaned pitifully. It took all of his willpower to tune her out and focus on his problem. Suddenly an idea occurred to Benedict and a bizarre plan formed in his mind. It might not work. He didn't have time to think it through now. He would figure out if it made sense after he'd given the idea an objective, unemotional analysis, but there were some things he would have to do now if it was going to work.

"Please, Charlie, I'm dying," Carrie managed. "Take me to the hospital. I won't tell what happened."

"I'm so sorry. I'm going to help you."

"Thank you."

Benedict looked around until he spotted Carrie's purse. It was lying on the couch. He opened it and found the key to her Porsche and a ring that held many more keys. Benedict dangled the key ring in front of Carrie's eyes.

"Which key opens your front door?"

"What?" Carrie asked dully. She was having trouble focusing.

"We're going to the hospital, but you have to tell me what key opens your front door so I can help you."

Carrie stared at Benedict. He wasn't making sense, but she was also finding it hard to think clearly. She pointed to her house key.

"Are any of these other keys for a car Horace drives?"

"Jesus, it hurts."

"Focus, Carrie. Are any of these keys for a car Horace drives?"

Carrie started to gag but she forced herself to point to a key.

"What car is this key for?" Benedict asked.

"Bentley," she gasped.

"Good girl. Now let's take care of you."

Benedict picked up the wounded prosecutor. She was heavy, and it was a struggle to get her down the steps to the garage. He opened the Porsche's trunk and dropped her in it.

"Oh, God!" Carrie shouted.

Benedict grabbed the towel, rolled it in a ball so that Carrie's blood was on the inside, slammed the lid of the trunk, and raced upstairs. As he climbed the stairs he could hear Carrie pounding on the inside of the trunk. It was unnerving, but Benedict forced himself to ignore the sound. The farther he got from the garage, the more distant the thump-thump-thump became until the sound disappeared completely by the time he entered his kitchen.

Benedict found a Tupperware container and put the rolled-up towel in it. He sealed the lid, opened the freezer, and stashed the container in the back of the compartment. Then he grabbed some ice cubes and closed the freezer. His heart was racing. He dropped the ice cubes into a glass and fixed a stiff drink. He pressed the cold glass to his forehead and took deep breaths until he was calm. As he relaxed, Benedict remembered how Carrie's naked body had looked when he maneuvered her so the sex would look real in the DVD.

"What a waste," he thought as he surveyed his living room. He'd have to clean up the pieces of the broken vase. He didn't see any blood, but there might be hair or fibers on the couch where Blair had sat when she viewed the DVD. He'd have to do something about that. His Dustbuster came to mind.

The alcohol he was drinking started to have the desired effect. When Benedict was calmer he began to fine-tune his plan. It was no secret that the Blairs' marriage was on the rocks. He wondered how many people at the Rankin, Lusk cocktail party had seen them argue. But many married couples argue without resorting to murder to settle their differences. What made the Blairs' situation different was their prenup. Had Carrie lasted until the end of this week, it would have cost Horace Blair twenty million dollars, and twenty million dollars was an excellent motive for murder. While Carrie was bleeding out in his living room it had occurred to Benedict that no one would suspect him of killing Carrie if Horace Blair was sent to prison for murdering his wife.

Charlie was very good at developing his own magic tricks. Plotting Horace Blair's downfall was a lot like storyboarding a large illusion, like the one David Copperfield had created when he made the Statue of Liberty disappear. Benedict got a legal pad from his home office and started writing an outline. He'd have to get rid of the body, and he'd have to leave clues in the grave that would point to Blair. One clue would be the bullet that killed Blair's wife. It would be found during an autopsy.

Of course the police would need the murder weapon to make the match, and they would have to find it where it would implicate Blair. That's why he'd asked Carrie about the key to Horace's Bentley.

Working on his illusion relaxed Benedict, and he was totally calm by the time it was complete. He had a good idea of where to bury Carrie. He'd had a brainstorm about a clue he could leave in the grave shortly after he'd given her the towel to stop the bleeding. Making this part of the plan work would be tricky, but tricks were a magician's stock-in-trade. He checked his watch. It was only one a.m.—

hard to believe that so little time had passed since he'd shot Blair.

Benedict reviewed his notes. He would have to wait until the stores in the mall opened in the morning before he could start to create his illusion. Benedict took a deep breath. He felt in control of the situation. He would sweep up the shards from the vase, use the Dustbuster to vacuum the hairs from the couch, and then get a good night's sleep.

An hour later, when his head touched his pillow, Charles Benedict slept like a baby.

Chapter Eleven

Horace Blair had a full head of snowy-white hair, weighed only seven pounds more than he'd weighed in college, and looked ten years younger than seventy-four, thanks to upgrades to his facial features by the finest plastic surgeons.

Blair's massive home, modeled after the mansion of a British earl, was the centerpiece of a magnificent estate whose rolling lawns and well-tended woods were enclosed behind a high stone wall. The mansion's wide terraces overlooked an Olympic-size swimming pool, tennis courts, and a man-made lake.

When he was home, Horace woke up at five every morning except Sunday and swam a mile in the indoor lap pool. After finishing his swim, he would shower, slip on a terry-cloth robe, then seat himself in a glassed-in kitchen nook. The nook looked out on a splendid garden that was pleasing to the eye even in foul weather, thanks to the efforts of an army of gardeners.

Each morning, Blair's personal chef would set the

table in the nook with a glass of freshly squeezed orange juice, half a grapefruit, a freshly baked croissant, and a cup of coffee brewed from a blend that was specially prepared for the master of the house. Stacked beside the food would be several newspapers including the *Wall Street Journal*, the *Washington Post*, and the *New York Times*. After breakfast, Horace would drive his Bentley to the Blair Building, where he would oversee his international business empire. Blair employed a chauffeur but enjoyed driving too much to use his services unless he needed to work on the way to the office.

Horace's morning routine usually soothed him, but Wednesday morning it had done nothing to alleviate the tension that had robbed him of a good night's sleep. On Thursday his prenuptial agreement with his wife would terminate and he would have to pay her twenty million dollars. Blair could afford the money. He made that much in interest every week. What galled him was not getting his money's worth from his loveless marriage.

In business, Horace Blair never acted rashly, but his personal life had been one series of blunders after another, and his marriage to Carrie Trask may have been his most foolish and impulsive mistake.

Ten years ago, Horace entertained a group of Japanese businessmen at his country club. Despite being tipsy, he had driven home in one of his prized possessions, a bright-yellow Diablo 6.0 Lamborghini with a top speed of 200 miles an hour. The alcohol he had imbibed had affected his judgment and he was cruising along at 120 miles an hour when a policeman pulled him over and cited him for driving under the influence and reckless driving.

Horace Blair never caved without a fight, and he'd hired Bobby Schatz, Washington, D.C.'s top criminal defense attorney, to represent him. When Horace Blair walked into Judge Hugo Diaz's courtroom in Lee County, Virginia, he had been prepared to do anything, including lie, to win his case. When he left the courtroom he was floating on air, and it wasn't because Judge Diaz had been so impressed by his honesty that he had imposed the least serious sentence possible after Horace changed his plea to guilty in the middle of the prosecutor's cross-examination.

Horace had shed his third wife eight months before in a bloodless coup. He'd grown tired of her and he wasn't sorry to see her go, but even though he was sixty-three, he was still vigorous and in need of female companionship. Carrie Trask, the prosecuting attorney, was a goddess. She had sleek blond hair, translucent gray-green eyes, high, sculpted cheekbones, and a smile that could light up a city. Once he saw her, Horace Blair knew he had to possess her, and what better way to make an impression than to help her win her case?

Blair was unconcerned about the consequences of a conviction. His lawyer had explained that there would be no jail time for a first offense, any fine would be a fly speck on his bank balance, and he had a chauffeur who would drive for him if the state took his license. Yes, there would be a conviction on his record, but that was a small sacrifice to make for love.

Taking the stand had given Blair a chance to talk to Carrie, though he had to admit that that was the weirdest first date he'd ever been on. Still, he'd seen the confusion on Carrie's face when he'd opened his heart to her and told her that her opening statement had made him realize how dangerous his actions had been. Then he had looked deep into Carrie's eyes and told her that he would not play games and was ready to pay the price for his actions. Carrie had not been able to hide her surprise at this unexpected turn of events, and Blair had been thrilled by what he perceived to be a successful first step in his campaign to win the prosecutor's heart.

Blair had waited to ask Carrie out until after he fulfilled the conditions of his probation and paid his fine. He wanted Carrie to see he was serious about being a good citizen and a good person. Carrie had turned him down the first time he had asked her to dinner, but he pursued the young prosecutor with a vengeance and finally wore her down. It proved a Pyrrhic victory.

Everyone but Horace knew that he had been foolish to marry Carrie. The age difference was too great; and it was obvious that Carrie didn't love him, and equally obvious that she was wedded to her career more than she was to him.

Horace had been married several times before. Those wives had been members of his country club set. They cooked for him, they went to social functions with him, and they kept his bed warm when he wanted sex. None of them worked. None of them wanted to work. Horace wanted a wife who would be there for him when he needed her. He realized his mistake in marrying Carrie when it dawned on him that she was rarely going to be where he wanted her to be if she was involved in a case. And she was always involved in a case.

It wasn't as if Horace hadn't been warned. Carrie had told him what was in store for him on the evening he proposed. But Horace was besotted, and he'd convinced himself that he could bring Carrie around. He had tried to convince Carrie to leave the commonwealth attorney's office. He had explained that there was no reason for her to put in long hours at a government job when he was so wealthy that she could do anything else she wanted to do. But prosecuting criminals was the only thing Carrie wanted to do.

On Wednesday morning, Blair sipped his juice and tried to enjoy the view, but he could not relax because thoughts of the prenup kept intruding. It had been Jack Pratt's idea. At first, Horace had rejected his corporate lawyer's suggestion, but he caved when Pratt reminded him that his first wife had taken him to the cleaners because he did not have a prenuptial agreement and that his prenups with numbers two and three had saved him.

If Horace thought that Carrie would sign the prenup without a fight she quickly disabused him of this idea. Carrie was not like his other wives. She had graduated near the top of her class at Georgetown's law school and was just as smart as Pratt. She had agreed to sign the prenup only if it included a guarantee that she would receive twenty million dollars at the end of the first ten years of their marriage if she did not divorce Horace or sleep with another man. Horace had agreed but had added the condition that she would lose everything if she revealed the details of the agreement.

Horace was trying to distract himself from thinking about the prenup by reading a business article when his houseman interrupted him.

"There's a detective at the front door who wishes to speak to you."

Blair frowned. "What does he want?"

"It's a woman, a Detective Stephanie Robb. She says it's about Mrs. Blair."

"What about Carrie?"

"She wouldn't tell me."

"Very well. Show her in."

Everything about Stephanie Robb was square and thick. Her short-cut dirty-blond hair framed her face in a cube shape. Her body had no waist and was short, muscular, and squat like a power lifter's.

The butt of the detective's gun peeked out of the brown jacket she wore over a white blouse. A brown skirt and comfortable brown shoes completed the ensemble.

"Thanks for seeing me, Mr. Blair," Robb said as she held out her ID so Blair could inspect it.

"My houseman said this concerns my wife."

"Yes, sir," Robb said.

"What about Carrie?"

"We want to know where she is," Robb said.

"I don't understand."

"No one has seen Mrs. Blair since Monday afternoon."

"She hasn't been at work?"

"No, sir."

Blair's brow furrowed. "That's strange. If there's one thing I know about my wife, it's that she's completely dedicated to her job."

"That's why we're worried. She's missed several court appearances, and she has an important trial coming up. But no one knows where she is."

"She didn't call in?" Blair asked.

"No, sir."

"I'm fairly certain she isn't here."

Now it was Robb's turn to furrow her brow. "You don't know?"

"Carrie and I don't see much of each other," he said brusquely. "This is a big house. She has her rooms and I have mine."

"Could you have someone check to see if Mrs. Blair is home?"

"Certainly."

Blair signaled for the houseman.

"Walter, when is the last time you remember seeing Mrs. Blair?"

"She was here Sunday for dinner but Monday was my day off. I visited my mother in New Jersey and I left here Sunday night and caught a late flight. I didn't see her on Tuesday."

"Can you please check Carrie's rooms, and see if her cars are in the garage."

As soon as the houseman left, Robb asked if Blair had seen his wife on Monday.

"No. I saw her last Thursday. Then I was in New York on business until Monday morning. If she came home Monday I didn't see her."

"Does Mrs. Blair have friends she may be visiting?"

"Carrie has never been very sociable. The friends I know about all work with her. I do have a question, though."

"Yes?"

"Why did the commonwealth attorney send a detective to check on Carrie instead of a patrol officer? Isn't that unusual?"

"Yes, sir, it is, but the circumstances warrant a broad inquiry. Your wife has prosecuted some very dangerous people."

"You think harm may have come to her?" asked Blair.

"We have no evidence to support that conclusion. Quite honestly, we're stumped."

The houseman reentered the kitchen. "Mrs. Blair's Porsche is not in the garage, and her bed doesn't appear to have been slept in."

"Thank you, Walter," Blair said to the houseman. "This is very upsetting," he told Robb.

"Can you describe Mrs. Blair's Porsche?"

Horace described the car and gave the detective the license plate number.

"Please keep me up to date on your investigation," Blair said.

"I'll definitely keep you in the loop. And you let me know if she gets in touch."

The detective handed Blair her card and left. Blair stared at it. Robb was with homicide. She had not told him that, probably because she didn't want to worry him. And Horace was worried. He and Carrie may have fallen out of love, but he had been in love with her once upon a time. The marriage had withered, and Horace was bitter because of the prenuptial agreement, but he didn't hate Carrie, and he hoped that nothing serious had happened to her.

Chapter Twelve

As soon as he arrived at his office Horace Blair plunged into a meeting to discuss plans to merge one of his companies with a British telecom company. The issues were complex, and Carrie and the prenup were soon forgotten. By the time the meeting adjourned, at nine in the evening, Horace was exhausted and could not wait to get into bed. As he pulled his Bentley into his four-car garage, Blair was surprised to see a strange car parked near his front door.

When Blair entered the house, Walter was waiting for him.

"Has Mrs. Blair come home?" Horace asked his houseman.

"No, sir, and she hasn't called."

"Then whose car is that?"

"It belongs to a Mr. Charles Benedict. Normally I wouldn't have let him wait, but he said it concerned Mrs. Blair."

"What about her?"

"He wouldn't give me any specifics."

"Very well, Walter. Where did you put him?"

"In the library."

Blair walked down a hall that led to the back of the mansion and entered a room lined with bookshelves. Charles Benedict was sitting in front of a fire Walter had laid for him, reading a biography of Harry Houdini. He stood when his host walked in.

"Mr. Blair, I'm Charles Benedict. I apologize for intruding but I'm in possession of information that will save you millions of dollars."

"If you're selling something, stop right now."

"This concerns your prenuptial agreement with your wife. I know it terminates tomorrow and I know you'll have to pay Carrie twenty million dollars—two million for every year she's been married to you—if she's remained faithful."

Blair flushed with anger. "How do you know the details of our agreement?"

"Carrie told me after we'd slept together."

"What!"

"I'm an attorney, Mr. Blair. My specialty is criminal defense. Your wife and I have tried cases against each other. One evening, we met in her office after one of our trials recessed." Benedict shrugged. "One thing led to another and we made love. After that, we started meeting regularly."

"Can you prove any of this?"

"Oh, yes. Take me to your front door. I have something to show you."

"My front door?"

"You'll understand in a minute."

Blair was about to say something. Then he changed his mind and led the way to the front hall. The lawyer opened the front door.

"Please give me your front-door key."

Blair looked confused, but he fished his keys out of his pocket and took the front-door key off of his key chain.

"I'm going to step outside and close the door. When I'm outside, check the door to make sure it's locked."

Benedict stepped outside and closed the door. Horace tested the door to make sure it was locked. Moments later, Benedict opened the locked door.

"What does this prove?" Blair asked.

Benedict handed Blair the key he held in his hand.

"Most of the time, Carrie came to my condo when we made love," Benedict said as Horace put the key back on his key chain, "but she was into risk and we made love here on several occasions when you were away. I would wait until she called me and I'd drive over. Carrie gave me this."

Benedict took a key out of his pocket that was identical to the key Blair had given him. He opened the front door again.

"Make sure it's locked," Benedict instructed before he stepped outside and shut the door. Moments later, he reentered the front hall.

"This is your proof?" Blair asked. "No court will rule that Carrie violated the prenup because you have a key to my front door."

Benedict removed an envelope from his inside jacket pocket.

"I also have a DVD showing Carrie and me making love. Would you like to see it?"

Blair's shoulders sagged and he suddenly looked his age. His marriage to Carrie had disintegrated but he was still shocked that he had never suspected that she was cheating on him.

"How much do you want, Mr. Benedict?"

The lawyer looked confused. Then he looked offended.

"You think I came here to ask for money?"

"Well, I . . . naturally."

"No, no, I should have made myself clear from the start. I was in love with Carrie, and I thought she cared for me. She told me she had to stay with you because of the prenup, but she swore she loved me and would marry me when she got your money and could divorce. Then she dumped me."

Benedict looked down. "She said she'd found someone else. She said she was bored with me. I couldn't believe how callous she was. She'd been using me all along, Mr. Blair, the same way she used you.

"No, Mr. Blair, I don't want money, I want her to pay for the way she treated me. Carrie took advantage of both of us and I want to see her suffer the way she's made me suffer."

Benedict held out the sex tape. "This DVD is my gift to you. Make good use of it."

Benedict and Blair shared a drink and talked for another half hour. As soon as the lawyer left, Horace phoned Jack Pratt, his attorney at Rankin, Lusk, and told him to come to his estate. It was late, and senior partners at Rankin, Lusk rarely made house calls, but Horace had been one of Pratt's best clients for years.

As soon as Walter showed Pratt into the library, Horace motioned the lawyer toward the armchair Charles Benedict had recently vacated and handed him a glass of the aged single-malt scotch the attorney favored.

It would be difficult to guess that Jack Pratt was in his mid-sixties. He worked out every day in the firm's gym with a personal trainer. His suits, which were hand-tailored in London, fit like the proverbial glove, his teeth gleamed, and not a strand of his sleek, expertly dyed black hair was out of place. Pratt had cultivated manners that would have met with approval in the home of a British royal, and even though he was ruthless in legal matters his adversaries rarely disliked him.

"I've received some very upsetting news, Jack."

Blair, who was not given to emotional displays, was visibly upset.

"What happened?" Pratt asked.

"Carrie has disappeared."

"What do you mean?"

"Exactly what I said. This morning, I received a visit from a Lee County homicide detective. No one has seen Carrie since Monday afternoon. She hasn't come home or to her job, and no one knows where she is."

"You said a homicide detective. Do they think she's been murdered?"

"They don't know. She's just disappeared."

Pratt frowned. "This can't be good, Horace. Carrie has every reason to be here this week."

"Yes, she does, and the prenup is the reason I called you. I had a visitor this evening. Do you know a lawyer named Charles Benedict?"

"I don't know him, but I've heard of him."

"What's his reputation like?" Blair asked.

"I really don't know. He practices criminal law, so we don't run in the same circles. Do you want me to check him out?"

Blair nodded. Suddenly Pratt smiled.

"What's so funny?" Horace asked.

"I just remembered. Benedict is an amateur magician. I saw him perform at a Virginia Bar Association awards dinner a few years ago. He did card tricks, and he was pretty good."

"There's nothing funny about what happened tonight. Benedict knows about the prenup."

Pratt stopped smiling. "How did he find out?"

"Carrie told him after they . . ." Horace flushed. "He was screwing her, Jack. She cheated on me, and Benedict isn't her only lover." Horace held up the DVD. "He gave me this. It's a recording of them . . . doing it. I want you to take it and put it somewhere safe. I don't know why she's gone missing but she's going to show up again to demand her money."

Blair paused. Pratt could see that he was furious. "She is not to get one penny, Jack. Not one red cent."

Chapter Thirteen

Vancouver, British Columbia, was a symphony of towering snowcapped mountains and picturesque bays that made its setting one of the most beautiful in North America. On Tuesday, Dana phoned Margo Laurent from Seattle before driving there, but the call went to voice mail. She phoned again after she checked into her hotel in Vancouver, with the same result.

On Wednesday morning, Dana caught the 6:00 a.m. ferry to Victoria. One and a half hours later, the ferry docked in Swartz Bay. She drove south until she arrived at the Empress, a massive, elegant Edwardian-style hotel that would have been at home in England. The glass-and-steel building where Dana was headed was only a few blocks from the Empress, but centuries away architecturally.

Dana walked through the revolving door into a thoroughly modern lobby at five to nine. A security guard and a desk clerk examined her closely.

"Will you please tell 515 that Dana Cutler is here?"

Five minutes later, the doors of Dana's elevator

car opened into a living room that was almost as big as Jake's house. The blond giant who had followed her from Rene Marchand's office was waiting for her. He was wearing Nike trainers, pressed jeans, a black turtleneck, and a shoulder rig. The butt of a .45 automatic protruded from the holster attached to the rig. Behind the bodyguard, through floor-to-ceiling windows, Dana saw a seaplane landing in the Inner Harbor.

"The countess is ready for you," the blond said in German-accented English. He reminded Dana of the Nazis in World War II movies. She was tempted to ask him if he was just following orders when he tailed her in Seattle, but she tamped down the desire to crack wise.

The Aryan turned his back to her and walked to the far end of the living room, where a stunning blonde was seated. The countess had high cheekbones and iridescent blue eyes and looked to be an inch or so taller than the detective. She was dressed in a black-and-red body-hugging, floor-length, high-necked silk cheongsam decorated with flowers and dragons that made her look like a madam in a Shanghai brothel.

"I am Countess Carla Von Asch, Miss Cutler. Please sit down. Can Kurt get you something to drink?"

Once again, Dana heard a German accent.

"I'm good," Dana said as she sat in a comfortable armchair opposite the countess. "Let's discuss the scepter? Do you have it?"

"If we can agree on a price I will be able to secure it for your client."

"So you don't have it?"

The countess smiled. "Let's leave any discussion of the location or ownership of the Ottoman Scepter until you can assure me that your principal is willing to pay for it."

"Okay. What's your price?"

"Ten million dollars."

It took all of Dana's self-control to keep from reacting. "I'll tell my client. How can I get in touch with you?"

"I will be here on Friday morning. Let's agree to meet at the same time."

"What if my client isn't willing to pay that much? Do you have a cell phone or e-mail?"

The countess smiled. "This is not a negotiation. If your client wishes to meet my price you will be here on Friday morning and we will work out the details of the sale. If you are not here I will know your client has declined."

The bodyguard escorted Dana to the elevator. On the way down, the private investigator was overcome once more with a feeling that something was not right. As soon as the doors opened, Dana walked over to the desk clerk, who was manning the desk by himself.

"This is some place," she said, smiling.

He nodded but didn't say anything.

"What does one of these condos go for?"

"You'll have to talk to the rental agent. I don't have that information."

"Yeah, good. Can you give me the agent's name and number?"

The clerk handed Dana a card.

"I was just in 515. Does the countess own that or is she just renting?"

"I can't tell you that information."

Dana had anticipated this type of response. She placed her palm on the counter and pulled her hand away, revealing four fifty-dollar bills.

"Are you sure you can't help me?"

The clerk eyed the bills greedily. Then he looked down the hall across from his station, on the alert for the security guard. When he was certain they wouldn't be disturbed he leaned toward Dana and whispered, "The woman and a blond guy checked into the condo yesterday, but she doesn't own it."

"Who does?"

"Horace Blair."

Dana had never heard of Horace Blair.

"Thanks," she said. "One more thing." She slid another fifty onto the pile. "What car is the woman in 515 driving? A license number would be great if you have it."

Dana staked out the condo's garage. Ferries left for Vancouver every hour. If the countess was headed back to the mainland she would be leaving soon.

Two hours later, a Volvo that had seen better days drove out of the garage with the countess at the wheel and the bodyguard in the passenger seat. The arrangement struck Dana as odd, and the car was not of the sort she was expecting a countess to own.

Dana let several cars get between them. She followed the Volvo to Swartz Bay and drove onto the ferry just as the countess and her companion were getting out of their car to go to an upper deck. The bodyguard was still dressed in jeans and a turtleneck, but he wasn't packing. The countess had pulled her hair back into a ponytail and was wearing jeans and a green cable-knit sweater.

Dana decided to stay in her car during the trip to Vancouver. She didn't want to risk being seen. While she waited, she reviewed everything that had happened in the past few days, starting with her meeting with Margo Laurent. What was her first impression of her client? She remembered thinking of her as a French femme fatale, a character out of some old mystery novel. Dana frowned. Now that she thought about it, every person she'd dealt with was like a character out of some old mystery novel. Professor Pickering was an oddball who lived in an eerie mansion on a spooky island. Captain Leone had reminded her of a pirate captain. And there was definitely something odd about Rene Marchand. A high-end antiques dealer would want to impress wealthy clients. Marchand's office looked as if it had been thrown together hastily. It didn't even have a phone, and she didn't remember seeing a computer. Finally, there was Countess Von Asch with her slinky Chinese dress and Teutonic bodyguard.

But most of all, there was the case itself. In real life, private detectives were not tasked with finding golden scepters belonging to Ottoman sultans. Was it possible that none of this was real? When she thought about it, her adventures were like something out of a 1940s pulp magazine, or . . . Dana's jaw dropped. It was like that old movie that Jake loved. They'd watched it on the Turner Classic Movies channel during an evening devoted to Humphrey Bogart. What was it called? *The Maltese Falcon!* That was it. This case was exactly like that movie.

But someone had tried to murder Otto Pickering, and the money was real. Margo Laurent had given her twenty-five thousand American dollars and a first-class ticket to Seattle. If it wasn't so she could find the Ottoman Scepter, what was it for? Still, the whole setup didn't feel right. When they docked, Dana planned to follow the countess. Maybe she would see something that would help her make sense of the Case of the Ottoman Scepter.

Chapter Fourteen

Shortly after the ferry docked, Dana was driving south on I-5 toward Seattle, a few car lengths behind the Volvo. Several hours later, the Volvo got off the interstate at the Mercer Street exit and Dana followed it up Queen Anne Hill until the Volvo pulled into a parking space in front of a tavern. Dana cruised by and saw the countess and her bodyguard walk into the tavern. Then she found a parking space a block away that gave her a clear view of the tavern's front door.

While she waited, Dana got her laptop and searched the Internet for Countess Carla Von Asch. She came up blank. She also drew a blank with Margo Laurent, Otto Pickering, and Rene Marchand. Then she tried Horace Blair, and got several thousand hits.

It didn't take long for Dana to learn that Horace Blair was the multimillionaire head of a conglomerate with tentacles in shipping, scrap metal, real estate, and other lucrative enterprises, but nothing she learned helped her understand why Margo Laurent, or whoever she was, had sent her across a continent in search of a golden scepter.

Was the scepter even real? Dana hadn't questioned its existence until now. It didn't take her long to confirm a part of the story Margo Laurent had told her. Mehmet II had given a gold, jewel-encrusted scepter to Gennadius after bringing him to Constantinople on a horse from the imperial stable that was outfitted with a silver saddle. But she could find no further reference to the scepter.

Dana looked up to make sure the countess and her bodyguard weren't leaving the tavern. After watching the door for a few minutes, Dana got another idea. She typed in Isla de Muerta and brought up a website run by the island's chamber of commerce. The Stanton's B&B was recommended as a place for tourists to stay and she learned that sport fishing trips and nature hikes were among the island's draws.

Dana clicked on a section that gave a history of the island and learned that it had indeed gotten its name from the men who'd died on the ships that had wrecked on the rocks surrounding it. She was about to leave the history section, but she paused when she saw a paragraph mentioning famous people who had vacationed on Isla de Muerta. Horace Blair owned one of the summer homes on the island. Dana bet she knew which one. This was the second time Horace Blair's name had come up. What did he have to do with a golden scepter?

Dana was about to research the millionaire in more depth when Otto Pickering walked into the tavern. Pickering had told her that he didn't know who owned the scepter, so this was either an amazing coincidence or Pickering had lied to her.

Dana got out of her car and headed for the tavern. When she walked inside she saw the bodyguard and the countess seated at a table talking to Professor Pickering and Rene Marchand. The bodyguard said something that made the others laugh. Dana was willing to bet that the joke involved her.

"Hey, guys," Dana said as she walked toward them, "I'm looking for the Maltese Falcon and the Treasure of the Sierra Madre. Do any of you know where I can find them?"

Heads swung toward her, and Rene Marchand said, "Uh-oh."

Dana pulled a chair over to the table and sat down.

"So, who are you really?"

They looked at one another, unsure of what to do. Then the bodyguard shrugged.

"I guess the cat is out of the bag."

Dana heard a bit of the South where his Teutonic accent had been.

Otto Pickering held out a handbill that announced that the Queen Anne Players appeared Fridays and Sundays in LaRosa Restaurant's Interactive Comedy Mystery Dinner Theater.

"You're actors?" Dana said, not really surprised.

"Part time," Pickering said.

"Am I safe in guessing that none of you are who you said you were?"

The professor held out his hand. "Ralph Finegold, at your service. I teach chemistry at the university."

"Patty Weiss," said the countess without any trace of a German accent. "I'm a student."

"George O'Leary, accountant," the bodyguard said.

"And I'm Marty Draper," said the antiques dealer. "I own an art gallery, and I do sell antiques through it."

"And who is Margo Laurent?" Dana asked.

"Ah," said Ralph Finegold. "That we can't tell you."

"Can't or won't?" Dana asked.

"Can't. We have no idea who she is," Patty said.

"We got a call on the Queen Anne Players' answering machine, last Thursday," Ralph said. "The woman had a French accent and she said she was willing to pay twenty thousand dollars and expenses if we would role-play a mystery. That definitely got our attention.

"I called her back and she said she wanted to play a practical joke on a friend who was a real private eye. She said that two of us would have to go to Isla de Muerta. One of us would wait in a summer home for you and the other person would wait outside and shoot into the house. George and I went up and

Captain Leone took us across. He runs the only taxi service to the island."

"So he's for real?" Dana said.

"Yeah," George laughed. "You couldn't invent a character like that."

"The Stantons were in on the prank, too," Ralph said. "Mr. Stanton unlocked the house where we met and hid George after he shot at you."

"That was pretty stupid," Dana said to O'Leary. "You could have hurt one of us and I would have shot you for real if I'd caught up with you."

George shook his head. "You were never in danger. I was in the army and I'm a very good shot. If you examined the bullet holes, you would have seen that they were very high and very wide.

"I also had the distances worked out and I left my car engine running. I was pretty sure you wouldn't just charge out, and I was pretty certain you wouldn't get to me before I drove off."

Dana didn't challenge him. The incident was in the past and there was no way to know what would have happened if she'd reacted a little quicker.

"What was the point of the joke?" Dana asked, still mystified.

"We don't know," Marty answered. "We were just told to run you around until Friday. Then we wouldn't have to do anything else."

"Why Friday?" Dana asked.

"Laurent didn't say," Ralph answered.

"How did you choose your characters?" Dana asked.

"Laurent sent us a scenario with a sketch of every character and what we were supposed to do," Marty said. "The condo in Victoria and the house on the island were arranged in advance. I had to find an office to rent and I had to get the stenciling put on the door. Otherwise, we just played our parts."

"And you did a good job," Dana admitted.

"Not good enough," Patty said ruefully. "How did you figure it out?"

"You may be phony mystery characters but I'm a real live private eye. Though I do have to admit you had me going for a while. Then I realized that the plot and your characters were right out of a potboiler. So I tailed you and George here from the condo in Victoria."

"Do you have any idea who Laurent is or why she's playing a practical joke on you?" Ralph asked.

"I haven't a clue. I live outside of Washington, D.C. Laurent—or whoever she is—met me at a D.C. restaurant and told me she'd pay me twenty-five grand plus expenses to recover this Ottoman Scepter."

Ralph whistled. "You got twenty-five grand and expenses and we got twenty and expenses. That's an expensive joke."

"Exactly what I've been thinking, but I may have dug up a clue as to the person behind it. The house on the island and the condo in Victoria are both owned by Horace Blair, and Blair is a multimillionaire. Do any of you know him?"

"I do," Marty Draper said.

"How?" Dana asked.

"I haven't seen the Blairs in a while, but I've sold them art for their home on Isla de Muerta. His wife, Carrie, has been in the gallery a few times."

"This makes no sense," Dana said.

"Do you think Horace has it in for you? Was he involved in some case you worked on?" Patty asked.

"I've never met Horace Blair. I've never even heard of him. And I can't think of any case I worked on where his name came up. Besides, this prank doesn't smell like revenge. I'll come away with almost twenty-five thou for a few days' work. He could have hired someone to hurt me for a hell of a lot less than that."

"You said you're from D.C.?" Patty said.

"Yeah."

"Maybe Laurent needed to get you away from the East Coast. She sent you three thousand miles from home and told us to run you around until Friday."

"I can't think of any reason for her to do it. I don't have anything going on this Thursday." Dana shook her head. "None of this makes any sense."

"I can't agree more," Ralph said with a cheerful smile. "And there's no sense brooding over it. We've all made a nice fee for very little work, and I for one am not going to complain."

There was a pitcher of beer sitting on the table.

Ralph pointed to it. "Can we treat you to a pint and dinner? It's the least we can do."

"Beer and a cheeseburger sounds great," Dana said. "Maybe if I get good and drunk, this caper will make some sense."

Chapter Fifteen

On Wednesday afternoon, Sarah Gelfand rushed from her part-time bookkeeping job to the grocery store. She was almost at the checkout counter when she remembered that Bob, her husband, wanted her to buy chips and salsa because he was having some of his buddies over to watch football on Sunday.

By the time she found the chips and bought a jar of salsa it was almost time to pick up her eight-year-old twins from their karate class. She arrived at the dojo just in time, drove home, and was starting to unload the groceries from the station wagon when Bob pulled into the garage. He was helping her carry the groceries into the kitchen when the phone rang.

"Is this Sarah Gelfand?" a man asked when Sarah picked up.

"Yes."

"My name is Stuart Lang. I manage the River View Mall. Your father, Ernest Brodsky, rents space from us."

"Yes?" Sarah said. She was not certain why Lang

was calling her, but the mention of her father worried her. He'd had some problems with his heart lately.

"I apologize for calling you but Mr. Brodsky's rent is way overdue. I talked to him about it at the beginning of the month and he assured me he would pay me today, but there was no check in the mail and his shop was closed when I went by."

"What time was that?"

"I stopped by twice. Once around eleven, when the mail was delivered. Then I went back at three-thirty."

"And it was closed both times?"

"Yes. I could see mail on the floor just inside the store."

Sarah was concerned. "Dad never misses a day."

"Do you have any idea where he is?" Lang asked.

"Have you called his apartment?"

"I called the number on the rental agreement." He rattled it off.

"That's Dad's number. Was he there?"

"That I can't say. But he didn't answer the phone. I wouldn't have bothered you but this isn't the first time he's been late with the rent, and he was very specific about paying today. I have someone who's interested in the space and I need to know what Mr. Brodsky is planning to do."

"I understand. I haven't talked to my father since last Tuesday. I'll try to reach him and I'll tell him you called."

"Who was that?" Bob asked as soon as Sarah hung up.

Sarah told her husband about the phone call.

"Call your dad," he said. "Maybe he has a cold and skipped work."

"A cold has never stopped him before," Sarah said. She dialed her father's number and got his answering machine.

"I'm worried," Sarah said.

"Then you better get over there. I'll watch the kids."

Sarah grabbed her coat and sped across town to the garden apartment where her father was living. She parked in front in his reserved space, worried because the space was not occupied.

Wednesday's *Lee County Journal* was lying on the doormat, which meant that her father had not been home since Tuesday.

Sarah rang the doorbell twice, then knocked twice more. She shouted her father's name. When there was no response, she opened the door with the key her father had given her. Her father was a good housekeeper and the kitchen looked clean and tidy. Sarah walked through the living room and found nothing amiss. In the bedroom, the bed was made and she didn't think any clothing was missing from her father's closet or drawers. She looked in the hall closet and found his suitcase.

Sarah sat down on the sofa in the living room. Why wasn't her father home and why hadn't he gone to work? Where was he? If he'd gone on a trip he would have called her so she wouldn't worry. Something was wrong. She hoped he had not had a heart attack. She worried that he was in a hospital somewhere.

Sarah had met the neighbors who lived on either side of her father. They were both friendly with Ernie, but neither one knew where he was. Sarah decided to drive home and ask Bob if he thought they should file a missing-person report.

Part II

The Key

Chapter Sixteen

Dana got a seat on a red-eye out of Seattle. She tried to sleep on the cross-country flight but she couldn't stop thinking about the way she'd been played. Why hadn't she seen that Laurent's story was ridiculous? The obvious answer was the twenty-five grand. It wasn't logical to think that someone would pay that much money to play a joke on her. But someone had paid her twenty-five thousand dollars, and the Seattle actors another twenty thousand, to make sure that she would run around in circles for a week. A person would only pay that much to send her on a wild-goose chase if they were going to make a hell of a lot more money if the prank was successful.

A cab let Dana off at her house an hour before the sun rose on Thursday morning. She dropped her duffel bag in the entryway and was about to turn on the lights when her instincts told her that something was wrong. She looked around. At first, nothing seemed amiss. Then it dawned on her that there should have been mail lying on the mat under the mail slot.

Dana closed the door quietly, took out her gun, and looked around the living room. Nothing. She slid around the wall into the kitchen and again sensed that something was wrong. It took a moment before she figured out what was bothering her. When she'd left for Seattle, all four chairs had been pushed in at the kitchen table, but one of the chairs was a few inches away from the table now. She surveyed the kitchen slowly. Nothing else was out of place.

Dana took a deep breath and edged down the hall, hugging the wall on the same side as the bedroom door. When she reached her destination, Dana crouched low to make a smaller target and spun into the room. Her eyes had adjusted to the dark and she could make out a shape on the far side of the bed. In one smooth motion, Dana flipped the light switch and aimed her gun.

Jake Teeny rolled on his side and squinted at her for a moment. Then he flashed a sleepy grin.

"I didn't know you were into role-playing. What are we doing, the lady cop and the handcuffed prisoner? Personally, I prefer woman in chains and the sex-crazed warden."

Dana expelled a breath and the hand holding the gun dropped to her side.

"Why are you home?" she asked, angry at Jake for scaring her, and angrier at herself for almost shooting her lover.

"It's great seeing you, too."

It occurred to Dana that she should be happy that Jake was home and safe.

"I'm sorry. I wasn't expecting you for two more weeks and I thought someone had broken in."

"I left a message on the machine. Didn't you get it?"

"No. I've been out of town on a really weird assignment."

"Oh?"

"I'm too beat to talk about it now, and I'm really glad you're home, but why aren't you freezing your ass off in the Arctic?"

"The whole expedition was a disaster," Jake said as he sat up and leaned against the headboard. "There was bad weather, then one of the scientists broke his leg."

"Did you get some good pictures?"

"Yeah, but I don't think they'll publish an article, so the magazine probably won't use them."

"Maybe you can put them together for a show."

"Maybe."

Dana put her gun on the end table, dragged herself across the bed, and kissed Jake.

"I missed you," Dana said.

"I'm glad," Jake said as he nuzzled her neck.

Dana laughed. "Down, boy. I was on a red-eye—I smell, and I haven't slept a wink in twenty-four hours—so I'll take a rain check on the sex until the morning."

"Nuts."

"I plan to make it up to you, so you'd better get plenty of rest, because you're going to need it when I wake up."

Dana and Jake slept until a little before noon and were still in bed at twelve forty-five. They made love again in the shower. Then Jake headed for the kitchen so he could start breakfast, although, as Dana noted, it was technically the afternoon.

Dana had a big smile on her face when she followed the delicious scent of freshly brewed coffee into the dining room, where a full mug and the morning paper were waiting for her. She was so glad to have Jake home. She really loved him, and it didn't hurt that he was one of the sexiest men she'd ever seen. Jake, who was in his mid-thirties, was an inch shorter than Dana at five nine, and had wavy brown hair and liquid brown eyes. His skin was always tanned because he was outdoors so much of the time. Jake's job could be physically demanding, so he stayed in shape. Dana grinned as she remembered the feel of his rock-hard body.

Jake saw how happy Dana looked, and he couldn't help smiling, too. Not so long ago he had wondered if he would ever see her smile again.

"So, what's this weird case you were working on?" Jake asked as he set down plates loaded with scrambled eggs, bacon, and buttered toast at their places.

Between bites, Dana told Jake about her meeting with Margo Laurent, her trip to the West Coast, and her discovery that the search for the Ottoman Scepter was a prank.

"I think calling what happened to you 'weird' is an understatement. The whole thing is downright bizarre."

"I agree."

"Are you going to try to figure out what happened and who was behind it?"

"When I can. I had to put several cases on the back burner, and I've got to dig myself out."

Jake grabbed the sports section so he could catch up on what happened to his favorite teams while he was away. Dana took the first section and read the depressing news about the Middle East, the failing economy, and congressional gridlock. When she got to the part of the paper that reported on local news, she found herself looking at a picture over a headline that read: COMMONWEALTH ATTORNEY STILL MISSING. Dana was struck by the resemblance the prosecutor in question bore to Margo Laurent. Then she froze when she learned that the missing woman was Carrie Blair, wife of industrialist Horace Blair.

There was that name again.

The article told how Carrie Blair became the "Society Prosecutor" and concluded by stating that the last time anyone had seen the missing woman was Monday afternoon. Dana felt very uneasy. The last time she'd talked to Margo Laurent was Friday. After that, all of Dana's calls had gone to voice mail.

"What's up?" Jake asked when he noticed the intensity with which Dana was reading the story about the missing prosecutor.

"My weird case just got a whole lot weirder."

Dana walked down to her basement office and booted up her computer. She found a good photograph of Carrie Blair on the Internet and used Photoshop to change Carrie's blond hair to black and add dark glasses. When she was through, Dana maneuvered the before and after photos so they were side by side.

Jake walked in carrying two coffee mugs. He set one down next to Dana and pulled up a chair.

"I think I've found my mystery woman," Dana said. Then she told Jake about the missing prosecutor.

"Horace Blair owns the house on Isla de Muerta and the condo in Victoria. It's too big a coincidence. I think Margo Laurent is really Carrie Blair."

"Do you know the Blairs?" Jake asked.

"Not that I remember."

"So what's going on?"

"I have no idea. This whole business is giving me a headache."

Chapter Seventeen

Charles Benedict's office was in a two-story house with a wide front porch that stood on the border between the commercial and residential sections of downtown Crestview, Lee County's county seat. It had been built as a residence in 1875. When Benedict bought it, 130 years later, he kept the exterior but completely remodeled the interior.

Nikolai Orlansky loved meeting at Benedict's office because nothing he said there could ever be used against him. Benedict had the house swept for listening devices every time Nikolai dropped by for an attorney-client conference but Nikolai was paranoid and he imagined that government agencies using NSA/CIA-developed technology were probably listening in. He delighted in pressing his finger to his lips, giving Benedict a wink, then spewing out confessions about the Kennedy assassination and any other weirdness he would think up on the spur of the moment.

Benedict put up with Orlansky's shenanigans because he was a steady source of income and a good person to know if you needed untraceable weapons, high-grade narcotics, and beautiful young whores, or had a desire for animate or inanimate objects to disappear.

Nikolai Orlansky didn't look like a crime lord or a psychopathic killer any more than his dapper lawyer looked like a hit man. The Russian did not have an imposing physique or cold, heartless eyes. If anything, he looked nonthreatening; a roly-poly fellow with a kind smile, a full head of floppy black hair, and a hearty laugh.

Orlansky and Benedict had met when Nikolai hired Charlie to represent a trusted lieutenant who was facing a murder charge. Two unimpeachable witnesses had been making out in a car two down from the scene of the crime. Orlansky's man had not seen them, and he had been standing in a pool of light, so the witnesses had been 100 percent certain when they picked him out of a lineup.

Orlansky was a realist. He knew the prosecution had an airtight case. He told the lawyer that he did not expect miracles and had hired Benedict out of loyalty to a friend who had been at his side since they were teenagers in the Ukraine. Benedict had listened carefully. When Orlansky was through, he told him that he could make the friend's problem disappear for an additional thirty thousand dollars.

"These people cannot be bribed," Orlansky said.

"I don't intend to bribe them," Benedict had said.

Then he'd held out his palm, dropped a quarter into it, and closed his fist. When he opened his fist, the quarter was gone.

"I said I would make the problem disappear. Once I have the cash, the witnesses will join the quarter in never-never land."

Orlansky had missed the literary reference but had gotten the idea. Two weeks after he paid Benedict, the witnesses failed to appear for a court hearing and the charges against his man were dismissed. The witnesses were never heard from again.

Benedict had a real knack for practicing law, and he won a lot of his cases fair and square. But every so often he needed an edge. Nikolai was prepared to pay extra for special services, and Charlie loved being the recipient of his largesse, but today they were meeting because Orlansky's lawyer needed a favor.

"I can do this," Orlansky said when Benedict finished his explanation. "In fact, I have someone in place."

"Oh?"

"You know Gregor?"

Benedict smiled.

"He beat up some asshole in a bar. I am pissed because it was not business, but who can talk to Gregor?" Nikolai shrugged. "So I don't bail him out. Is a lesson."

"Gregor is perfect."

"So, it is done," Nikolai said. "But we are in

America, Charlie, the land of the capitalist, where no lunch is free."

Charlie wrote a figure on a piece of note paper, which he planned to burn as soon as Nikolai left. He anticipated collecting a lot more from Horace Blair when the millionaire hired him to defend him against a charge of murder.

Nikolai steepled his fingers and stared into space. Then he crossed out Benedict's number and wrote another that was two thousand dollars higher. Charlie had anticipated Orlansky and even with the new number he was one thousand dollars ahead of what he'd been prepared to pay.

"Done," Benedict said.

"I like doing business with you, Charlie. You are a no-bullshit guy. So, when do you need this favor?"

"Soon. I'll let you know."

Nikolai stood up. "Good, and you got that atomic bomb planted at Langley for me, the one disguised as a meatball hero?"

Benedict shook his head. "I wish you wouldn't do that shit. One of these days, guys in Ninja outfits are going to crash through my windows and smoke both of us."

"Ah, but that would prove I was right and you were wrong about the bugs, so I would have the last laugh."

Chapter Eighteen

Stephanie Robb's divorce attorney had phoned her while she was eating breakfast to tell her that her asshole husband was threatening to fight for custody of their daughter. The idea of Vince-as-full-time-parent was laughable, and Stephanie was furious at his transparent ploy to get her to reduce her demand for child support.

The homicide detective had vented to Frank Santoro during the drive from police headquarters. Robb's partner was a stocky Italian with curly black hair who was usually calm and did not act without first thinking through the problem at hand. He was a good counterweight to his smart but excitable partner, who was prone to making snap decisions. Santoro had developed an ability to tune out Robb's tirades, which he'd been forced to endure ever since she had caught her "scumbag husband" and his "skank" girlfriend making the beast with two backs on her living room floor three months ago.

Stephanie was still fuming when Frank parked the car at the barrier the forensic team had erected to keep sightseers from the field where the body had been found.

"We're here," Frank said.

Robb looked at the path that led into the field as she traded her shoes for boots. They'd been warned that the field where the corpse had been dumped had been turned into a bog by yesterday's heavy rain.

"I hate fucking nature," she swore.

"I'll send a memo to our perps asking them to take your feelings into account when they're disposing of a body."

"Fuck you, Frank."

"Hey, Steph, lighten up. I'm not trying to get custody of Lily. I don't even like kids."

Robb glared at Frank, but her partner didn't notice since he was already walking across the field toward the milling crowd of forensic experts and uniformed officers who had beaten them to the scene.

Stephanie surveyed the area. On one side of the road was a fence that delineated the boundaries of the McHenry farm. The low grassland where the body had been dumped ran between the other side of the road and a narrow, winding river. Woods surrounded the tract. Under other circumstances, the tranquil beauty would have been perfect for a nature hike, but the weather was cold, damp, and blustery, and the idea of dealing with a rotting corpse spoiled the mood. Robb stuffed her hands in her pockets and trudged after Santoro, who was talking to the medical examiner when Stephanie caught up to him.

"The deceased has been out here a few days," Nick Winters was saying. "It looks like he was stabbed in the heart. One wound, and I'm guessing the killer knew what he was doing because it's the only entry wound I could see with the vic clothed. I'll know more after I get him on the table."

"Who found him?" Frank asked.

Winters threw a thumb over his shoulder. "That's the McHenry place. Their kid was taking the dog for a run and the dog sniffed him out."

"How come he didn't find the body before today?" Robb asked.

"He doesn't walk the dog in this field every day. The last few days, he ran him in the woods on the other side of the farm."

"Where's the kid?" Frank asked.

"Home. He was pretty shook up. There's a policeman with him."

"Okay," Frank said. "We'll talk to him when we're through here."

"Do we have an ID?" Robb asked.

"Not so far. There's no wallet. I'll take his prints."

Stephanie edged past two uniformed cops who were sipping hot coffee from a thermos and got her first look at the corpse. She figured the man for five eight or nine. He had been dumped on his back, and his legs and his left arm shot out at odd angles. The right hand was trapped under his body. Parts of the face had been eaten by animals but the patches of hair that were still attached to the scalp were mostly gray. She figured he was probably in his late sixties.

Robb walked around the corpse, working angles in hopes that something she saw would inspire her. The man was wearing tan chinos and a blue work shirt. His brown shoes were scuffed and stained with mud and the rain had leached out some of the color from the red stain that had spread across the fabric that covered his heart.

Robb squatted next to the corpse. The left arm was lying on the grass and the hand was palm up. It looked calloused. A working man, not an office guy; blue collar. She stood up.

"Poor bastard," Robb murmured. She wondered what he'd done to deserve an end like this. Probably nothing, though you could never tell. Maybe drugs were involved or some other criminal activity. Maybe John Doe wasn't blameless. With luck, they'd eventually know his story, and the identity of the person who had ended it so abruptly.

Chapter Nineteen

When Santoro returned from the crime scene he found a copy of the *Lee County Journal* on his desk with the headline circled in red. The story had been written by Art Suchak, the *Journal* reporter who covered crime. Santoro read it carefully before carrying the newspaper to Robb's desk.

"Read this," he said as he handed the paper to his partner.

The headline asked: DID MISSING PROSECUTOR AND BILLIONAIRE HAVE KILLER PRENUP? The story revolved around a rumor that Carrie and Horace Blair had entered into a prenuptial agreement. According to the rumor, the agreement terminated during the week in which the prosecutor had disappeared, and the terms would have forced Horace Blair to pay his wife $20 million—$2 million per year—if she stayed faithful to him during the first ten years of their marriage.

Robb looked up from the paper. "That is definitely a motive for murder."

"You think her husband killed her?" Santoro asked. "We don't even know if she's dead."

"Blair's reaction when I told him I was looking into his wife's disappearance was odd."

"How so?"

"At first, he didn't seem to care. He said he didn't even know if she was in the house or the last time she'd been home. Later, he acted concerned. It was like it suddenly dawned on him that it would look bad if he wasn't."

Santoro didn't say anything for a moment. Then he pulled out his phone.

"Suchak," the reporter answered when Santoro was put through.

"Hey, Art. It's Frank Santoro."

"To what do I owe this call?"

"Your excellent story in the morning paper. It was really brilliant. For years, I've been telling everyone that it's a shame you haven't won a Pulitzer."

Suchak laughed. "If you want something from me, Frank, feed me doughnuts, not bullshit."

"I was hoping you'd tell me how you learned about the Blair prenup."

"Alleged prenup. I don't know if they have one. If you'd learned to read, you'd know that its existence is only a rumor."

"Can you tell me how you heard about the rumor?" Frank asked.

"Quid pro quo, Frank. You show me yours and I'll show you mine."

"What do you want to know?"

"Is Carrie Blair alive or dead and is Horace Blair a suspect?" the reporter asked.

"The missus is missing. That's all we know. I'm not speculating on the state of her health or why she's missing. As of now, we don't have a crime. If we don't have a crime, we don't have suspects."

"Should I write that, as usual, Lee County detective Frank Santoro hasn't a clue as to what's going on?"

"Only if you want me to arrest you."

"Seriously, Frank, can you give me anything?"

"Not at this time, but I'll promise you a heads-up if we do get a break. That is, if you tell me why you think the Blairs have a secret prenup."

"Some guy phoned in the tip. And, no, he didn't give me a name. Also, he was trying to disguise his voice. So I called a source at Rankin, Lusk, the law firm that handles Blair's affairs. My source says that there was scuttlebutt when Blair married Carrie that she'd been forced to agree to a prenup."

Santoro asked Suchak a few more questions. Then he looked at Robb, who had been listening in. Robb shook her head.

"Thanks, Art. I appreciate the help," Santoro said.

"Just don't forget me when you get your break."

"You'll be the first to know when we've got something solid."

Santoro frowned as soon as he ended the call.

"Should we question Blair about the prenup?" Robb asked.

"Not yet. Let's wait until we have something more substantial than a rumor."

Chapter Twenty

Horace Blair was fuming when Jack Pratt returned his call.

"I assume this is about the *Journal* story," Pratt said.

"You've read it?"

"Yes."

"How did the reporter find out?" Blair demanded.

"It says a source gave him the information."

"How can that be? Only Carrie, you, me, and Benedict know about the prenup."

"I didn't leak the story," Pratt said. "What about Benedict?"

"What would he stand to gain?"

"I have no idea. But if none of us called the *Journal*, that leaves Carrie."

"Why would Carrie tell a reporter about the prenup? She loses everything if she talks about it."

"Maybe she's trying to frame you for murder," Pratt said.

"How would that benefit her? I'd have to be executed for her to inherit and she'd have to hide until then. And what if I didn't get a death sentence? It makes no sense."

"I'm just thinking out loud. And there is another possibility. You told me Carrie told Benedict that she was dropping him for someone else; and there could have been other lovers before Benedict. She might have let the existence of the prenup slip to any one of them."

"Could someone in Rankin, Lusk have learned about the document?" Horace asked. "You have secretaries, paralegals. There are janitors. Anyone who works at the law firm and has access to its files could have discovered the prenup."

"It's possible someone at the firm saw my notes, but I don't have a copy of the document. Remember, you insisted that only you and Carrie have copies?"

"That's true."

"Where are the copies?" Pratt asked.

"Mine is in my safety-deposit box. I have no idea where Carrie put hers."

Pratt thought for a few minutes and Blair waited.

"You should be okay, Horace," the lawyer said. "If the DA wants to use the agreement as evidence of motive he'll have to have the document. A rumor or anything Carrie told Benedict or anyone else about the prenup would be inadmissible hearsay. I can't be forced to testify about the document because of attorney-client privilege, and my notes are protected as work product. My advice is to go about your business the way you usually do. Worrying won't change anything."

Chapter Twenty-One

Barry Lester's nickname was Lucky, and he was lucky. Take his looks. Barry reminded some people of a ferret. He was short, skinny, and freckle-faced with watery blue eyes and spiky red hair that stuck out at odd angles no matter how often he combed it. But somehow he was always lucky with the ladies.

Then there was his career. Barry was a criminal who was not very good at the con games and petty thefts that were his bread and butter. Though he was arrested frequently enough, Barry usually managed to avoid punishment for his crimes; a DA would screw up, a witness wouldn't show up, or else he'd glom onto information about a more serious gangster he would trade for dismissal or an easy sentence.

Unfortunately, it looked like Barry's luck had finally run out. He had been the wheelman in a liquor-store robbery. When his equally inept co-conspirators jumped into his car, screaming, "Go, go, go," Barry tried to comply, but two blocks from the crime scene the car ran out of gas and everyone had been arrested. Barry called his attorney as soon as he had the chance, but his attorney was on vacation. The attorneys for the rest of the gang, however, were not, and they beat feet to the prosecutor's door to cut deals, which left Barry holding the bag. When Barry's attorney returned from Hawaii, tanned and rested, he informed his client that he was probably going to be spending the next few Christmases behind bars.

But Barry Lester wasn't called Lucky for nothing. Just when it looked like storm clouds were going to be a permanent part of his future, Tiffany Starr, Barry's girlfriend, came to see him, and those clouds parted and let in the sun. Two days later, Barry made sure his luck held up by picking a fight with an ultra-violent criminal named Gregor Karpinski.

Gregor Karpinski earned his living by inflicting grievous bodily harm on anyone Nikolai Orlansky told him to. He was six feet five inches tall, with muscles like concrete, an IQ just slightly above normal, and a very mean disposition. The inmates of the Lee County jail were allowed one hour of recreation each day, and Gregor spent his time pumping iron in a corner of the fenced-in, asphalt-paved area where other inmates played basketball or sat around smoking and talking. He was on his way to that corner when Barry Lester walked into him. The impact barely moved Gregor. Instead of running for his life, Barry glared at Gregor and barked, "Watch where you're going, asshole," which Gregor would normally translate to mean, "Please beat me until I resemble hamburger, then put ketchup on me and eat me." But he had his instructions, and instead of ripping Barry's head from his body, Gregor merely hoisted Barry into the air by his hair and broke his nose.

From that point on, Barry saw the world through a red haze. He remembered guards rushing to his rescue, and he definitely remembered begging the guards to take him out of population and put him in isolation, the section of the jail where snitches and inmates who were in danger of being killed or maimed by other inmates were held for their own protection. After a trip to the infirmary, where they worked on his nose, Barry Lester got his wish.

Chapter Twenty-Two

At dawn, Charles Benedict was parked where he could see the driveway of Horace Blair's estate. The area around the estate was populated with other large estates, so there was not much chance that he would be seen by a neighbor. Even if he was, Benedict's Mercedes was upscale enough that it wouldn't draw attention.

At eight-thirty, Blair's Bentley left the grounds and headed downtown. When Horace pulled into the Blair Building's parking garage, Benedict followed. Blair parked in his reserved spot, and the lawyer drove two levels down to the general parking area. Charlie was wearing jeans, a baseball cap, dark glasses, a bland, tan jacket, and latex gloves. When he got out of his car he was carrying several items, including a copy of the key from Carrie Blair's key ring that opened the trunk of the Bentley, a ziplock bag with the balled-up towel that was soaked with Carrie's blood, and another ziplock bag with hairs he'd pulled from Carrie's head before he'd buried her.

Benedict stuffed the bag with the hairs in his jacket pocket and concealed the other bag under his jacket. He waited until no one was around the Bentley to open the trunk. First, he scattered the hairs. Next, he pulled out the bag with the towel. The blood had frozen in the freezer and he'd stashed it in a cooler during the drive, but the heat from his body had defrosted it and it was wet when he smeared it across a section of the trunk near the edge. Benedict put the towel back in the bag when he finished with it. They would be incinerated before the day was out.

Several years ago, Benedict had been consulted by a potential client who was charged with stabbing his wife to death. The killer had wrapped the body in a tarp so it wouldn't leave any trace evidence in his trunk. When he pulled the body out of the trunk to bury it, a smear of blood had been left. It was a dark night and he hadn't noticed. It wasn't a large smear but it was enough to send him to prison for life. The man had gone elsewhere because he couldn't come up with Benedict's retainer, but Benedict remembered the damage a tiny smear of blood could do.

Before he closed the Bentley's trunk, Benedict took one last goodie out of his pocket. There was a golf bag and a pair of golf shoes lying in the back. Benedict moved the shoes and placed the .38 that had ended Carrie's life behind them, where it would be easy to find. The gun's serial numbers had been filed off, and there were no prints on the gun that could lead the police to Benedict. The gun would raise suspicions when it was found, and it would be powerful evidence of guilt when they dug up Carrie's body and a ballistics test matched the bullet that had killed her to the weapon.

Chapter Twenty-Three

Stephanie Robb came in late because Lily had been acting out in class and she had to meet with her teacher. Robb had read a few books about the effects of divorce on children. She had even spoken to a counselor her attorney had recommended. But she was still upset because her bastard husband had not read these books or talked to a counselor and was using their daughter as a football in the divorce proceedings.

Robb was still steamed when she walked into the detective division in time to see Frank Santoro hang up the phone.

"We have an ID on the John Doe who was found in that field by the river," Santoro said.

"Who is he?"

"Ernest Brodsky. He has a shop in the River View Mall, and a daughter, Sarah Gelfand. That was Kline. He broke the news to her. She's coming to the morgue in an hour to make a formal identification. We'll meet her there and see if we can learn anything."

Bob Gelfand put his arm around his wife and tried to comfort her. The couple was sitting on a bench outside the room in the morgue where Sarah had just identified her father's body. Her shoulders convulsed with each sob, and Frank Santoro and Stephanie Robb waited patiently until Sarah was calm enough to answer their questions.

"I'll try to make this fast, Mrs. Gelfand," Santoro said. "I know you want to get out of here and back to your children. But I want to catch the person who did this, and right now we don't have any leads. Any help you can give us will be greatly appreciated."

Sarah raised her tearstained face toward the detective. "I don't know how I can help. Dad didn't have an enemy in the world."

"I don't mean to be disrespectful but I have to ask. Did your father have any vices? A gambling problem? Drugs? Was he a drinker? Any problems with women?"

Bob Gelfand laughed. "No one who knew Ernie would ask a question like that. He was a sweet guy. Ernie is . . . was seventy-two, and totally devoted to his grandkids. He was married to the same woman for forty-three years. Martha died two years ago and he was very depressed but he didn't drink or take antidepressants or anything like that. And as for gambling, not a chance."

"What about debts? Had he borrowed money from someone, or does he owe money?" the detective asked.

Sarah dabbed at her eyes. "He was having trouble paying the rent on his store. The manager of the mall said he was behind in his rent. The store was locked and he couldn't get in touch with Dad. That's why I went over to his apartment."

"I'm way out in left field with this, but could he have gone to a loan shark for the rent?"

"No way," Bob said. "Ernie would have gone to a bank. If that didn't work out, I make a good living. He knows we would have helped him."

"What about his neighbors? Did he have a beef with any of them?"

"No," Sarah answered. "I've met some of them. They liked Dad, and he never mentioned anything like that."

Santoro sighed. "I'm going to let you go. I'm real sorry about your dad. He sounds like a great guy."

"He was," Bob assured Santoro.

Santoro and Robb walked the couple to the front door.

"What do you think?" Robb asked her partner when they were alone.

"If Brodsky was as saintly as they pictured him, this case is going to grow cold fast," Santoro said. "With the missing wallet it looks like a robbery."

"Yeah, probably," Robb agreed. "The only thing that bothers me is where we found the body. A mugger is going to grab the wallet and take off. That field was a long way from the River View Mall and Brodsky's apartment. He wasn't killed there, so the killer had to drive him to the spot, then risk being seen while he was dumping the body."

"That's a good point. Let's head for the mall and see if we can learn anything."

The River View Mall, an open-air complex of shops and restaurants, was a twenty-minute drive from the morgue. Stuart Lang, who managed the mall, was short, balding, and overweight. He was pacing in front of Mr. Brodsky's store and glancing at his watch when Robb and Santoro drove up.

"This is terrible," Lang said as soon as the introductions were completed. "We've never had a tenant murdered."

"Can you think of anyone who might have done this or any reason for Mr. Brodsky meeting with violence?" Santoro asked.

"No. He was a real gentleman, a very nice guy."

"I understand he was having trouble paying his rent," Robb said.

"That's true. I felt bad about it. I bent over backward to accommodate him because he's been a tenant for so long. The mall is owned by a Chicago company, and he was here when they took over, long before I started as manager."

"Were you going to evict him?" Robb asked.

Lang shook his head sadly. The concern seemed genuine. "I was very close to asking him to leave. We were trying to work things out, but his business was very slow. Ernie's wife died a few years ago and he closed the shop for a while. I guess some of his good customers went elsewhere and he was never able to get the business back on track."

"Can you let us in?" Robb asked. "There might be something inside that will help us."

Santoro handed Lang a copy of the search warrant they had procured earlier in the day. It also asked for surveillance tapes of the area around the shop.

"I've got the tapes in my office," Lang said as he unlocked the door. "You can pick them up before you leave."

"Thanks," Santoro said.

"There's one other thing," Lang said. "Mr. Brodsky's car was towed from the lot a few days ago. The security guard noticed it on his rounds on Tuesday, Wednesday, and Thursday after Mr. Brodsky disappeared. He's supposed to run the plate and try to notify the owner when a car is abandoned, but the guard is new and he was confused about the procedure. I called Mrs. Gelfand to give her my condolences after you called to tell me that the body had been identified and she mentioned that her father's car was missing. She wanted to know if it was in the lot. I checked with our security office and eventually figured out what happened."

"So he never drove away from the mall on Tuesday night?"

"Apparently not."

Lang returned to his office. Robb and Santoro spent an hour going through Brodsky's books and papers, but they came up blank.

"That was a waste of time," Robb said.

"Maybe we'll get lucky with the tapes," Santoro answered.

"We're going to need a break to solve this case," Robb said. "It has random robbery written all over it."

"You're probably right. What possible motive other than robbery could someone have for killing an elderly locksmith?"

Chapter Twenty-Four

At four-thirty, the receptionist buzzed Stephanie Robb to tell her that a man was calling with information about the Blair missing-person case. Robb sighed. She'd been fielding calls about Carrie Blair since the story broke, and none of the tips had gone anywhere. Still, there was always an outside chance that the caller really knew something that could move the investigation forward, so she had the call put through.

"This is Detective Robb speaking."

"I know what happen to Mrs. Blair."

Robb was certain that the caller was a man, but his voice was muffled.

"To whom am I speaking?" Robb said.

"No is important who I am. What I know is important."

Robb guessed the caller was Hispanic, or someone trying to sound Hispanic.

"And just what do you know?"

"I see him do it."

"Do what?"

"Put her in the trunk."

"You saw someone put Mrs. Blair in the trunk of a car? Is that what you're telling me?"

"*Sí.*"

"Who did you see putting her body in the trunk?"

"Mr. Blair. He no think anyone see him, but I see him."

Robb knew the make of all of Blair's vehicles. "What kind of car did he put the body in?" she asked.

"A fancy car, black. He take it to work sometimes."

Blair owned a black Bentley.

"When did you see Mr. Blair put the body in the black car?"

"Monday, late. Maybe it was Tuesday, after midnight. I no have a watch."

"Where did this happen?"

"Are you doing a track on me?" the man asked, suddenly panicky.

"No, sir. But I would like to meet with you."

"No."

"Can you tell me your name?" Robb asked, but the line was already dead.

The detective sat back and thought about the conversation. Did the caller really see Horace Blair put his wife's body in the trunk of a car? If he did see him, where did he see him? Robb remembered her visit to Blair's estate. The grounds were beautiful and very well tended. It would take an army of gardeners to keep a place like that looking good, and a lot of gardeners were Hispanic. Some of those Hispanics might be in the country illegally and wouldn't want to meet with an officer of the law.

Robb would love to look inside the trunk of Blair's Bentley, but there was no way she could get a search warrant with an affidavit supported only by the word of an informant who refused to give his name.

"Hey, Frank."

Santoro was writing a report. He held up a hand, finished a sentence, then swiveled his chair in Robb's direction. When she had his full attention she told him about the call.

"You think there's anything to it?" Santoro asked.

"I have no idea, but the guy sounded scared. He didn't sound like a crank."

"No judge is going to give us a warrant."

"I figured that out already. So what do we do?"

Santoro looked at the ceiling and spaced out. When he returned to Earth he said, "Why don't we drive to Blair's office and ask him if we can look in the trunk? See how he deals with that."

Horace Blair looked up expectantly when the two detectives entered his office.

"Do you have news about Carrie?" he asked.

"No, sir," Robb answered, "but we may have a lead."

"I'm Frank Santoro, Detective Robb's partner, and we have an odd request for you."

"Yes?" Horace said.

"You own a Bentley, right?"

"Yes?" Horace answered, slightly confused by the question.

"Where is it?"

"In the parking garage. I drove it to work today."

"Great!" Santoro answered. "Can we look in the trunk?"

"The trunk of the Bentley?" Horace repeated, not certain he'd heard the detective correctly.

"If it's no trouble."

"Why do you want to look in the trunk? I don't understand."

"We had a confidential tip, Mr. Blair," Robb answered. "I'm sorry, but we can't reveal the content. You understand."

"I understand why you can't reveal the content of a tip, but I don't understand how the trunk of my car can possibly be connected to Carrie's disappearance."

"If you open it for us, we may be able to clear up your confusion," Santoro said.

Horace hesitated for a moment. Then he stood up. "Come with me."

No one said a word during the elevator ride down to the parking garage. Blair led the detectives to his car. The detectives slipped on latex gloves while Horace used his key to open the trunk. Robb angled the beam of a flashlight around the interior. The light reflected off the irons in a bag of golf clubs. A baseball cap and a pair of golf shoes had been shoved in a corner. Robb had almost decided that she and Santoro were on a wild-goose chase when she played the beam along the edge of the trunk and saw a brown smear. She looked up at Frank, who was leaning over her shoulder.

"Is that blood, Mr. Blair?" Frank asked.

Blair bent over and examined the area illuminated by the flashlight.

"I don't know."

"Can you think of any reason why there would be a bloodstain in the trunk of your car?"

"No."

Blair sounded genuinely puzzled, but Santoro had dealt with criminals who were great liars, so he drew no conclusions.

"Frank," Robb said. She had shifted the flashlight beam and it now shone on two blond hairs. Frank focused on them.

"Your wife is blond, isn't she?" Robb asked.

"Yes."

"Mr. Blair, I'd like to have someone from our crime lab examine the trunk. It could help us find your wife. Would that be okay with you?"

Blair looked confused. He hesitated and the detectives waited.

"You think this will help you find Carrie?" he asked.

"It might."

"Then I guess it's okay."

"Thank you," Robb said.

While Santoro stepped away and punched in the number of the crime lab on his cell, Robb took another look in the trunk. She leaned in and moved the golf bag to see if there was anything under it. This dislodged the golf shoes, which had been leaning against the bag. Robb tensed. Her back was to Blair, and what she saw in the beam of the flashlight set off alarms.

Robb stood up casually as if she were through with the search. Then she turned away from Blair to shield her gun from him. When she turned back, she was pointing her service revolver at the millionaire.

"Mr. Blair, please raise your hands and take a step back."

Blair stared at the gun. "What the hell's going on here?"

Santoro looked at his partner as if she were crazy. "What are you doing, Steph?"

"Raise your hands, now!" Robb commanded.

Blair raised his hands. He looked confused and frightened.

"There's a gun hidden behind the golf shoes," Robb told Santoro.

Santoro leaned into the trunk and saw the gun. He picked it up by the trigger guard and dropped it in an evidence bag. Then he held up the bag so Blair could see what was in it.

"Is this your gun?" Santoro asked Blair.

Blair started to answer. Then it dawned on him that a homicide detective was holding a gun on him and a gun he'd never seen before had just been removed from the trunk of his car where bloodstains had also been found.

"I think I should confer with an attorney before this goes any further," he said.

"That's your right, Mr. Blair, but this is very suspicious. It would help if you explained what this gun was doing in your car," Santoro said.

"I want to speak to a lawyer before I answer any more questions," Blair said firmly.

"And I think we should continue this discussion at police headquarters," Robb said.

Chapter Twenty-Five

Horace Blair's panicked call to Charles Benedict had come in right on schedule. Benedict was certain Blair would call him as soon as the police followed up on the anonymous tip he'd phoned in to Stephanie Robb, and he was not disappointed. The ability to steer a mark toward a particular choice was a critical skill for a magician, and Benedict had perfected it. After he gave Blair the DVD, Horace had offered him a drink, and the two men had engaged in a lengthy conversation about Carrie and other topics, including Benedict's vast experience in criminal law. Normally, Blair would call upon one of his corporate attorneys when he had a legal problem, but Benedict had been certain that his emphasis on his criminal-law specialty would subliminally influence Blair's choice of an attorney when the police came calling, and he had not been wrong.

Benedict spotted Santoro and Robb when he stepped out of the elevator and into the Homicide Division.

"Hey, guys, what's happening?" he asked.

"What are you doing here?" Robb snapped.

Robb disliked Benedict because he'd skewered her during cross-examination in an armed-robbery trial involving muscle for the Orlansky mob. Benedict took Robb's bad manners as a compliment.

"Mr. Blair asked me to drop by," Benedict said.

"How do you know Blair?" Robb demanded.

"Uh-uh," Benedict answered as he wagged his finger at the detective. "Attorney-client confidentiality and all that."

"You're looking prosperous, Charlie," Santoro said.

"I can't complain."

"Not with clients like Horace Blair," Santoro said. "We'd like to talk to him."

"About what?"

"About some stuff we found in the trunk of his Bentley."

"Oh? What kind of 'stuff'?" Benedict asked.

"Blond hairs, blood, a gun, stuff like that. The lab is testing the hairs and the blood to see if they belong to his wife."

"What made you think to look in the trunk of Horace's Bentley?" asked Benedict.

"We got a tip."

"Did the tipster give a name?"

"No, it was anonymous."

"What was the tip exactly?"

Santoro smiled and shrugged his shoulders, trying hard to look sheepish.

"We'd like to tell you, but you know how it is early in an investigation. I'm afraid we have to keep it confidential as of now."

Benedict returned the smile, letting Santoro know that he was too polite to tell the detective that he was full of shit.

"Did you have a search warrant for the car?"

"Didn't need one. Mr. Blair gave us permission to look in the trunk. He was very cooperative."

"I don't suppose you Mirandized him or suggested that he speak to a lawyer?"

"There was no need. Mr. Blair wasn't a suspect."

"Then he's free to leave?"

"No, Charlie. We found a handgun in the trunk with the serial numbers filed off. That's a violation of the penal code. If we talk to him, he might clear up our confusion about the gun."

"I'll ask Mr. Blair what he wants to do."

Santoro led the way down a short hall and stopped on the other side of a holding cell in front of a metal door with a window three-quarters of the way up. Benedict peeked in and saw Horace Blair waiting in a narrow, claustrophobic room with stained white walls. He was seated in an uncomfortable wooden chair, leaning his elbows on a scarred wooden table. When the door opened, Blair looked up. He started to say something but Benedict shook his head sharply. Then the lawyer handed Santoro a letter.

"This is a formal demand that you not listen in or tape our attorney-client conference or speak to my client unless I'm present. So please turn off all of your recording devices."

"We don't have any on."

"Good. That means you won't have any trouble complying. And now I'll speak to my client alone."

Santoro shut the door and Benedict sat opposite Blair. The millionaire was dressed in an expensive suit, but it was rumpled. He looked furious.

"Do you know what the fuck is going on?" Horace snapped.

"Unfortunately, I do. The police have taken advantage of you, Horace. Robb and Santoro knew they couldn't get a warrant to search the Bentley because they didn't have probable cause, so they tricked you into letting them look in the trunk of your car."

"But they said it would help find Carrie."

"Your cooperation may help the detectives send you to jail," Benedict said in hopes of frightening Blair. The more Blair panicked, the easier he would be to manipulate. "If the hairs and blood they found in the trunk of the Bentley turn out to be Carrie's, they may arrest you for murder."

"That's ridiculous."

"I know Stephanie Robb. She has tunnel vision. Once she fixes on a suspect you can't reason with her."

"I can't be arrested. I have businesses to run. I have meetings scheduled in Europe and Japan."

"Robb won't care, but I do, and I'll do my best to

make sure that you make those meetings. You were wise to call me."

"I should have done it before I let those lying bastards search my car."

"Don't beat yourself up. You were worried about Carrie and that kept you from being cool and objective, the way you are when you make business decisions. Most people want to cooperate with the police, especially if they haven't done anything wrong."

"I haven't, and I have no idea why Carrie disappeared or where she is."

"Have they accused you of being involved in Carrie's disappearance?"

"No, but they've been acting like I'm a suspect ever since they searched my car. How can they arrest me? Don't they have to have evidence?"

"Unfortunately, the handgun they found in the trunk of the Bentley had its serial number filed off. That's illegal."

"I have nothing to do with that gun!" Blair shouted. "I've never seen it before!"

Benedict held up his hand. "Okay, relax. You have every reason to be upset, but before we talk about what they found in your trunk or Carrie's disappearance there are a few matters we need to get out of the way."

"Such as?"

"Do you want me to act as your attorney in this matter?"

"Yes. I need an expert in criminal law."

"Okay, then. If I'm going to be your attorney I'll need a retainer. Fifty thousand dollars will be adequate for now."

"That's fine."

"You understand that the fee will be much more if they charge you with murder."

Blair nodded.

"Good. Now you need to know some of the rules involving the attorney-client relationship."

"My corporate attorneys have told me about that."

"I'm sure they have, but I want to go over the rules again in the context of a criminal matter. Anything you tell me is confidential. I am forbidden by law to reveal the information to anyone, and no judge can ever force me to reveal it, even if you tell me you killed Carrie."

"I did not kill Carrie."

"Of course. I never thought you did. I'm just making a point. And another point I want to make is that no other person may have this same relationship with you. If you talk to a friend, your secretary, a member of your board of directors, and you say something that can be used by the police, those people can be subpoenaed by a grand jury and forced to reveal what you told them, no matter how much they like you and want to protect you. So, from now on, think of me as your protector and your shield. Do not speak to anyone about anything to do with this matter without consulting me first. Do you understand?"

"I understand completely."

Benedict smiled. Horace Blair thought the smile signified Benedict's satisfaction in knowing that he understood the information Benedict had just imparted, but Charles Benedict was smiling for a different reason. From this moment on, Horace Blair would be isolated from all outside influences and would do anything Benedict told him.

"Let's get down to business. The detectives want to interview you. I advise you very strongly to refuse to let them. But it's your decision."

"After the way they've treated me, the last thing I want to do is talk to those two. I'm a friend of the chief of police and I have a good mind to call him about their conduct."

"That might be a good idea somewhere down the line, but let's hold your contacts in reserve. Now, let's you and I discuss strategy."

"Is your client ready to talk?" Stephanie Robb asked as soon as Benedict stepped out of the interrogation room.

"Absolutely not," Benedict said. "And you two should be ashamed of yourselves for tricking Mr. Blair."

"Oddly, I'm not," Santoro said.

"I assume you're going to let my client leave now," Benedict said.

"You assume wrong, Benedict," Robb answered with a smirk. "He's going to cool his heels tonight.

Maybe after a taste of jail, your fat-cat client will be a little more cooperative."

Benedict was delighted. This was exactly what he'd hoped for.

"What's the charge?" he asked.

"We've got him dead to rights on the thirty-eight, Charlie," Santoro interposed so Robb would have a chance to cool down. "We're treating Blair no differently than we would any other person in the same situation."

"All right, Frank, but don't put him in the general population. Put him in isolation while I arrange bail."

"Why should we?" Robb asked belligerently.

"I'm doing this for you two," Benedict said. "You have no idea how well connected Mr. Blair is. I'm pissed at you for tricking him into opening the trunk, but I know you well enough to know that you thought you were doing the right thing. If this blows up in your face, it could jeopardize your careers."

"Is that a threat?" Robb demanded.

"No, it's me trying to help you."

"He has a point, Steph," Santoro said. "And Blair will be out on bail soon, in any event. There's no sense putting him in danger."

Santoro turned to Benedict. "I'll arrange for a cell in the isolation wing."

"Thanks, Frank. I'll let Mr. Blair know how considerate you were."

As soon as Benedict left, Robb turned on her partner.

"Why are you kissing Blair's ass?"

"There's a lot of evidence against Blair, but it's not enough for an indictment. We can't even prove that Mrs. Blair's dead. Blair's going to be furious anyway, but his lawyers will go ballistic if he gets hurt in population."

Robb calmed down long enough to see that Santoro was right.

"Okay, call the jail and get him a cell in isolation. But the gloves come off the minute we have probable cause to arrest Blair for killing his wife."

Charles Benedict was in a terrific mood when he left police headquarters. Everything was going according to plan. Carrie Blair's Porsche had been dismembered in one of Nikolai Orlansky's chop shops. Its parts were scattered across the United States, thus eradicating any evidence that it, and not the Bentley, had been used to transport Carrie's body.

Carrie's shallow grave was seeded with evidence that would lead to Horace Blair's conviction for murder at a trial in which he would be defended, for a hefty fee, by the very individual who was framing him for the killing. Only one thing remained to be done. The police had to find Carrie's grave, and that would be taken care of very soon.

Benedict looked at his watch. It was a little after

eight p.m. His timing was just right. Nikolai Orlansky had a man on his payroll at the jail who could
guarantee that Horace Blair would spend the night
in a cell next to Barry Lester. Benedict would take
his time arranging for bail to be posted. By the time
Blair was back on the street, his fate would be sealed.

Chapter Twenty-Six

The jailer opened the steel door and Horace Blair walked out. His face was drained of color and his shoulders were stooped. He looked very old, and Benedict guessed that he hadn't slept. As soon as he saw his attorney in the waiting area, Blair flushed with anger. He straightened up and started to speak, but Benedict held up a hand to stop him, telling him to wait to talk until they were safely away from the jail. Blair erupted as soon as he was in Benedict's car.

"What the fuck is going on? Why did I have to spend a night in jail?"

"Hey, I know it was tough being in lockup all night, but I made sure they didn't put you in population. Did they give you your own cell?"

"Yes, but this cretin in the cell next to mine wouldn't shut up. He kept asking why I was in jail. Then he started talking about how many women he fucked and how he could get me drugs. I tried to sleep but it was impossible."

"You didn't talk about your case, did you?" Benedict asked, pretending to be alarmed.

"No. I remembered what you told me."

"Well, you're out now."

"Why wasn't I released sooner? I told you to get Pratt on this."

"I did, but he said he couldn't do anything until the bank opened in the morning. So I called the bail bondsman I usually use, but he had a family emergency. Believe me, I got you out of there as fast as I could. I didn't get any sleep, either."

Blair stewed in silence for a while. Then he had another outburst.

"This is outrageous. No one treats me like this. Those detectives are going to see what happens when someone fucks with me."

"Someone is definitely fucking with you, and it's not just the detectives. Could Carrie have put the hairs, the blood, and that gun in the trunk of your car? Does she have a key to your Bentley?"

"You think she's behind this?"

"I have no idea. But someone is setting you up, and she's the most likely suspect, unless you can think of someone else."

"I have enemies. You don't run a business like mine without ruffling a few feathers."

"Is there anyone you can think of who hates you so much they would kill Carrie, then try to pin the crime on you? Anyone who lost out to you in a business deal, or someone in your company who wants you out?"

Blair grew quiet. "I've made some dicey moves in

the last two years. There were some very pissed-off Russians who lost out on a bid to build an oil pipe-line, and I engineered a leveraged buyout of a high-tech company in California. But that was business. I can't believe any of those people would try to get back at me by killing my wife."

"Can you make a list for me of people who might hate you enough to do something like this? We have to cover all the bases. The one thing we know for certain is that someone is definitely out to get you.

"But now my priority is to get you home, where you can take a shower, get some sleep, and eat a good meal. You're going to have to stay sharp if we're going to get you through this nightmare in one piece."

Chapter Twenty-Seven

Dana's jaunt to the West Coast had played havoc with her business. She spent the weekend writing the reports she'd put aside to go on her wild-goose chase. On Monday, she testified in an insurance case. Minutes after she left the courtroom she'd received a call from an attorney representing a Baltimore Ravens running back who had been accused of beating up his girlfriend. Dana usually refused to represent batterers, but the player swore he was innocent and Dana believed him by the time she finished talking to him at his lawyer's office.

After the meeting, Dana took the elevator to the garage under the attorney's building. She was getting into her car when her cell phone rang.

"Cutler," she answered as she slid behind the wheel.

"Hey, I'm glad I caught you. It's Alice."

Alice Forte was a divorce attorney who had hired Dana on several occasions.

"What's up?" Dana asked.

"Marta Osgood was just here. She thinks Theodore is skimming from the business and hiding assets in an offshore account."

"What do you think?"

"It's possible. He is a slimeball."

"Send me what you've got and I'll get right on it."

"Will do. Say, did that woman ever hire you?"

"What woman?"

"This was a week or so ago. She called me for a reference. I said you were pretty good when you were sober."

Dana laughed. "Thanks a bunch. What was her name?"

"I can't remember it." Forte paused. "She had a French accent."

Dana had started to put her key in the ignition but she stopped.

"Do you remember anything else about her?"

"Not really. She called me around ten last Thursday. She wanted to know if I would recommend you. I said you did a great job and had a terrific reputation, so she asked how she could get in touch. I gave her your number. That's about it."

"Was her name Margo Laurent?"

"Yeah, that's it, Laurent! So did she hire you?"

"Yes, she did. Thanks for the referral," Dana said, and ended the call.

Carrie Blair had called Alice and the Queen Anne Players last Thursday, so something must have happened on Wednesday or Thursday that prompted the calls. As Dana drove out of the parking garage she tried to remember what she'd been doing on those two days. Jake was away and she'd stayed home when she wasn't working, so the triggering event had to be connected to one of her cases. There was a drug conspiracy case in federal court and a state vehicular homicide, but she'd finished most of her work in the criminal cases. She was investigating two divorces for Alice and one for another attorney. Then there were several cases for United Insurance.

Dana frowned. Whatever happened had to have happened on Wednesday, because she had slept most of Thursday. Wednesday night and early Thursday morning she'd worked on an insurance case but that couldn't be it. The case was a big nothing. Lars Jorgenson was claiming that he'd been permanently injured in a car crash. He walked with a cane and had a quack for a doctor. The insurance company had dealt with this doctor before and they didn't buy it, so Dana had camped outside Jorgenson's apartment and had eventually photographed him jogging.

Then the crazy woman chased her!

That had to be it. Dana remembered taking pictures of Jorgenson jogging when this couple walked out of a condo. The woman had looked her way before screaming and running toward her. Dana had peeled out and had seen the woman stop in the middle of the street. Was the woman Carrie Blair? Had she been close enough to read Dana's license plate? If she got the number, finding the owner would be easy for someone in law enforcement.

Dana sped home and raced down to her office. She had sent the photographs from the Jorgenson case to the insurance company, but she had a duplicate set in her file. Dana found the Jorgenson file and took out the photographs. She spread them across her desk and examined them with a magnifying glass.

It was Carrie Blair. Who was the man? If she could find him he might be able to tell her what was behind Blair's scheme. She would have to blow up the photo so she could get a good look at the face of Carrie Blair's companion.

Chapter Twenty-Eight

Christopher Rauh's hamlike hands were clenched, his massive body leaned threateningly toward Stephanie Robb, and his face was beet red.

"Are you out of your fucking mind?" the man in charge of the Lee County Homicide Division asked, his voice only a few decibels below a scream.

"He killed her," Stephanie Robb answered defiantly.

"Do you have any idea how powerful Horace Blair is? I've had Ray Mancuso on my ass all morning," he said, naming the commonwealth attorney, "and he's had the mayor on his ass, and the governor has been screaming at the mayor."

"Powerful people don't get a pass in America, Chris," Robb argued. "You kill someone, you go down. Virginia isn't a banana republic."

Rick Hamada laughed. He was short and chubby and his sweater vest and slicked-down black hair made him look like a nerd, but in court, Lee County's chief criminal deputy was Attila the Hun.

"Blair's buddies live in the White House, Steph,"

Hamada said. "He has Supreme Court justices over to his house for brunch. He's a multi-fucking-millionaire who contributes to every influential politician in this state. For guys with Blair's influence, Virginia *is* a banana republic."

"We can nail him," Robb insisted.

"Not on what you've given me," Hamada said. "There's an old saying about not missing when you aim at a king. If you arrest Horace Blair for murder and the case blows up, you're going to be spending the rest of your law-enforcement career in animal control."

"It's her blood and her hair," Robb said. "Read the lab report. We have witnesses who will testify that the Blairs had a heated argument at the Theodore Roosevelt hotel a week before she disappeared. And don't forget the gun."

"Which you can't connect to a murder because you don't even know if Carrie Blair is dead," the assistant commonwealth attorney reminded Robb.

"You should never have made Blair spend a minute in jail," Rauh snapped. "You knew Benedict would get him out on bail."

"The gun gave us a legit basis for arresting Blair," Santoro said calmly, in hopes of lowering the temperature in the room.

"Were Blair's prints found on the gun?" Hamada asked.

"No," Santoro answered, "but neither were anyone else's. It was wiped clean."

"This could turn into a major cluster fuck," Rauh fumed. "But it won't, because we are going to dismiss this stupid gun charge. Then you are going to stay away from Horace Blair unless I tell you otherwise."

"So we're off the case?" Robb asked, making no attempt to hide her anger.

"No. You're on the case. But you will not—I repeat, *will not*—contact Horace Blair or anyone who knows him until you have cleared it with me. Is that understood?"

"That was pleasant," Frank said as the detectives walked back to their desks.

"Asshole motherfuckers," Robb muttered.

"They did make a few good points," Frank said.

Before Robb could reply, the intercom on Santoro's desk buzzed.

"Detective Santoro, there's an Arthur Jefferson out here," the receptionist said. "He wants to speak to you about the Blair case."

Robb started to say that they didn't have time, but Santoro held up his hand.

"Okay, send him in."

"Jefferson is a bottom feeder," Robb said as soon as Santoro let up on the button. "He barely makes a living off of court appointments and traffic cases. What could he possibly know about the Blairs?"

"Hey, we can use all the help we can get. And the tip about the Bentley panned out."

Arthur Jefferson was a skinny, light-complexioned black man with a wide smile and outsized gestures. He talked too loud, he swung his arms to emphasize his points, and he was quick to bend the truth. He also looked like he wasn't doing too well. His dark blue suit was shiny from wear, the collar of his white shirt was frayed, and his shoes were scuffed.

"How y'all doin'?" Jefferson asked when he drew in sight of the detectives.

"We're doing good," Frank answered. "How about you?"

"Can't complain, can't complain."

"So, Arthur," Robb began impatiently, "what brings you here?"

Jefferson grinned. "I am here to make your day. Yes, ma'am, I am here to make you one happy detective."

"And how are you going to do that?" Santoro asked.

"Y'all been lookin' for Carrie Blair, have you not?"

"We have."

"A client of mine can help you find her."

"Who is this client?"

Jefferson threw his hands out at his side. "Not so fast. We got to come to an agreement first."

"Keep talking," Santoro said.

"My client fell in with a bad crowd, yes sir, a bad crowd." The lawyer shook his head slowly to show

how bewildered he was that one so good could have
made such a tragic mistake. "Now he's facing some
jail time. If he helps you out, we'd like you to make
things right for him."

"And how exactly is he going to help us?" Santoro
asked.

"He's gonna tell you where Carrie Blair is buried."

Chapter Twenty-Nine

Frank Santoro held open the door to the interrogation room and Arthur Jefferson gestured Barry Lester inside. Lester had been brought to the Homicide Bureau so that other inmates wouldn't know he was snitching. He was dressed in an orange jumpsuit and his hands were cuffed. Santoro took off the cuffs and Lester flashed his most ingratiating smile as he and his lawyer took seats on one side of the room's only table. Robb and Santoro sat on the other side.

"I hope I can help you guys," Lester said.

"I checked you out, Barry," Santoro said. "It looks like you've made a habit out of helping the police solve crimes."

"Look, I know I've got a record, but I'm not a bad guy, and when I get a chance to pay back my debt to society by helping you guys solve a crime, I take it."

Lester shook his head in disgust. "That Blair is one sick puppy. Killing his wife, that's cold." He turned his attention to Robb. "The stuff I've done, none of it is violent. I don't go for that. And men who abuse women, well, I draw the line there. My mother—God rest her soul—taught me to respect women."

Robb's features hardened and her shoulders tensed. Stephanie hated ass kissers.

"That's good to hear," Santoro said to head off anything rash his partner might do. "So, Barry, your lawyer says you know where Carrie Blair is buried."

"I do."

"How did you learn this information?"

"Blair told me."

"Really?" Robb said, unable to mask her skepticism.

"They had him in isolation for the night, and he had the cell next to me. Man, was he scared. Here he is, a big-shot millionaire with Hong Kong tailors, and they put him in a jumpsuit two sizes too small, locked in with hardened criminals." Lester grinned. "So I calmed him down and we got real friendly."

"Blair is the head of a multinational corporation," Robb said. "He negotiates with the Communist Chinese and the Russians. I have a hard time believing that he would be stupid enough to tell you he'd killed his wife, then give you the location of her grave."

"But he did. Like I said, I got his confidence, and he admitted he did her. He said he put her in the trunk of his Bentley and drove her to this place and buried her."

Santoro and Robb didn't show any reaction, but

they both wondered how Lester knew that Blair had a Bentley and that the body might have been in its trunk.

"He just confessed and told you the exact spot where he dumped the corpse?" Robb asked.

"That's right."

"How do we know you didn't kill Carrie Blair?" she said.

"No way. I've been locked up since before she disappeared. Check the records."

Santoro leaned back and folded his arms across his chest. "What do you want, Arthur?"

"He leads you to the body and testifies, I think he's earned himself a 'Get Out of Jail Free' card."

"We'll talk about that with the commonwealth attorney if Mr. Lester takes us to the body."

The picturesque Blue Ridge Mountains are part of the larger Appalachian range. The densely packed trees release isoprene into the atmosphere, which creates a haze and makes the mountains look blue from a distance. But Stephanie Robb and Frank Santoro were not appreciating the beauty of the region as their caravan of police vehicles headed for the abandoned campground where Barry Lester claimed they would find Carrie Blair's grave. The lead car was driven by two uniformed officers. Lester was sitting in the back beside his attorney. Robb and Santoro were next, followed by a van from the crime lab. The morgue wagon, piloted by medical examiner Nick Winters, was also there in case Lester knew what he was talking about.

Santoro hadn't said a word since they'd left police headquarters, and Robb could tell that he had something on his mind.

"What's bothering you?" Robb asked her partner.

"Something about this case doesn't feel right."

"Like what?"

"I don't know. There's just a lot of odd stuff going on."

"Such as?"

"First we get an anonymous tip about the Bentley, and the paper gets an anonymous tip about a prenup. Then there's Blair; he's the head of a multinational corporation, he deals with heads of countries. You can't be a wimp and get where he's gotten. Can you see him spilling his guts to Lester?"

"Sometimes things are exactly as they seem, Frank. In real life, if the wife gets killed, it's usually hubby whodunit."

The lead car turned off the highway at a sign advertising Rainbow Lake Resort. The sign was weathered and the paint was peeling. The resort used to give guided trail rides, canoe trips, and provide a place for camping. Three years before, the owners went bankrupt and closed it down. Now the deserted camp was used by the homeless and rowdy teenagers.

Robb turned the car onto a dirt road. Vegetation

had reclaimed part of it and there were potholes to navigate. There had been heavy rains the week before that would have wiped out any trace of tire tracks. The lead car stopped in a gravel parking lot in front of an abandoned log cabin that had served as the office and rec room for the camp. Santoro could also see the empty stables and cabins. The area was surrounded by dense woods. Straight ahead, a sharp wind was driving the blue-green waters of a large lake onto a rocky beach.

The van from the crime lab and the morgue wagon pulled in. Robb parked next to the patrol car. When she got out of the car, the wind off the lake seared her cheeks. Robb turned up her coat collar before opening the back door of the car that had transported the prisoner. Jefferson got out. Then Lester edged across the seat and stood up. He was handcuffed and his ankles were secured by manacles. Santoro watched him carefully when Robb unlocked his shackles.

"Thanks," Lester said as he shook out his hands and hopped up and down for a few seconds.

"Where is the body, Barry?" Robb asked.

Lester turned in a circle and stopped when he spotted the lake.

"Okay. We go along the woods on the left toward the water. He said there was a trail."

"Lead on," Santoro told him. Lester started walking with his lawyer close behind and the detectives on either side. Nick Winters and an assistant from the morgue followed the forensic experts. The officers who had driven Lester took shovels out of the trunk of their car and brought up the rear.

A narrow hiking trail led into the woods a few yards from the lakeshore.

"Let the people from the crime lab go first," Santoro ordered. A man and two women worked their way cautiously down the trail, recording everything with a video camera.

"He said he buried her about a quarter of a mile in on the left side of the trail," Lester said.

He scanned the underbrush, then stopped suddenly and pointed to another trail that led into the forest.

"This should be it," Lester said. "The grave shouldn't be too far in. Blair told me he got tired carrying the body. That she was heavy, so he couldn't go too far."

"Wait here," Santoro said as he and Robb followed the techs down the new trail. They had not gone far when they saw a cleared area with dirt that looked freshly turned. As soon as the forensic experts finished, Santoro ordered the officers with the shovels to get to work.

"And be gentle," he said. "Treat this like an archaeological dig. The lab techs will supervise."

The officers had moved a small amount of dirt off the grave when one of them stopped and pointed at something shiny that was half buried under some soil.

"What's that?" he asked.

The woman from the forensic team used a light whisk broom to brush away the material covering the object. She was wearing gloves. She picked up the object and placed it in an evidence bag held by one of the other techs. The third forensic expert photographed the whole thing with a video camera. The technician with the envelope held it up. Santoro peered through the plastic at a key that looked very similar to the one he used to open his front door.

It didn't take much more digging before a blood-less white knuckle was uncovered. The policeman who had exposed it called over the lab techs, and everyone else gathered at the edge of the grave.

"I told you," Lester said, pleased as could be. Everyone else was somber.

As more dirt was tossed out of the grave, more and more of Carrie Blair was revealed. The blood that stained the front of her white blouse had dried and looked brown and flakey. Her face was drained of color and patches of skin had rotted away, revealing bleached bone and tissue. Santoro looked away out of respect. Robb stared hard and seethed.

"It looks like Mr. Lester came through for us," Santoro told Jefferson, who was keeping his head up and his eyes away from the corpse.

"Indeed he did, indeed he did. Now it's your turn to come through for him," the lawyer said.

"You know that only a prosecutor can make that call, but I'll tell him to do the right thing."

"If he does," Lester said, "I'll sweeten the pot by telling you why Blair popped his wife."

Robb had been listening to the conversation. She turned quickly and stared at Lester menacingly.

"You've been holding out on us?" she asked.

"Not at all," Lester said, holding up both hands to placate the angry detective. "I promised to tell you where Blair buried the body, and that was all I promised. This info is a bonus. If you come through for me."

Chapter Thirty

"Fuck, fuck, *fuck*," Christopher Rauh said as he stomped around his office.

"I know exactly what you mean," Rick Hamada said. "But there is definitely enough to go to a grand jury. Especially now that we have the ballistics report on the bullet that was found during Carrie Blair's autopsy."

Robb and Santoro were smart enough to say nothing. They had already laid out their case and it was up to their superiors to decide what they wanted to do with it.

"Arrest Blair for murder and there is going to be a shit storm," Rauh said.

"Which I am going to have to weather," Hamada reminded him. "I'll be prosecuting, which means I'll be hit with the fallout if Blair walks."

"So you're okay with going for a murder indictment?" Rauh asked.

"We have a body, a motive, strong forensic evidence, and the murder weapon. Yeah, I'm good to go," Hamada answered.

Rauh looked down at his desk. Then he looked at Santoro and Robb.

"You did good work. I'm proud of you. You didn't let me stop you from going after Blair."

"Thanks," Santoro said. Robb didn't say anything. She was still pissed off at Rauh.

"Okay. You two work with Rick to get the case in shape for the grand jury. If we get an indictment, you get to make the collar."

The meeting broke up and Hamada followed the two detectives into the hall.

"I second what Chris said," Hamada told them. "Let's meet tomorrow morning and work up this sucker."

Robb smiled but Santoro didn't. Stephanie had pushed to go to Rauh and Hamada as soon as they received the ballistics report. On paper, the case looked solid. But Santoro wondered if the case wasn't too solid. He hadn't voiced his doubts because Robb's arguments for going after Horace Blair were based on solid evidence, and his doubts were based on a queasy feeling.

Stephanie had a meeting with an assistant commonwealth attorney, so she walked with Hamada to the prosecutor's office. Santoro went to the jail and asked the officer who was manning the reception desk for the visitors' log for the time Barry Lester was incarcerated. Arthur Jefferson had visited several times.

Most of those visits had been in the past few days, which was not surprising. Lester's only other visitor was a woman named Tiffany Starr. That sounded like the type of phony name a stripper or hooker would use, which meant that Miss Starr probably had a rap sheet.

When he returned to his office, Santoro ran Starr's name and discovered that she was on parole for a narcotics offense. Parole and Probation was on the floor below the Homicide Bureau. Half an hour later, Santoro returned to his office with a copy of Tiffany Starr's pre-sentence report. Reading a tale of another wasted life was depressing.

Tiffany's given name was Sharon Ross and she was the daughter of Devon and Miranda Ross. The Rosses were well off, and Sharon had gone to private schools, where her grades were mediocre. Her first brush with the law came as a juvenile, when she ran away from home. Shoplifting charges soon followed. The pre-sentence writer suspected that Sharon was using cocaine as early as the eighth grade and was stealing to finance her habit.

In her sophomore year of high school, Sharon spent two months at a fancy clinic, but rehab didn't take and she was readmitted in her junior year. She dropped out of school at the beginning of her senior year and married Fredrick Krantz, an auto mechanic who was also a drummer in a rock band that played in one of the clubs Sharon frequented. They ran away to Oregon, where the marriage unraveled.

Sharon returned to Virginia, where she faked a résumé and got a job as a bookkeeper. She was fired soon after for embezzling money.

Sharon received probation with a requirement that she go into rehab for her drug problem. When she violated the conditions of her probation, the judge sent her to prison in hopes that tough love would work where all else had failed. In prison, Sharon developed a heroin habit. After leaving prison, Krantz adopted the name Tiffany Starr and began dancing at various strip clubs. That is where she met Barry Lester.

Santoro was about to put the pre-sentence report away but he hesitated. He had the feeling that something he'd read was important though he didn't know what it was. He started rereading the report from the beginning, and it didn't take him long to see what he'd almost missed. Sharon Ross's father was Devon Ross, and Kyle Ross was Sharon's brother. On the Monday that Carrie Blair disappeared, everyone had been talking about *Commonwealth v. Kyle Ross*. Santoro tried to remember why. He recalled that there was something about evidence that had gone missing. Then Carrie disappeared and the case was quickly forgotten.

Santoro called the Narcotics Unit and learned that Mary Maguire was the prosecutor who had tried the Ross case. Maguire's secretary told the detective that Maguire was handling a pretrial matter on the second floor of the courthouse.

Santoro walked over to the courtroom where Maguire was working and sat in the rear. When court was over, Maguire stuffed her paperwork in her attaché and Santoro intercepted her outside the courtroom.

"Judge Stiles can be a real hard-ass. I thought you handled him nicely."

"Who are you?" Maguire asked, not bothering to hide her impatience.

Santoro showed her his ID. "I'm a detective over in Homicide."

"Homicide? How can I help you?"

"I wanted to ask you about a case you tried, *Commonwealth v. Ross.*"

Maguire flushed angrily. "Thanks for ruining my day."

"Pardon?"

"I was hoping never to hear about *Commonwealth v. Ross* ever again."

"Why is that?"

"I had the single most embarrassing moment I've ever experienced trying that case."

"What happened?"

Maguire told Santoro about the cocaine that was mysteriously transformed into fizzing baking soda.

"And Charles Benedict was the lawyer?"

"I'm certain he switched the cocaine, and Carrie was convinced she knew how."

"Carrie Blair?"

"She was my supervisor. The judge had her come

down so she could decide whether to dismiss. She was furious. She told me not to blame myself because she knew what happened."

"And what was that?"

"She never told me."

"But she suspected Benedict?"

"I can't remember if she came right out and said it, but I'm sure she was convinced that Benedict engineered the switch."

"Has anyone followed up on the investigation?"

"No. Carrie was going to do it. Then . . . well, you know."

"Yeah."

"Why did you want to know about the Ross case?"

"It came up in something I'm working on."

"Something involving Benedict?"

"I can't answer that right now, sorry."

"I get it, but I wish the worst for that bastard."

Santoro had discussed *Ross* with Maguire as he walked her to her office. The important additional information he'd gotten from the young prosecutor was that Carrie Blair seemed angrier at Benedict than Maguire would have expected. On the way back to his office, Santoro wondered whether Blair and Benedict had a history. He also wondered if Benedict, whose specialty was drug cases, had ever represented Kyle Ross's sister.

When he got to his desk, Santoro looked up the

court records for Sharon Ross's cases. Charles Benedict was listed as the attorney of record in her last two brushes with the law.

Santoro let his mind wander. It seemed far-fetched, but Santoro was nagged by the idea that Charles Benedict might have something to do with Carrie's murder. He wondered if Carrie had come in contact with the attorney after court on the day she disappeared.

Santoro swiveled toward his desk and searched his file for the log of the information found on Carrie Blair's office and home computers and Carrie's phone records. He didn't find any calls or e-mails from Carrie to Benedict, but he did note that Carrie had run an Internet search on a private investigator named Dana Cutler a few days before she'd disappeared. Why was Blair interested in a private investigator?

Shortly before Carrie conducted the Internet search for information about Cutler, she had called the Department of Motor Vehicles. Then she called a lawyer named Alice Forte and a number in Seattle, Washington. When Santoro dialed the Seattle number he was connected to an answering machine for the Queen Anne Players. Now Santoro was thoroughly confused.

Chapter Thirty-One

Dana meant to get in touch with the detectives in charge of the Blair case but she had been on the go, constantly building a defense for the football player who had been accused of beating his girlfriend. The evening after Carrie Blair's body was unearthed, Dana staggered home at ten thirty and collapsed on the couch to watch TV while she ate chicken lo mein out of a take-out carton. The lead story on the news killed her appetite.

On the screen, Horace Blair was being perp-walked to a police car by a stocky woman in a brown suit. A voiceover informed Dana that Carrie Blair's body had been found in the Blue Ridge Mountains and that her husband, Horace Blair, had been accused of her murder. Before she could think too much about Blair's arrest, her cell phone rang.

"Cutler," she answered.

"I hope I'm not calling too late," a vaguely familiar voice said.

"Who is this?"

"Marty Draper." There was a pause. "Rene Marchand."

"Oh, hi, Marty. What's up?"

"I was watching CNN and they had a story about the Blairs."

"He's been arrested for his wife's murder."

"I know. They showed her picture and it made me remember something. Did you know that Carrie was an actress?"

"No, I didn't."

"There was one time when she came to the gallery without Horace. I was getting ready to close and go to a restaurant down the street from the gallery. I asked her if she wanted to join me. She seemed grateful for the company.

"Anyway, we both had a little more wine than we should have and we got to talking about our childhoods. Mine was a little rocky, but hers was bad."

"Oh?"

"She told me that she never dreamed of being a lawyer when she was young. Her exact words were, 'I was too busy trying to survive.'"

"What did she mean?"

"Her mother was an alcoholic. She abandoned Carrie when she was eleven. That was after her father died of a heart attack while he was serving a prison sentence for auto theft. Carrie said that Children's Services shuffled her around through a series of foster homes. She didn't go into detail, but I got the impression that she was sexually and physically abused. That's where the acting came in.

"Carrie said she ran away when she turned sixteen. She ended up in Hollywood, planning to become a movie star. She said she made money any way she could, but she didn't go into detail.

"You only saw Carrie in her disguise, but she was really beautiful. She told me that she was cast in minor roles in a few low-budget films. I think one was a vampire flick, and there was another one about a giant alligator at a summer camp for teens. But she caught on pretty quickly that the directors who offered her the roles didn't do it because she was a talented actress. When she finally came to grips with the fact that she was not going to be the next big thing, she married another bit player for security, but her husband was abusive and the marriage didn't last very long."

"How did she get to be a lawyer?"

"It's a great story. After getting divorced, Carrie worked low-paying jobs and barely got by. One day it dawned on her that education could be a way out of her situation. She got a GED, graduated from a community college, and ended up at Berkeley, where she graduated summa cum laude with a degree in history. That got her into Georgetown Law School, which is how she ended up on the East Coast.

"Anyway, the reason I called you was to tell you about the acting."

"Did you tell her about the Queen Anne Players?" Dana asked.

"I definitely mentioned it."

"Then that's the link."

"Carrie would know how to fake a French accent," Draper said, "and how to disguise herself as this Margo Laurent woman."

Chapter Thirty-Two

The next morning, Santoro had to be at the courthouse at nine to testify in a motion to suppress. He was at the office of the prosecutor who was handling the hearing forty-five minutes before court was to start. They went over the evidence and walked up to the courtroom together. Santoro had his cell phone turned off while he was testifying. When he left the stand, he walked into the hall outside the courtroom and checked for missed calls. Stephanie had phoned him twice.

"Where are you?" Robb asked as soon as Santoro called her.

"I was in court on the Danny Fong case. I told you."

"You did. I forgot. Can you meet me at Horace Blair's estate? I'm on my way."

"What are we going to do there?"

"I have an idea and I want to see if it pans out."

Robb was parked on the side of the road next to the gate to the Blair estate. Santoro parked behind her. Sitting beside Robb was Wilda Parks, a feisty woman in her early sixties who had been working in the crime lab since well before Santoro joined the force. Santoro walked over to Robb's car. She rolled down the window.

"Why are we here?" Santoro asked.

"Wilda found Horace Blair's prints on the key from the grave."

"So?"

Parks was holding three plastic evidence bags in her lap. Robb pointed to one bag which held a single key.

"That's the key we found in the grave," she said.

She pointed to another bag which held a key ring with several keys.

"That's the key ring we found in the purse that was buried with Carrie Blair.

"And these," she said, pointing to the third bag, "are the keys we took from Horace Blair when he was booked into the jail."

Santoro looked confused. "What are you going to do with these keys?"

"There is a key on Carrie Blair's key ring that looks exactly like the key we found in the grave. What if they both open a specific door in the Blair house but none of Horace's keys open that door?"

"You think Blair dropped the key in the grave by accident?" Santoro asked.

"It's possible. If he buried Carrie at night he might not have noticed."

Santoro pointed to a key on Horace Blair's key ring. "That key looks exactly like the key we found in the grave."

Robb shrugged. "I could be wrong. If I am, we wasted a trip out here. Hop in and let's see what happens."

Robb pressed the button on an intercom attached to the wall next to the gate. Moments later, Walter Paget, Blair's houseman, answered. Robb identified herself and asked to be admitted to the estate.

"I can't let you in without Mr. Blair's permission."

"Actually, we don't need his permission, Walter. I have a search warrant that authorizes me to enter the grounds. If you don't open this gate right now, I'm going to arrest you for obstruction of justice, your choice."

The houseman was silent. Robb waited patiently. Moments later, the gate opened and Robb drove up the driveway to the front door. Walter was waiting for them.

"Thanks for letting us in," Robb said as she showed him the search warrant.

"How can I help you?" Walter asked in a tone that could only be described as frosty.

"We want to see if a few keys fit any of the doors in the house," Robb answered.

"What doors?"

"We're not certain but we might as well start with the front door," she said. "Can you close it and lock it for us, please?"

Paget hesitated for a moment before stepping inside and closing the door. Robb took the key that had been found in the grave out of the evidence bag and Parks began filming the proceedings.

Robb held up the key. "I am Lee County detective Stephanie Robb and I'm standing at the front door of Horace Blair's house. This is a key that was found in the grave where Carrie Blair's body was discovered. The crime lab found prints matched to Horace Blair on this key. I am going to insert it in the front door of Horace Blair's home."

Robb bent down and inserted the key in the front door lock while continuing to describe what she was doing for the camera. She twisted the key and opened the front door. Parks caught the expression of surprise on the detective's face. Obviously Robb never thought it would be this easy.

Robb put the key back and removed the keys found in Carrie Blair's purse. She selected the key that looked identical to the key found in the grave and identified it for the camera. Then she put it in the lock and opened the front door. Finally, Robb took out the keys on Horace Blair's key ring and tried the key that looked like the key found in the grave. It looked newer than the key from the grave and the key found in Carrie Blair's purse. Santoro frowned as Robb tried the key. It did not open the front door. Robb tried every other key on the chain. None of them opened the front door.

Robb told Parks to stop filming. Then she smiled. "We got him. Blair fucked up."

"That's what it looks like," Santoro agreed, but he didn't sound completely convinced. Robb was too excited to notice.

Chapter Thirty-Three

Three days in jail had done the damage Charles Benedict had anticipated. Blair's complexion was pasty and he looked every day of his seventy-four years. With Carrie dead and Blair in jail, there was only a skeleton staff at Blair's estate. Blair had given Benedict the security code for the front gate and the house so he could pick out clothing for Horace to wear at court appearances. Benedict had brought a beautifully tailored suit to the jail but Horace had lost so much weight that the suit looked like it was draped on a wire hanger.

"How are you holding up?" Benedict asked. He sounded deeply concerned but he was really delighted.

"Am I going to get out today?"

"I hope so. Gardner is tough but Jack Pratt has lined up several prominent witnesses who will vouch for you."

Before Benedict could say anything else, the Honorable Preston L. Gardner III emerged from his chambers.

"We're here for a bail hearing in *Commonwealth v. Blair*," Gardner said as he took his seat on the dais. "Are the parties ready to proceed?"

"Rick Hamada for the commonwealth. We're ready, Your Honor."

"Charles Benedict for Mr. Blair. The defense is ready."

"I don't need any opening statements," the judge said, "so let's get this show on the road. You've got the burden, Mr. Hamada."

Rick Hamada began his presentation by calling Frank Santoro. He used the first few minutes to establish the detective's credentials before asking questions that would allow him to argue that the defendant should be held without bail.

"Detective Santoro," Hamada asked, "can you please summarize the evidence that led you to the conclusion that there was probable cause to arrest the defendant for murder?"

"Yes, sir. First off, there was the motive. There were newspaper reports about a prenuptial agreement—"

"Objection! Irrelevant," Charles Benedict said as he sprang to his feet. "This court shouldn't be using unfounded rumors to decide an issue as serious as bail."

"The rumor is just one piece of the decision to arrest," Hamada replied. "It's background and was just part of the big picture."

"There's no jury here, Mr. Benedict," Judge

Gardner said. "I'll allow the testimony and take it for what I deem it's worth."

"Go ahead, Detective," Hamada said.

"The newspaper reported that the defendant and his wife had signed a prenuptial agreement before their wedding. According to the story, Mr. Blair was going to have to give Mrs. Blair twenty million dollars the week she disappeared."

"Please tell the judge if any physical evidence caused you to suspect that Mr. Blair may have killed his wife," Rick Hamada said.

"There was the evidence we found in the trunk of Mr. Blair's Bentley," Santoro answered.

Hamada turned to Judge Gardner. "For purposes of this hearing only, Mr. Benedict has agreed that we can present the following testimony without calling experts from the crime lab or the medical examiner."

"Is Mr. Hamada correct?" the judge asked.

"He is," Benedict agreed.

"Proceed, Mr. Hamada," Judge Gardner said.

"Detective Santoro, please tell the court about this evidence and its significance?"

"Okay, well, we found blond hairs in the trunk. The crime lab performed a DNA test on the hairs and concluded that they belonged to the victim, Mrs. Blair. So that was evidence that suggested she may have been in the trunk.

"Next, we found a blood smear in the trunk. The lab concluded that the blood was from Mrs. Blair by doing DNA testing. That suggested that Mrs. Blair may have been wounded or deceased when she was in the trunk."

"Did you find a gun in the trunk?" Hamada asked.

"We did, a .38 pistol."

"Was there anything unusual about the gun?" the prosecutor asked.

"The serial numbers had been filed off."

"Why was that significant?"

"We see this commonly in guns that are sold illegally on the street and used to commit crimes."

"Objection," Benedict said. "Irrelevant, and the prejudice outweighs any possible relevance."

"Sustained."

"After you discovered this physical evidence in a car belonging to the defendant did you discover the body of the victim in this case, Carrie Blair?"

"We did."

"Where did you find it?"

"It had been buried in a shallow grave in the woods at an abandoned resort."

"Did the medical examiner determine the cause of death?"

"Yes, sir. Mrs. Blair was shot and the bullet caused massive internal injuries."

"What type of bullet caused the damage?"

"A semi-jacketed hollow-point."

"Where was this bullet discovered?"

"The medical examiner found it in Mrs. Blair's body while he was performing the autopsy."

"Why didn't the bullet exit the body?"

"A semi-jacketed hollow-point has a soft point. It's designed to mushroom inside the body when it hits bone. That's why there was so much damage to the internal organs."

"Was the bullet sent to the crime lab?"

"It was."

"Did the ballistics expert at the crime lab draw a conclusion concerning the gun that fired the bullet?"

"Yes, sir. He concluded that the gun that was found in the trunk of Mr. Blair's Bentley fired the bullet that killed Mrs. Blair."

"One more thing, Detective Santoro. Did you find some keys in Mrs. Blair's grave?"

"We did."

"Where did you find the keys?"

"Mrs. Blair's purse was found in the grave, and there was a key ring in the purse. Then there was a single key that was unearthed when we began digging."

"The key was just lying there?" Hamada asked.

"Yes, sir. It looked like it may have fallen in the grave by accident."

"Objection! That's pure speculation," Benedict said.

"Sustained."

"Was the crime lab able to connect the single key to the defendant?"

"A forensic expert found a fingerprint on the key and matched it to the defendant."

"Did you conduct an experiment with the keys?"

"My partner, Detective Stephanie Robb, did. I was also present at the defendant's estate, and so was Wilda Parks, the forensic expert who raised the print. We had in our possession the single key, the keys from Mrs. Blair's purse, and the keys that were in the defendant's possession when he was arrested."

"What did Detective Robb do when you arrived at the estate?" the prosecutor asked.

"She tried the single key in the front door of the defendant's mansion, and it opened the door," Santoro replied.

"So the key turned out to be the defendant's front door key?" Hamada asked.

"Objection," Benedict said. "There is no evidence that the key belonged to Mr. Blair. That's speculation. It could have been Mrs. Blair's key and Mr. Blair may have touched it at some point. You can't date fingerprints."

"I'll sustain the objection," Judge Gardner ruled.

"I'll rephrase the question, Detective. Did the key that you found in the grave that bore the defendant's fingerprint open the front door to the defendant's mansion?"

"Yes, it did."

"Did any key on the key ring you found in the victim's purse open the front door?"

"Yes, one of the keys on the key ring found in the purse did open the front door."

"What about the defendant's keys? Did any of them open the front door?"

"No. We tried them all and none of them worked."

Horace Blair leaned into Benedict. "That's impossible," he whispered furiously.

"We'll talk about this at the break," Benedict said. "Let me listen to the testimony. I don't want to miss anything."

"What conclusion did you draw from this experiment?" Hamada asked.

"We thought it was unlikely that Mrs. Blair had two keys to her front door, though that is certainly possible. We thought that it was more likely that the key on her chain, which bore her fingerprints, was Mrs. Blair's house key and the single key belonged to someone else, who had accidently dropped it in the grave while he was digging.

"The most likely owner of the single key was the person whose prints were found on it, the defendant. That conclusion was strengthened by the discovery that none of the defendant's keys opened the front door of his house."

"Thank you, Detective. I have no further questions."

Charles Benedict was certain that Hamada did not plan to put Barry Lester on the stand. Hamada would have no idea how Lester would stand up under cross, and he wouldn't want Benedict to get his hands on a transcript of sworn testimony that could be used to contradict Lester at trial. Benedict was also certain that Hamada was laying a trap for him, and he looked forward to falling into it.

"Detective Santoro," Benedict said, "what prompted you to go to Mr. Blair's place of business and ask him if he would let you look in the trunk of his Bentley?"

"We received a tip from someone who claimed to have seen the defendant put Mrs. Blair's body in the trunk of his car."

"What is the name of the good citizen who came forward with this information?"

"It was an anonymous tip."

"I see. Now there was no way that you could have gotten a judge to issue a search warrant for the trunk based solely on an anonymous tip, was there?"

"No, sir."

"Then how did you get to see the inside of the trunk?"

"Mr. Blair opened it for us."

"He could have refused, couldn't he?"

"Yes."

"And there was nothing you could have done about that if he had said that he was not going to let you search the trunk, was there?"

"No."

"Mr. Blair is the head of a multinational business empire, is he not?"

"Yes."

"He has degrees from two Ivy League universities?"

"I believe so."

"All of which point to Mr. Blair being highly intelligent?"

"I guess so."

Benedict pointed at his client. "So, Detective, you're telling Judge Gardner that this highly intelligent executive who deals with problems on a global scale killed his wife, went to great lengths to hide her body, then willingly let you look in the trunk of his car, knowing that the murder weapon was in it and that there might be other evidence that would incriminate him?"

"The defendant let us look in the trunk," Santoro responded.

"Let's talk about these keys. It was pretty convenient finding the key with Mr. Blair's print in that grave, wasn't it?"

"I don't know about convenient. It was there."

"Dropped accidentally by the murderer?"

"That was a possibility."

"Mr. Blair had a key chain with his keys on it when he was arrested, did he not?"

"Yes."

"The keys on the chain were for his cars, the side door to his house, and his office, right?"

"Yes."

"Isn't it normal to keep your house key on the ring with the rest of your keys?"

"I don't know what's normal."

"Do you keep the key to your front door on your key chain with the rest of your important keys?"

"Yes."

"How did the key you found in the grave get off Mr. Blair's key ring and into the grave? Do you think it just hopped off?"

"I don't know how it got in the grave."

"What possible reason would Mr. Blair have to take his front door key off of his key chain while digging that grave?"

"I have no idea."

"Now, Detective, if I have this right, Mr. Blair's motive is based on a rumor spread by an unknown source; you asked to search the car based on a tip from someone who refused to identify himself; then you conveniently found Mr. Blair's key in the grave where the killer buried his wife. Isn't one explanation for what is going on here that the real killer spread the rumor about the prenuptial agreement, then called you with the tip about the Bentley and planted that key to frame Mr. Blair?"

"That's a possibility, but it's been my experience that murderers—even those with above-average IQs—often make stupid mistakes, and we often receive anonymous tips from good citizens who want to help solve a crime but don't tell us their name because they are afraid the criminal will seek revenge, or for some other reason."

"Tell me, Detective Santoro, did another anonymous tipster tell you where to find the place where Mrs. Blair was buried?"

"No, sir," Santoro responded.

"Then how did you know where to look?"

Rick Hamada fought hard to restrain himself from leaping up, pounding his chest, and howling like a wolf that has just vanquished his prey. Frank Santoro's face showed none of the joy Hamada felt.

"An inmate was housed in the cell next to the defendant during the period when Mr. Blair was incarcerated," Santoro said. "Mr. Blair confessed to him that he had killed his wife so he wouldn't have to pay her twenty million dollars when their prenuptial agreement terminated. Then he told him where the body was buried."

"Lester lied!" Blair shouted as soon as Benedict closed the door to the jury room where they were conferring during a recess. "I hardly spoke to him. He's a lying son of a bitch."

"And we'll prove that," Benedict said. "I'll have my investigators digging into his background immediately. The cops put snitches in isolation to protect them. I'm betting that Lester has a history of getting out of trouble by testifying for the police.

"The good news is that if we unmask him in front of the jury, we'll blow apart the state's entire case."

"Is this going to prevent me from getting bail?" Blair asked anxiously.

"I don't know," Benedict said.

"The whole case makes no sense," Horace said. "I would never have let those detectives look in the trunk if I'd killed Carrie."

"I agree, and Gardner is smart enough to get that," Benedict said.

"What I can't understand is how my house key ended up in Carrie's grave. After you used the key on my key ring to open the door I put it back on the key ring."

"I can think of an explanation, but I hope I'm wrong."

"What is it?"

"Your wife was a longtime prosecutor, Horace. She had many opportunities to make enemies in the law-enforcement community. And she also had friends who are cops. The killer would plant the key to frame you, and a friend of Carrie's who thought you killed her would plant the key to make sure you were convicted."

"You think I was set up by the police?"

"It's possible."

"But the key would have to have been put in the grave when Carrie was buried. I still had it when she disappeared."

"The police took your keys when you were booked into the jail on the gun charge. If the person who killed Carrie planted the key, he could have gotten it from the property room and put the key in the grave. Or the key could have been dropped in the grave while the grave was being uncovered. The key is small. It would fit in a palm. You could let it fall in one section and cover it with dirt while the diggers were working on another section. "

"But that means Detective Robb or Santoro might have killed Carrie."

"Or anyone else who was at the grave site."

"Robb and Santoro put me in isolation. Either one could have made sure I was put in a cell next to Lester."

"Good thinking," Benedict said. "I hope we're wrong, but I'm going to have my investigators look into Robb's and Santoro's backgrounds to see if either one had a grudge against Carrie or was particularly close to her."

Chapter Thirty-Four

Dana Cutler decided that she couldn't put off telling the detectives in charge of the Blair case about the Ottoman Scepter any longer, so she drove to Lee County to watch Horace Blair's bail hearing, certain that one of them would be a witness. The courtroom was packed and the only seat Dana could find was a narrow space in the last row of the spectator section between a slovenly, obese man in a malodorous tracksuit and the bright-eyed assistant commonwealth attorney who had created the space by edging away from her foul-smelling benchmate. The young prosecutor was one of several who were in the courtroom to watch Rick Hamada in action.

When Dana finished wedging herself in place she shifted her attention to the front of the room, where a guard was escorting Horace Blair to the defense table. Charles Benedict walked over to his client, giving Dana her first chance to get a good look at Horace Blair's lawyer. She studied him closely and could not shake the notion that he looked just like the man Dana had seen with Carrie Blair when

Dana was working the Lars Jorgenson insurance case.

Dana had a copy of the photograph she'd taken of Carrie and the mystery man on her phone so she could show it to the detectives. She found it and compared the man with Carrie to Charles Benedict. There was no question in her mind that Carrie's companion and Horace Blair's attorney were the same person.

Why would Horace Blair's lawyer and Horace Blair's wife be together so early in the morning? There was one obvious answer, and Dana realized that she had more to talk about with the detectives than she had thought when she entered the courtroom.

Dana listened intently to Frank Santoro's testimony. When the lawyers were through with him, Judge Gardner called a recess. Santoro spoke briefly with Hamada before heading up the aisle. Dana intercepted him at the courtroom door.

"Detective Santoro, my name is Dana Cutler. I'm a private investigator and I'd like to talk to you about the Blair case."

Santoro remembered Carrie's Internet search for information about the investigator. Then he remembered something he had read about Dana and he frowned.

"You write stories for that supermarket tabloid *Exposed*, don't you?"

"I don't want to interview you. I'm not writing a story. I have information about this case you should know. There's no quid pro quo involved."

"What kind of information?"

"Look, it's complicated. Can we meet after court?"

Santoro hesitated.

"I was a cop before I went private, Detective. I'm not going to jack you around. You have my word."

"Okay. There's a coffee shop about two blocks from here, Fallon's. I'll meet you there when we break for lunch, and I'll bring my partner."

"See you then," Dana said.

Dana was in a booth, sipping a cup of black coffee, when the detectives walked in.

"It's an honor," Stephanie Robb said as she and Santoro slid into the bench seat across from Dana.

Robb had just made detective when Dana butchered the bikers who gang-raped her. That act made Dana a hero to Robb, and to many other women in law enforcement.

Dana nodded but didn't say anything. She hoped Robb was referring to the case involving President Farrington and not the incident with the bikers. She'd been insane when she killed the meth cooks, and she'd killed to survive. Fortunately, the waiter appeared, so Dana was able to change the subject.

"You told me that you have information about the

Blair case," Santoro said when the waiter left with their orders.

"I do, and it's pretty weird. I don't know what you'll make of it, but I felt I had to tell you what I know."

The detectives listened intently as Dana told them about her quest to find the Ottoman Scepter and her discovery that the assignment had been a hoax perpetrated by Carrie Blair. The waiter brought their food just before Dana finished her tale.

"Why do you think Carrie paid you and those actors all that money?" Robb asked when Dana finished.

"You think the prenup is the motive for the murder, right?"

Robb nodded.

"I think Carrie got me away from D.C. because she thought I had information that Horace Blair could use to void it."

"What information?"

"Before I tell it to you I'd like you to answer a question for me."

"Shoot."

"Have you seen the prenup? Can you prove it exists?"

"We're having trouble confirming its existence," Santoro told her. "Horace's lawyer won't let us talk to him about it and Jack Pratt, his civil attorney, refuses to meet with us. But if you were in court during my testimony, you heard that we have an informant who will testify that Horace told him he killed Carrie because he didn't want to pay her twenty million dollars when the prenup ended."

"What were the conditions Carrie had to meet to get the money?" Dana asked.

"The informant says that Blair told him she would get the money if she didn't divorce him or cheat on him during the first ten years of the marriage," Santoro said.

"We don't know if that clause is really in the prenup since we haven't seen it," Robb said, "but it makes sense."

"What I know might blow a hole in your theory."

Dana showed the photograph of Carrie and Benedict to the detectives.

"That's Carrie Blair and Charles Benedict outside Benedict's apartment shortly before seven a.m. on the day Carrie contacted me, pretending to be Margo Laurent."

Wheels turned in Robb's head as soon as she realized what the photo implied. "You think Benedict was fucking Carrie Blair?"

"I was in a car, taking pictures of an insurance cheat for United Insurance. I didn't know who Carrie Blair or Charles Benedict were. But Blair went ballistic when she spotted me. She started screaming and she charged at my car, so I took off. Blair acted the way a person with a guilty conscience would act. It's definitely the way I would act if I thought a PI had caught me cheating on my husband, especially if cheating on my husband was going to cost me twenty million dollars.

"I think Carrie Blair memorized my license plate and used it to figure out who I was. Later that day, she called Alice Forte, a lawyer I work for, and got my phone number. Then she called me, pretending to be Margo Laurent.

"Here's your problem," Dana concluded. "Horace Blair would have no reason to kill Carrie if he knew she'd violated the prenup."

"Blair may not have known that his wife had something on the side," Robb said. "If he didn't know she was cheating, he'd still have a motive to kill her."

"That's true," Dana said, "but the odds are good that a person with Horace's resources *would* know that Carrie was having an affair."

"That still doesn't let Blair off the hook," Robb countered. "Husbands kill cheating wives all the time. Maybe he's just a jealous husband. But there's something else that makes me think that Blair definitely didn't know about his wife and Benedict."

"What's that?" Dana asked.

"If Benedict was having an affair with Horace's wife, and Horace knew about it, why would he hire Benedict to defend him? Doesn't that tell you that Horace didn't know about the affair?"

"That's a good point." Dana shrugged. "Look, I've been pretty busy making up for lost time since I got back from my 'quest,' so I haven't spent a lot of time thinking this through. I just thought I should tell you about the scepter and Benedict."

Santoro looked at his watch. "Court is going to start in ten minutes. We've got to get back."

The waiter brought the bill. Santoro took out his wallet, gave him cash, and laid his wallet next to himself on the seat.

"Thanks for lunch," Dana said.

"Thanks for talking to us," Santoro said.

The detectives left and Dana picked up her sandwich. She felt relieved that she had fulfilled her duty as a citizen and could put the Blair case behind her. The feeling lasted the length of time it took Frank Santoro to reenter Fallon's and walk back to her booth. He reached across the bench on which he'd been sitting and picked up his wallet.

"I left this here so I'd have an excuse to come back," Santoro said as he slipped the wallet into his back pocket. "I need to talk to you and I don't want Steph to know. Is there someplace we can meet tonight?"

Chapter Thirty-Five

Dana had discovered Vinny's while working undercover in narcotics for the D.C. police. Several things recommended it for a clandestine rendezvous. First, Vinny's was in a rather disreputable section of the capital, making it highly unlikely that anyone Dana or Santoro knew would wander in. Second, the chef's hamburgers and fries were outstanding.

Santoro showed up twenty minutes after Dana ordered. He spotted her through the haze created by the illegally smoked cigarettes that were part of the bar's ambience.

"Sorry I'm late," Santoro said. "Traffic."

"Not a problem." She pointed at her food. "Order yourself a burger and fries. You'll thank me."

"I can also use a beer. Court gave me a migraine."

Dana signaled to the waitress, then pointed at her burger, fries, and beer.

"Did Gardner give Blair bail?" Dana asked.

"He's going to rule in the morning."

"So, why the secret meeting?" Dana asked.

"How much do you charge?"

"You want to hire me?"

"Maybe. Let's see what you think when we're done."

Dana told Santoro her hourly rate.

"I can do that," Santoro said, "but before I talk to you, I want your promise that you'll keep what I say to yourself."

"Okay."

"I have doubts about the case against Blair."

"Have you told your partner?"

"I've tried, but Steph is so certain Blair murdered his wife that she can't hear what I'm saying. That's why I need to have someone without any preconceived notions look at the case. Do you think you can do that?"

"I can try. So why do you have doubts about Blair's guilt?" Dana asked just as the waitress placed Santoro's beer in front of him. He took a long drink before answering.

"You heard the testimony, right?"

"Most of it."

"Okay, well, first off, there are all these anonymous tips. The tip to the paper about the prenup was anonymous. The tip about Blair putting his wife's body in the trunk of his car, anonymous. And why would a guy as smart as Blair let us look in the trunk if he knew the gun was still in there?

"Then there's that key. How did it get in the grave? Benedict was right. Most people keep their house key on their key chain, so how does Blair's house key get off the chain and into the grave?

"Finally, there's our jailhouse informant, Barry Lester. I have a hard time believing Blair would give him the time of day, let alone confess to murder— *and* tell him where he buried the body."

"Could Lester have killed Carrie?"

"No, he was in jail when Mrs. Blair was killed."

"So how did he know where the grave was if Blair didn't tell him?"

"Either the person who killed Carrie Blair told him or the killer had someone else tell him."

"Have you checked to see who visited Lester since he's been locked up?"

Santoro nodded. "The only visitors were Lester's girlfriend and Arthur Jefferson, his attorney. Lester's girlfriend is a stripper. Her stage name is Tiffany Starr—and that's what she calls herself—but she was born Sharon Ross. She's divorced, and her married name was Sharon Krantz."

"Do you have phone numbers and addresses for Starr and Jefferson?"

"Yeah."

Santoro pulled out his notebook and rattled off contact information for Tiffany Starr and Arthur Jefferson.

"Tell me a little about Barry Lester and his girlfriend," Dana asked as soon as she'd stored the information in her phone.

"Starr has a record for kiting checks, and she embezzled from a company she worked for as a book-keeper."

"Let me guess. She needed the money to buy drugs?"

Santoro nodded. "Heroin and cocaine, mostly, but she's used other stuff. She's been in and out of rehab, usually as a condition of probation."

"Got it. And Barry Lester?"

"Lester is a small-time punk with an aversion to work. He's a high school dropout who's supported himself with con games and petty, nonviolent crimes. The guy lives on the fringe. Occasionally he'll work a low-paying job when he can get one, but he can't say no to easy money. This last time he really fucked up. He drove the getaway car in a liquor-store robbery. No one was hurt, but his buddies cut deals. If he hadn't agreed to rat out Blair he'd be looking at serious time."

Santoro hesitated. Suddenly he looked nervous.

"There's someone else I need you to look at."

"Who?"

"Charles Benedict. This is the real reason I want to hire you. Horace Blair is incredibly rich and very well connected. We caught hell when we booked him on the gun charge. If I investigate Blair's defense attorney and he discovers what I'm up to he'll scream bloody murder and claim we're harassing him. We'd risk having the case dismissed for prosecutorial misconduct."

"You think Benedict might be involved in Carrie's murder?"

"If he was Carrie's lover he might have a reason to kill her."

"That's quite a leap."

"What do you know about Benedict?"

"Nothing really."

"I've always thought he was shady. You know who Nikolai Orlansky is, right?"

Dana nodded.

"A lot of Benedict's clients are connected to Orlansky, and a few of his cases have ended in strange ways."

"Such as?"

"Witnesses and evidence have disappeared, or a witness changes his story."

"That's not evidence that he killed Carrie Blair."

"You're right. But Blair and Benedict had a run-in shortly before she disappeared."

Santoro told Dana about the Ross case.

"Now, here's something I found out," Santoro said. "Kyle Ross isn't the only member of the Ross family Benedict represented. He was Sharon Ross's attorney on two of her drug cases."

"You think Benedict told Tiffany the location of the body?"

"It's a possibility. And there's something else. Benedict worked awfully hard to convince us to put Blair in isolation."

"That's something any defense attorney would do if he had an elderly, well-heeled client who would be dog meat in population."

"That's true. But . . ." Santoro shook his head. "I

just have this feeling that something about this case is not right. I may be way off base, but I'd feel better if you told me that after you investigated."

"Okay. I'll take a shot at it."

"How much do you need for a retainer?"

"Forget about the money. Carrie Blair paid me a bundle for a few days' work. If her husband didn't kill her, I owe it to Carrie to find out who did."

"At least let me cover your expenses."

"We can talk about that when I finish my investigation."

"Okay. So, what do you think?"

"If Benedict had Tiffany Starr tell Lester where the body was buried, it would explain a lot. What's got me puzzled is the key you found in the grave. How did it get there? If Horace Blair didn't murder his wife but the key is Blair's house key, the killer had to get it from . . . Blair. And I . . ."

Dana stopped in midsentence because Santoro's mouth was open and it was clear he was not listening.

"What's the matter?" Dana asked.

"Something has been bothering me ever since Steph conducted her experiment with the keys at Blair's estate, and I just realized what it is."

Santoro stood up. "I'm going to my office to get something. Here's my address. I'll call my wife and tell her you're coming. She'll put on some coffee. We're going to have a long night."

Chapter Thirty-Six

Frank Santoro met Gloria when she was working as a dispatcher. She understood his hours and never got on him about the time he spent on the job. Frank adored Gloria, and he appreciated how lucky he was to have someone who understood the demands of police work. His first marriage had gone on the rocks because of the time Frank spent on his cases and the shitty mood he could be in after a shift dealing with the dregs of society.

Dana liked Gloria as soon as the heavyset brunette opened the door and flashed a big, warm grin at her. By the time Frank pulled into his driveway, the two women were chatting away over coffee in the living room. Frank knew they had been talking about him when the women worked to stop smiling as he walked in carrying a briefcase.

"Don't believe a word she says," Frank told Dana.

"Who says we were talking about you?" Gloria said. "You men always want to be the center of attention."

Frank kissed Gloria on the cheek, then told her

that he and Dana were going downstairs to review surveillance tapes. Gloria handed Dana a thermos filled with coffee.

"If you want something to eat, give a holler," she said as Dana and her husband vanished down the steps to the basement.

"Why am I here, Frank?" Dana asked as Frank pulled a DVD out of his briefcase and put it in his laptop.

"Something has always bothered me about the keys. You weren't close enough in court to see them, but there are three that are important. The key in the grave with Horace Blair's prints on it and the key on the key chain we found in Carrie's purse—they both opened the front door to Blair's mansion. But they had something else in common. They were both dulled by wear. Then there's the key on Horace's key chain that didn't open the front door: it *looked* like the other keys, but it was newer.

"Around the time Carrie disappeared on Monday there was another homicide. The guy's name was Ernest Brodsky. He was in his seventies, didn't have any vices, and everyone liked him. We figured it for a killing in the course of a robbery, but there was one odd thing about the case. Brodsky had a shop in the River View Mall, and the evidence points to the crime occurring on Tuesday night in the parking lot of the mall, but his body was found in a field miles away. If Brodsky was robbed and killed at the mall by some junkie, why move the body? It didn't make sense until I remembered what Brodsky did for a living."

"And what was that?" Dana asked.

Santoro grinned. "He was a locksmith, and he had equipment in his shop for making copies of keys! If a locksmith made a key that looked similar to Blair's front door key but wouldn't open the door, that key would look newer."

"And the tapes?" Dana asked.

"They show what went on in the mall on Monday and Tuesday."

The last time anyone had seen Carrie Blair was after court on Monday afternoon, so Santoro and Dana watched the DVD for Monday until Brodsky closed his shop. After Brodsky left the mall Santoro skipped through Monday evening and started watching again when Brodsky opened up on Tuesday morning.

"There!" he said a few minutes after they started watching in real time.

A man in a hooded sweatshirt, jeans, and sneakers walked into the picture and opened the door to the locksmith's shop. He kept his face out of view of the surveillance camera, as if he knew where it was and didn't want to be identified.

Santoro zoomed in. The picture was in black and white, but the resolution was grainy.

Dana squinted at the screen. "I think he's Caucasian," she said, "but that's about all I can tell."

The man stayed in the store for twenty minutes and came out holding a small paper bag.

"That's about the right size for a few keys," Santoro said just as the man walked out of the picture.

There was another set of tapes that covered the parking area near Brodsky's shop. Santoro cued up the DVD for Tuesday morning and stared hard at the screen. Suddenly a Porsche drove into a spot around the corner from Brodsky's place of business, even though most of the lot was empty.

"Carrie Blair drove a Porsche," he said. "And it's missing."

Santoro froze the screen and enlarged the picture. Part of the license plate was visible.

"I can only make out two letters," Santoro said. "What about you?"

Dana shook her head. Santoro checked his notebook.

"The L and the Q are in the right spot for her plate," he said.

Santoro pressed PLAY and the man in the sweatshirt got out of the Porsche, working hard at keeping his head down so that his face wouldn't show.

Santoro watched him walk around the corner, and kept watching until he returned to the car and drove off.

The man didn't return on Tuesday and Santoro fast-forwarded through the day. Dana and Santoro watched Brodsky lock the door of his shop at 5:30 p.m. and walk into the lot. The cameras didn't cover the whole lot and Brodsky had parked out of the camera's range.

It was after midnight and Santoro's eyes were about to fall out of his head. He leaned forward to turn off the machine just as a Mercedes drove across the screen. Santoro froze the picture and ran the DVD back.

"Can you make out the license?" he asked.

"No," Dana answered. "The car's going too fast. I couldn't see who was driving, either."

"Too bad. But this wasn't a total loss. Charles Benedict drives a Mercedes-Benz."

"Tell me what you're thinking, Frank."

"After Benedict kills Carrie, he decides to frame her husband for the crime by leaving a clue in her grave that points to Horace. He takes Carrie's house key off of her key chain, drives Carrie's Porsche, with the body in the trunk, to Brodsky's store in the mall. Benedict has Brodsky make a key that looks like the real house key but won't open the front door to the Blair mansion. After he buries Carrie, he figures out a way to switch the key that won't work for Horace's front door key, which has Horace's fingerprints on it. Benedict puts Carrie's house key back on her key chain before he buries her. Then he returns to the grave and plants Horace's house key in the grave where we'll find it. Now, the key in the grave opens Blair's front door, but no key on Blair's key chain opens the door, and we are going to conclude that Blair must have lost the key when he was burying his wife."

"That makes sense, but how did he switch the keys?" Dana asked.

"That is the million-dollar question."

"Which we won't be able to answer as long as Benedict represents Horace Blair."

Chapter Thirty-Seven

The next morning, before breakfast, Dana and Jake loosened up with calisthenics before running five miles. Dana had gotten home from Frank Santoro's house a little after one in the morning and she was groggy during their workout. Jake showered first, then made breakfast. When Dana came into the kitchen, her hair was damp from her shower and she was dragging.

"Have I told you recently that you are a genius?" Jake asked.

Dana perked up. "No. What did I do that's so smart?"

"Remember telling me that I should use my photographs from the Arctic expedition for a show? Yesterday, I phoned Louis Riker at the Riker Gallery. He called back while you were in the shower, and we're meeting this morning."

"That's great!" Dana said, breaking into a grin.

"It's not a done deal."

"I'll keep my fingers crossed."

After breakfast, Jake left for his meeting and

Dana went down to the basement office. She booted up the computer and did an Internet search for "Charles Benedict." There were several articles about cases in which he had served as defense counsel. There was also a piece in the *Washington Post* that had been written in connection with one of the attorney's high-profile cases.

Dana had no trouble learning that Benedict was a member of the D.C., Maryland, and Virginia bars and had earned a degree in economics from Dickinson College in Pennsylvania. At the University of Virginia Law School, Benedict made the law review and graduated fourteenth in his class. He should have been able to land a judicial clerkship or a position as an associate in a high-powered law firm, but he chose to hang a shingle and specialize in criminal defense. By all accounts, he had been a success from the get-go, experiencing none of the hardships usually encountered by sole practitioners.

What Dana found odd was that no article contained an account of Benedict's life before college. She was unable to find out where he was born and grew up, or anything about his parents. It was as if Charles Benedict did not exist before he went to Dickinson.

Dana called the *Washington Post* and asked to speak to Shawn DuBurg, the reporter who had written the profile of Benedict. After introducing herself, Dana explained why she was calling.

"Yeah, I remember writing the piece. Why are you interested?" DuBurg asked.

"I'm working for a client who's thinking of hiring Mr. Benedict and he asked me to check him out."

"Everything I know is in the article," DuBurg said.

"I was interested in what wasn't in it. For instance, you didn't write about Mr. Benedict's childhood, where he grew up, that sort of thing."

"That's because it wasn't relevant to the article. It was about his legal career."

"I'm having a hard time finding out anything about Mr. Benedict before he went to college. Do you know any of that stuff?"

DuBurg was quiet for a moment. "You know, I think I did ask him but he said he'd had a rough childhood and didn't want to discuss it. Like I said, I was mainly interested in his legal career, so I didn't push him."

Dana thanked the reporter and ended the conversation. She tried to think of ways to get what she needed but every idea she had was a dead end, so she called Andy Zipay.

Zipay was an ex-cop who had left the D.C. police department under a cloud while Dana was still on the force. Dana had been one of the few officers who had not shunned him, and she'd sent business his way when he went private. When Dana got out of the mental hospital and decided to work as an investigator, Zipay returned the favor by sending her work. It was one of the assignments Zipay had referred to her that eventually led to Dana's discovery that the president of the United States was involved in a series of murders. Zipay was a very good detective and an excellent person to present with a puzzle.

Dana listened to the radio during the drive to Zipay's office. She turned up the sound when the announcer said there was a decision on bail in Horace Blair's case.

"Judge Gardner agreed with the defense that Mr. Blair was a prominent member of the community but he cited several reasons for denying bail. The judge held that the evidence produced by the commonwealth pointed to a strong possibility that Mr. Blair would be convicted of the murder charge. He recognized that the defense might call this evidence into question at trial but he said that he was forced to decide the issue of bail on the evidence presented in court.

"Another factor that Judge Gardner said weighed heavily in his decision was the possibility that Mr. Blair might be a flight risk. Mr. Blair's business takes him to all parts of the world, including countries without extradition treaties with the United States. Assistant Commonwealth Attorney Rick Hamada produced evidence that Mr. Blair had homes in many foreign countries and assets overseas that would enable him to live a life of luxury as a fugitive.

"Charles Benedict, Mr. Blair's attorney, said that he planned an immediate appeal of the court's decision."

Dana was a little surprised that the judge had denied bail to a person as powerful as Horace Blair, but Gardner, who had a reputation for being arrogant and self-important, also had a reputation for integrity.

Andy Zipay worked on the third floor of an older building with a respectable address. Dana was expected and Zipay's secretary sent her into Zipay's office as soon as she arrived. The investigator was seated behind a large oak desk in a small office cramped by metal filing cabinets and secondhand bookshelves. He was a few inches over six feet tall and had a pasty complexion. A narrow mustache separated a hook nose from a pair of thin lips, and his black, slicked-down hair was showing some gray.

"Long time no see," Zipay said with a smile.

"Too long, and I apologize for asking a favor the first time we're getting together."

"You stood by me when everybody else treated me like shit, so I'm always gonna owe *you*. What's up?"

"Have you heard of a lawyer named Charles Benedict?"

"Sure."

"What have you heard about him?"

"Nothing good. When I was in vice and narcotics his name would pop up on occasion, mostly in connection with the Orlansky mob. But the guy is smooth and no one ever got anything on him. Why do you want to know?"

"His name has come up in a case. I tried doing background on him and I've run into a stone wall."

"How so?"

"There's plenty about him from college on, but I haven't been able to find anything on him before then. I thought you might have a bright idea."

"You looked for a birth certificate, high school records?"

"I got nada. It's like he was born on his first day of school."

Zipay spaced out and Dana sat back and let him think. Suddenly, Zipay smiled.

"Maybe you're looking under the wrong name."

Chapter Thirty-Eight

Dana decided to talk to Barry Lester's girlfriend before attempting to talk to his lawyer. Guilty or innocent, Arthur Jefferson, a member of the bar, would refuse to divulge attorney-client communications, or anything that could harm his client. Tiffany Starr's only connection to bars was the time she'd spent behind them or danced in them.

Dana used false names and disguises on occasion because she had gotten a lot of publicity from the stories about her cases that had run in *Exposed*. Before leaving home, Dana put on glasses and a blond wig. Tiffany Starr might spot the wig, but Dana guessed that a stripper would wear one from time to time and wouldn't think anything of it.

Dana parked on a litter-strewn street in one of D.C.'s seamier neighborhoods. Starr lived on the third floor of a five-story brick apartment house decorated with gang graffiti. The elevator was broken and the odor of garbage and bad cooking permeated the stairwell. Dana held her breath until she was in front of Starr's apartment.

A rail-thin woman with straight blond hair opened the door an inch and peered at Dana over the security chain. Cigarette smoke curled up from somewhere behind the door.

"Tiffany Starr?" Dana asked.

"Who wants to know?" the woman asked. There were dark circles under her eyes and her skin had a sickly pallor. Dana thought that Starr might have been attractive once upon a time, before drugs and hard living blunted any appeal she may have had.

"My name is Loren Parkhurst and I'd like to talk to you about Barry Lester's case."

"Why should I talk to you?" Starr asked.

"I'd prefer to tell you inside, where the neighbors can't hear, if you know what I mean."

Starr hesitated. Then she slipped off the chain and opened the door. She wore a T-shirt that stretched across breasts Dana was certain had once been smaller. The tight T-shirt and tighter jeans were knockoffs of high-priced brands. The tip of a tattoo peeked above the top of the T-shirt but Dana couldn't make out what it was.

The apartment's tiny front room was surprisingly tidy. The furniture was cheap but Monet and Picasso prints hung from walls with peeling paint. The pictures hinted at a past far different from the stripper's present. Dana also noticed editions of *People* and several screen magazines stacked on an end table along with a Danielle Steel novel. That gave her an idea.

"You have a nice place here," Dana said to break the ice when she was inside with the door closed.

"What's this about Barry?" Starr asked, ignoring Dana's attempt at small talk.

"Do you read *Exposed*?"

"Yeah, once in a while."

Dana handed Starr a business card that identified Dana as a reporter for *Exposed* named Loren Parkhurst.

"I'm working on a story we plan on printing."

"About Barry?"

"And you."

"Me?" Starr said. Dana could see the woman's eyes widen at the idea that she might become a celebrity.

"Would you mind if we sent a photographer up here to take some shots?"

"Uh, that would be okay, I guess," Starr answered, trying to stay cool even though Dana could tell that she was thrilled by the attention she thought she'd receive from a national publication.

"Great. When is a good time? I know you're probably busy."

"I work nights, so I'm home most of the day."

"Oh, where do you work?"

"A club. I'm a dancer. That's how I met Barry."

"Okay, then. I'll have Oscar call to set up the shoot."

"So, what's this story about?"

"Do you mind if we sit down?" Dana asked.

"Take the sofa," Starr said. A recliner faced the TV. Starr sat on it and looked expectantly at Dana, who sighed and suddenly looked very serious.

"I don't want to alarm you, Tiffany, but you could be in trouble."

"What are you talking about?"

"Barry told the police that Horace Blair confessed to him that he killed his wife, then told him where Carrie Blair was buried."

"So?"

"We find it hard to believe."

"That's Barry's business."

"That may be true, but you can see that it's important that we get your side of the story to set the record straight."

"There is no 'side.' Barry got himself in this mess. I don't know anything about it."

"Don't you?" Dana asked.

"What would I know?"

"There are two possibilities here, Tiffany. One is that a prominent and powerful businessman with degrees from Harvard and Princeton confessed to a man he barely knew that he murdered his wife. That, to put it mildly, is highly unlikely."

"Barry's very persuasive. You can't believe how good he is at conning people."

"Horace Blair deals with the top executives in corporations and heads of state. I find it hard to believe Barry could convince Blair to spill his guts in the space of a few hours. But Barry would know where Carrie's grave was hidden if someone told him where she was buried. You and his attorney are the only people who visited him at the jail."

Starr took a drag on her cigarette. Dana could almost see the wheels turning.

"Horace Blair has powerful connections, Tiffany. If the authorities find out that Barry set him up, it will go hard on Barry, *and* anyone who helped him. If that someone is you, you can save yourself by coming clean."

"I have nothing to say because I didn't do anything," the woman insisted, but Dana didn't believe her.

"Did Charles Benedict ask you to talk to Barry?"

As soon as Dana asked the question she knew she'd made a mistake. Starr's already pale complexion lost any color it had and she jumped to her feet.

"I want you to go. *Now.*"

Dana rose, too, and looked Starr in the eye. "My number is on my card. Think about your situation and call me if you want to talk. It will be easier talking to me than the FBI."

Dana was halfway out the door when Starr asked, "Is that photographer still coming?"

"From what you've told me, there's no story. If you change your mind, you know where to reach me."

The door closed behind Dana, and Starr put her eye to the peephole. When Cutler started down the stairs, Tiffany started pacing. She hadn't signed on for this, she told herself. All she was supposed to do was tell some stuff to Barry that was going to help him get out of jail. Nothing was supposed to happen to her. Reporters weren't supposed to be coming around. Parkhurst had mentioned the FBI, for Christ's sake. No one had said the FBI was going to be involved.

Starr lit up a cigarette and wished she had some blow in the apartment. Fucking rehab! She really wanted to get away from that shit, but a little powder would calm her down, and she needed to be calm to think this through.

Starr flopped onto the recliner. She stared at the ceiling as if she believed an answer might appear there. She took a deep drag on her smoke and thought about the FBI. She definitely did not want anything to do with the FBI. Someone was going to have to fix this because she was definitely going to look out for number one if the F-fucking-B-fucking-I came to call. And there was only one person who could fix this, the person who had gotten her into this mess in the first place.

Starr levered herself out of her chair and grabbed her phone.

"We have a problem," she said as soon as Charles Benedict answered. "I just got a visit from a reporter for *Exposed*. She knows I talked to Barry at the jail."

"I don't think it's wise to discuss this matter over the phone, do you?"

"What I don't think is wise is for me to go down for Barry's shit."

"Let's meet someplace and talk about this calmly."

"I'll meet, but you better be prepared to sweeten the pot, because the reporter was talking about the FBI, and she mentioned your name."

"She mentioned me?"

"Yeah, Charlie. She wanted to know if you told me to talk to Barry."

"I'm sorry if the reporter bothered you, but you have nothing to worry about. I'll take care of you. I have meetings all afternoon, but we can meet tonight. That will give me time to go to the bank."

Starr hung up. The possibility of getting some cash got her worked up. She was almost sorry Barry would be getting out, too. All Barry had brought her was trouble. She danced her ass off at the club and brought home peanuts, which that son of a bitch always managed to sweet-talk her into giving him. And there were his big schemes, the sure things, get-rich-quick plans that never panned out.

Tiffany was sick of being broke, and she knew Barry screwed anyone who'd let him. Fucking Barry. He was the root of all of her problems. Maybe she should rat him out. If she made a deal with the feds they could put her in witness protection. She'd be able to get out of this shithole. Maybe they'd send her someplace nice, like Hawaii or Las Vegas. She really liked Las Vegas.

Tiffany made a decision. She'd meet with Benedict and see what he had to offer. If it wasn't enough, she'd call the reporter, rat out Barry, and get the fuck out of Dodge.

Chapter Thirty-Nine

Nikolai Orlansky put up Gregor Karpinski's bail as a reward for beating up Barry Lester. A few nights after getting out of jail, Gregor showered, shaved, and dressed in his flashiest clothes. Then he headed for The Scene in College Park, Maryland, a nightclub owned by Orlansky that catered to the students at the University of Maryland. Orlansky used it to launder money, and Gregor worked as a bouncer at the club on the weekends. During the week, he tried his luck with the college girls who frequented the bar. Nikolai gave Gregor permission to screw these girls as long as the sex was consensual. Nikolai did not want the club getting any bad publicity, so rape and roofies were a no-no. Gregor followed Orlansky's rules scrupulously, ever since he had been forced to watch Nikolai use a scalpel, pliers, and a power drill on a colleague who had raped a coed he had picked up at the club. The girl had been paid off, the incident had been hushed up, and the fish off the coast had been treated to a multi-course meal.

When Gregor got to the club he headed for a

booth on a platform elevated above the main floor that was reserved for members of Orlansky's crew. The booth gave its occupants a good view of the dance floor and bar so they could spot trouble before it went too far. It was also a good place to scope out pussy. Gregor started up the stairs to join his friends when his cell phone vibrated.

"Yeah," he said.

"Meet me in the parking lot. I'm in the back row by the fence."

Gregor wondered what Charlie Benedict wanted from him, but he had made out okay whenever Nikolai told him to do something for the lawyer.

Gregor looked for Benedict's Mercedes in the back of the lot, but he didn't see it. Then the headlights on a dull-brown Ford came on, blinked twice, then went dead. Gregor walked to the driver's side. The window was rolled down and Benedict was sitting behind the wheel, wearing a hooded sweatshirt. He grinned.

"Good to see you're out, Gregor. Hop in."

Benedict reached across and opened the passenger door. Gregor walked around the car and sat down beside the lawyer. He was curious about the car and the way Benedict was dressed, but he knew better than to ask questions.

"You did great with Lester," Benedict said. "I told Nikolai that."

Gregor wasn't big on idle chatter so he held his tongue. The lawyer would tell him what he wanted when he was ready. Sure enough, Benedict cut to the chase.

"I've got a job for you. Are you interested in some easy money?"

"I must hear what you want me to do."

"I need you to talk to someone, a woman. She's been asking questions about Barry Lester. I want you to convince her to stop."

"Nikolai is okay with this?" Gregor asked. Nikolai had made it very clear that members of his crew did not freelance unless they had his permission.

"Of course," Benedict lied. After his meeting with Tiffany Starr he realized that he would have to act quickly, and there had not been enough time to clear with Orlansky what he wanted done.

"How bad you want the woman hurt?"

"Rough her up enough to scare her. Get sexual. You know, cop a feel, put your hand between her legs and rub a little. Do enough so she gets the idea. Wear a ski mask, black. I want her to fear you. I want you to tell her you'll come back if she doesn't back off. Get it?"

"Yes, I see what you want."

Benedict handed Gregor an envelope stuffed with cash. Gregor noticed that the lawyer was wearing gloves. It was dark but he thought he saw specks of blood on the leather between the thumb and forefinger.

"So, we're good?" Benedict asked when Gregor was done counting the money.

"Yes, we are good."

"Okay, the woman's name and phone number are in the envelope. You make sure she keeps her nose out of the Blair case."

"How fast do you want me to do this?"

"I need it yesterday, Gregor. She's already forced me to do something I didn't want to do."

Gregor nodded and got out of the car. He looked at his watch and sighed. If he did this tonight he would not have time to get laid, but Benedict said it couldn't wait. Gregor went to his car, where he would have some privacy. He turned on an untraceable cell phone he used when he was making drug deals for Nikolai and dialed the number Loren Parkhurst had given to Tiffany Starr.

Chapter Forty

Dana headed home after leaving Tiffany Starr's apartment. She was pulling into her driveway when her phone rang. Dana parked and fished the phone out of her pocket.

"You owe me a dinner, Cutler," Andy Zipay said.

"I thought this was a freebie."

"Yeah, the work is. You're paying for the honor of being in the presence of pure genius."

"Okay, you get dinner . . . if your info is good."

"Good? It's great! I have a contact from the old days who works at an intelligence agency which shall remain nameless. He did an in-depth search using some software from outer space. You couldn't find out anything about Benedict before he went to college because Charles Benedict didn't exist until two years before he registered at Dickinson. His admission application to college shows that he never graduated from high school. He has a GED under Benedict."

"Dickinson is a pretty decent college. How did he get in with a GED?"

"Well, that is interesting. My buddy got into his college file. Benedict had close to perfect scores on his SAT exams. But that wasn't the most interesting thing my buddy discovered. The year before he got the GED he changed his name legally to Benedict from Richard Molinari, and Richard Molinari's name came up in a newspaper story about a double murder in Kansas City."

Dana ate a hasty dinner, then went on her computer and read the story to which Zipay had alluded. Twenty-five years ago, two drug dealers had been tortured and murdered in Kansas City. Their bodies had been found in an abandoned barn in the countryside. The police theorized that they had been killed for the money they were going to pay for cocaine. Richard Molinari had been arrested shortly after the murders but he had been released.

Dana found a few more references to the case but learned nothing new. She was about to try a different approach when the cell phone with the "Loren Parkhurst" number rang.

"Barry Lester is lying," a man said.

"Who is this?"

"Not on the phone. I must meet you."

Dana hesitated. Then she asked, "Where?"

The man told her before disconnecting. Dana sat back and thought. Tiffany Starr was the only person connected to the Blair case who had this number, so the man had to have gotten it from Tiffany. Who would she have told? Charles Benedict was a possibility, but the man who called had an accent, possibly Russian. He wanted to meet in an industrial park, which would be deserted at night. That was not a good sign. Still, Dana could not pass up a possible lead, so she collected several weapons and headed out the door.

Dana braked Jake's Harley, stopping at the curb in front of a vacant lot. She took off her helmet and hooked it on the motorcycle's handlebars. The lot was in the middle of an industrial park. Darkened warehouses and deserted offices crowded around the rubble-filled space. A cold wind whipped through the empty streets. Dana did not like the setup. Just as she was wondering if she should leave, the headlights on a parked car came on and the car's engine started. Moments later, a black Cadillac Escalade parked in front of her bike and a man got out.

Dana's first thought was that he was huge and thick, like a professional wrestler. Then he raised his head and she saw the ski mask. Before Dana could react, Gregor was on her. She kicked at his leg but the blow had no effect. Gregor punched Dana in the chest. Her motorcycle jacket absorbed some of the blow, but it was so strong that she found herself on the ground gasping for air. Gregor pulled her to her feet. When she was standing, he wrapped a thick, gloved hand around her throat and pushed her against the side of the SUV.

"Nice," he said. His voice was low and sensual, and the sound made Dana's skin crawl. Then Gregor's tongue flicked out of the hole in the ski mask and he licked her cheek.

"You are tasting very sweet, very fuckable."

Dana's heart surged in her chest. Nightmarish memories of the gang rape flooded her. Gregor's other hand found its way between Dana's legs and he began to rub rhythmically.

"This is feeling good, no? You are getting hot. Soon you will be wanting me to fuck you, no?"

Definitely Eastern European, maybe Russian, Dana thought as she slipped her hand behind her back.

"Please don't hurt me," she whimpered, words she knew her attacker wanted to hear.

"Listen good." Gregor tightened the grip on Dana's throat. "You have been asking questions about Barry Lester. This you do not do no more. If you don't stop putting your nose where it do not belong I will fuck you until you bleed. You understand?"

"Please," Dana begged.

Gregor grabbed Dana's crotch hard and she winced.

"You no like pain? *I* like pain. No more questions, understood? No more Blair case for you, understood?"

Gregor loosened the grip on Dana's throat.

"Tell me you understand."

"I understand," Dana said.

What Gregor did not understand was Dana's natural reaction to being accosted sexually. The last four men who had done that to her had died hideously, their bodies chopped in pieces by ax blows.

"If I hear you have not obeyed me, I will come to your house in the middle of the night and I will—"

Gregor stopped making sense as his threat became a high-pitched scream. His hands fell away from Dana and he staggered backward. Dana's knife was jammed to the hilt in his crotch and she followed him, twisting the blade viciously before pulling it free.

Gregor lurched backward. He was in shock. The pain was unbearable. Dana smashed her fist into Gregor's nose. She didn't know if it was the blow itself or the pain that brought him to his knees. She didn't care. She kicked him in the temple with the steel toe of her boot, then stomped his head against the sidewalk until she was certain that he was unconscious. She was about to land a blow that would finish Gregor when she stopped in mid-strike. She wanted to kill, but the time she'd spent in therapy at the mental hospital saved Gregor Karpinski's life. The man was not planning to kill her or rape her. He was a messenger sent to scare her, and that crime did not carry a death penalty.

Dana's chest heaved and she brought her breathing under control. Her attacker's crotch was damp with blood and she knew he would die if he didn't get medical help quickly. Dana couldn't use her own phone because the call could be traced to her. She searched the man's jacket pocket and found a cell phone. She used it to call for an ambulance.

What should she do next? If she stayed and the man died, she would be out of commission for as long as it took for the DA to decide that her use of force had been justified. She could not afford to be idle. She had to find out who sent her attacker.

What would happen if she left? She was wearing gloves, and the man had not drawn blood, so there would be no prints or DNA to connect her to the scene. If the man died, she would be home free. If he lived, he wasn't going to give her up. To do that, he would have to confess to attacking her.

Leaving was a no-brainer, so Dana straddled her bike and drove off. When she felt safe she called Frank Santoro.

"Who is this?" the detective asked. His angry tone told Dana that Santoro had been asleep.

"We have to meet right away," Dana said.

"It's after midnight. I just fell asleep."

"Tough. I just escaped being raped by someone connected to Horace Blair's case."

Chapter Forty-One

"Come on in," Santoro said as soon as he opened his front door.

"Do you have any scotch?" Dana asked.

Santoro filled a glass with a little bit of ice and a lot of Johnnie Walker and handed it to Dana. She sat on the sofa in the detective's living room and downed half of the glass.

"Are you ready to tell me what happened?" Santoro asked.

"Can you promise me you'll forget you're a cop?"

Santoro hesitated. Then he nodded.

"I might have killed someone tonight."

Santoro stayed calm. "Might have?"

"He was alive when I left but there was a lot of blood."

"Why don't you start at the beginning and tell me what happened?"

"I talked to Tiffany Starr yesterday but she wouldn't tell me anything. Around eleven I got a call from a man who told me he would prove Barry Lester was lying if I met him at an empty lot in an industrial park. When I got there he threatened to rape me if I didn't stop investigating the Blair case and Barry Lester."

"What did you do?"

Dana looked down. Now that the adrenaline had worn off she felt sick about what had happened.

"Dana?"

"I stabbed him in the crotch."

"Holy shit!"

Dana's head snapped up and she looked fierce. "I did what I had to do to save myself, and I'd do it again. It was a clear case of self-defense, but I would have been answering questions and put on ice for who knows how long if I'd stayed, and I can't afford that."

"So you just left him to die?"

"No. The man was just a messenger. I called 911, but I left before the ambulance arrived, so I don't know what happened to him."

"What do you want from me?"

"I have to find out who sent the man who attacked me so I can neutralize the threat."

Santoro had done some checking on Dana Cutler, including a look at the police file that detailed how Dana had dealt with the bikers who had kidnapped her. There were crime-scene photos in it. Santoro had seen some bad shit over the years, but these photos almost made him lose his lunch. After seeing the photos there was no doubt in Santoro's mind what Dana meant when she used the word "neutralize."

"There's no way I'm going to help you kill someone," he said. "If that's where this is going, count me out."

Dana stared into space for a moment. Then she nodded.

"What can you tell me about your attacker?" Santoro asked.

"He wore a ski mask. I was so anxious to get away that I didn't take it off, so I can't tell you what he looks like. But you shouldn't have any trouble identifying him. The guy is huge. Not fat. Well built, like a heavyweight boxer. And you shouldn't have any trouble finding him. He'll be in a hospital or the morgue."

"Is there anything else you remember? Any scars, tattoos?"

"I'm pretty sure he's Russian or from somewhere in Eastern Europe."

"Now, *that* is interesting," Santoro said. "The odds are that Russian muscle would be connected to Nikolai Orlansky, and Charlie Benedict has represented members of Orlansky's crew."

"I'd forgotten that."

"Yeah, well, you had other things on your mind."

A sudden thought occurred to Santoro. "Do you think Tiffany Starr might be in danger?"

Dana turned pale. "I'm sure this guy came after me because Tiffany told someone about my visit. The person she talked to is probably the person who told her where Carrie Blair was buried."

Dana looked worried. "Tiffany is a junkie, and junkies can't be trusted. If I killed Blair and Tiffany told me a reporter had come around asking questions, getting rid of Tiffany would be my top priority."

Santoro stood up and walked toward his bedroom.

"Where are you going?" Dana asked.

"I'm getting dressed. We're going to drive to Starr's apartment and see if she's okay."

Tiffany did not answer her door.

"She's a stripper. She could be at a club," Dana said.

"I hope so. Because she could also be dead."

Dana thought for a moment. "Wait in the stairwell."

"Why?"

"You don't want to know."

Dana had been inside Tiffany's apartment so she knew it didn't have an alarm system, and the bolt was pathetic. As soon as Santoro was out of sight, Dana jimmied the lock. Twenty minutes later, Dana was walking downstairs with the detective.

"She's not in the apartment but I did find an ATM receipt of a recent two-thousand-dollar deposit."

"A payoff for telling Barry Lester what to tell the cops?"

"Could be."

"Did you see anything that made you think Starr was in danger?"

"There wasn't any sign of a struggle or blood, if that's what you mean."

"Look, Dana, I've been thinking. If Nikolai Orlansky sent the guy who attacked you, you're in a lot of trouble. Orlansky is completely ruthless, he has no conscience. He views killing people as a business strategy."

"But he wouldn't know I'm involved. I used a false name when I talked to Starr."

"Then how did this guy get your number?"

"I gave her a business card identifying 'Loren Parkhurst' as a reporter for *Exposed*."

"Orlansky is smart, Dana. With the lead to *Exposed* he'll figure it out."

"What are you suggesting?"

"I'm suggesting that you leave town for a while. I know how tough you are but it will be next to impossible for you to get to Orlansky, and he can get to you anytime he wants."

"I'm not going to run. And what about my boyfriend? I'm living with someone I care about. If Orlansky is as ruthless as you say and he can't find me, he might try to get at me by threatening Jake."

"Good point, but I think I know a way to protect both of you. Is there any part of this investigation you can do out of town, because I'll need a little time to see if it works."

"There's something I was going to do that would take me away from D.C."

"Then do it. I'll let you know when it's safe to come back. It shouldn't be long."

Chapter Forty-Two

Dana got home a little after two-thirty. Jake woke up when she entered the bedroom. Dana sat on the side of the bed.

"We have to talk," she said.

The only light in the room came from the moon, so Dana's face was in shadows. Jake couldn't see her expression, but he could hear the tension in her voice. He sat up.

"What's wrong?"

"I was attacked tonight."

"Are you okay?"

"I'm fine, and the man who attacked me isn't. I took care of him. But he was working for someone who wants to scare me off a case, and I'm worried that they might try to get at me through you."

Jake was wide awake now. "How serious is this?"

"Very serious."

"Shit."

"I'm sorry, Jake. I'd never have gotten involved if I had any idea I might put you in danger."

"I know that."

"I'm working with a homicide detective who told me to go out of town for a day or so. He's working on something that he thinks will make the threat go away. Why don't you come with me?"

"Where are you headed?"

"Kansas City. We'll leave in the morning."

Dana was packing when Frank Santoro called.

"There have been two developments," the detective said. "Neither one is good, but one is interesting."

"Tell me."

"Tiffany Starr is dead." Dana felt the air go out of her. "A jogger found her body in Rock Creek Park. Stabbed in the heart. It looks like a robbery—her purse is missing and she wasn't wearing any jewelry."

"But you don't think robbery was the motive?" Dana asked as she shut down her emotions.

"It's too much of a coincidence," Santoro answered.

"You said there were two developments."

"Last night, a man named Gregor Karpinski was admitted to Georgetown Medical Center. He'd been stabbed in the balls and had his head kicked in. The beating was pretty brutal."

As soon as Santoro detailed Karpinski's injuries Dana's pulse shot up.

"There's a connection between Karpinski and Barry Lester," Santoro continued. "Lester was in general population in the jail. Then he was placed in isolation because he had a run-in with Karpinski. Karpinski is a beast, six five and solid muscle, and he works as an enforcer for Nikolai Orlansky. Barry Lester is a little shit with almost no muscle and no record of violence. The jail incident report states that Lester bumped into Karpinski, then called him an asshole."

"You think the fight was staged to get Lester into isolation?"

"That's precisely what I think. Karpinski doesn't breathe unless he gets permission from Orlansky, so either Nikolai wanted Lester in isolation or he was doing a favor for someone."

"Have you asked Karpinski if he was ordered to beat up Lester?"

"He isn't in any condition to answer questions."

"Will he pull through?"

"The doctors can't say yet. There's something else. Four years ago, Karpinski beat an assault charge. Do you want to guess who his lawyer was?"

Chapter Forty-Three

Kansas City, Missouri, was founded in 1838 at the confluence of the Missouri and Kansas Rivers and had grown into a picturesque city of boulevards, parks, and fountains. Dana and Jake had checked into a hotel a few blocks from the Plaza, an upscale, outdoor shopping and entertainment district that was famous for being the first suburban shopping center in the United States specifically designed to accommodate shoppers arriving by automobile. The blighted urban area into which Dana was driving seemed as far from the condos, museums, upscale restaurants, and nightclubs of the Plaza as Earth was from the moon, but it was only a short distance by car from the heart of downtown.

Dana had dressed in a severe business suit but she wondered if she was overdressed. The neighborhood she was in was a strange mixture of lots filled with abandoned tires and rotting furniture that were patrolled by feral cats, well-tended single-family dwellings, and trashed, ruined, and looted homes with shattered windowpanes. Sullen young men stared at her as she drove by, and she spotted gang colors she'd learned to identify during her stint with the D.C. police. What she did not see were happy couples strolling behind baby carriages or neighbors talking over white picket fences. Why make yourself a target?

Just as she'd given up on the neighborhood, Dana suddenly found herself in an oasis of modern middle-class homes with newly mown lawns. Dana parked in front of a fifties ranch-style home with a peaked roof and stone-and-wood siding. The house was set back from the street, and a slate path led across a manicured lawn. A minute after she rang the bell the door was opened by a slender African-American man with close-cropped salt-and-pepper hair, wearing a Kansas City Chiefs sweatshirt and neatly pressed jeans.

Dana had seen Roger Felton's name in the newspaper article detailing the execution murder of the two drug dealers. She had gone to police headquarters in Kansas City and learned that Felton was living with his elderly father in the neighborhood where Felton had grown up.

"Detective Felton?" Dana asked.

"I was," Felton answered as he eyed Dana suspiciously. "I'm retired. How can I help you?"

"My name is Dana Cutler." She held out her identification. "I was a police officer in Washington, D.C., but I'm private now. I'd like to ask you about a case you worked on about twenty-five years ago."

Felton scrutinized her ID before stepping aside

and ushering Dana into a large living room that was illuminated by the sunlight that streamed through high picture windows. An elderly man who was breathing from an oxygen tank sat in a wheelchair across from a stone fireplace.

"That's my dad," Felton explained. "I live in Florida, but he had a stroke and I'm back here to help him out.

"This is Dana Cutler from Washington, D.C.," Felton told his father. "She wants to ask me some questions about an old case."

Felton turned back to Dana. "He has trouble speaking, but Dad is still sharp."

Felton sat in an armchair and motioned Dana onto an identical chair that was standing on the other side of a walnut end table. A photo of a much younger man who strongly resembled Felton's father and a smiling, heavyset black woman stood in the center of the end table next to a lamp.

"So, what do you want to know?" Felton asked.

"Do you remember Anthony Watts and Donald Marion?"

"Sure," Felton said without a second of hesitation.

"I'm surprised you recall a case that old so easily," she said.

"There are some cases you never forget. I'm certain I know who killed those two but I could never prove it, and it's always bothered me. Why do you want to know about Watts and Marion after all these years?"

"Richard Molinari has become a person of interest in a case I'm investigating."

A cloud passed over Felton's features. "Richard, huh. That's a name I never hoped to hear again. What's he involved in now?"

"Some very interesting stuff, and he doesn't go by Molinari anymore. He changed his name to Charles Benedict, and he's a criminal defense attorney."

"You're kidding me?"

"Molinari moved from here to Pennsylvania and changed his name. Then he earned a GED, went to college, and graduated from law school at the University of Virginia, with honors."

"I'll be damned. I never saw that coming."

"What can you tell me about Molinari?"

"He's a stone killer, that's one thing I can tell you. You've probably noticed the racial makeup of this neighborhood. It's mostly black and Hispanic, and it has a very high crime rate. I tried to get my father to move to Florida because it's not safe, but he's stubborn. Even this area, which is mostly middle class, has more than its fair share of crime.

"There are a lot of gangs operating here, and it was worse twenty years ago. The most powerful gangs were African American, so figure out how tough a white boy would have to be to earn the position of enforcer in the Kung Fu Dragons, the dominant gang in the neighborhood. That was Richard. He was devoid of a conscience, owned a very high IQ, and was totally ruthless. No one wanted to fight him because you had to kill him or he'd never stop coming after you.

"Let me give you an example. Molinari's family moved from somewhere back East when he was sixteen. The first day in high school three kids beat him up. After that, Molinari gave them his lunch money and generally acted like a coward toward them, but before the month was out, two of the boys were beaten with a baseball bat. The brain damage was so bad that they were useless as witnesses. The third boy was burned to death in a house fire that killed his entire family. The day after the assault and the arson, Richard showed up at school with a baseball bat. He never said anything, but word got around the school that he was not someone to fuck with, if you'll pardon my French."

"Was he arrested?"

"The principal told us the boys had beaten up Molinari, and about the bat, so Richard was our main suspect, but the kid was too smart for us."

"Did you take a look at the bat he brought to school?"

"Sure, but it wasn't the bat he used. That bat was found on the front steps of the burned-out house, covered with the victims' blood but wiped clean of any prints. Someone, probably Molinari, spread the word around school that the kids had been beaten silly with a baseball bat."

"How did he get into the gang if he was white?"

"The rumor was that he made a deal with the leader of the Dragons to take out the leader of a rival gang that was trying to take over the crack cocaine trade in the area."

"He killed him?"

"We don't know. No one could prove he was murdered because he just vanished. After that, everyone started calling Molinari 'the Magician.'"

"Because he made his victims disappear?"

"That was part of it, but he actually was an amateur magician."

"If he was in so tight with the Dragons, why did he take off?"

"The Dragons were dealing for a Mexican drug cartel. Marion and Watts were emissaries from a gang in Cleveland that was going to do a drug deal with the Dragons. We had a snitch who told us that the deal was bigger than usual and there was a substantial amount of cash involved. Watts and Marion were supposed to make a swap in one location but they never showed up. We think Molinari lured them to an abandoned barn, killed them, then hid the money. We arrested Molinari but we couldn't hold him. The day he left the jail was the last day anyone saw him in Missouri."

"Fascinating."

"Isn't it. And what you've told me makes sense. Even as a teenager, Molinari was the smartest criminal I'd ever dealt with. He was definitely smart enough to know he had no future with the Dragons after he ripped them off, and smart enough to know he had to disappear, like a card in one of his tricks."

Chapter Forty-Four

Frank Santoro had a friend in Organized Crime in the Department of Justice who owed him a favor. According to Santoro's friend, Nikolai Orlansky was always accompanied by several bodyguards and his armor-plated car had bulletproof glass. Orlansky varied his routes from his home to his businesses and never visited the businesses in any predictable order. The crime lord did have one weakness, however—women.

Nikolai changed mistresses frequently. This was not a problem, since one of his businesses was prostitution and new young bodies regularly flowed from Eastern Europe to the brothels he controlled. Orlansky rarely kept company with one woman for very long, but he used the same penthouse apartment in a high-rise condominium in D.C. for his assignations. Santoro's friend said that Orlansky was known to have a very healthy sex drive and rarely remained celibate for more than a few days. According to the latest surveillance information, Orlansky's wife had just left for a shopping spree in

Manhattan and the Mafia chief had not visited his current mistress in several days.

Nikolai Orlansky's driver parked in a reserved spot next to an elevator that went straight to the penthouse. A second car filled with bodyguards made certain that their boss was safe before motioning him out of the car.

Santoro watched the ritual from the front seat of his car. As soon as Orlansky got out, Frank walked toward the gangster with his badge held high.

"Lee County police," he proclaimed in a loud voice.

The bodyguards swiveled toward him and several guns pointed at various parts of his body.

"Mr. Orlansky," Santoro said, "I'm unarmed and I'm not wearing a wire. I just want to talk. If you'll give me a few minutes of your time I'll be out of your hair."

Orlansky assessed the situation before telling his men to stand down.

"Frisk him," Orlansky told a slender man with a narrow mustache and watery eyes. Santoro had read several files on Orlansky, and he recognized Peter Perkovic from a mug shot. Perkovic was a ruthless killer and Orlansky's right-hand man.

"He's clean," Perkovic said after a thorough pat-down.

"Come in the car," Orlansky said. He slid across

the backseat, and Santoro sat next to him. Perkovic shut the door but watched the detective through the window.

"So, Detective . . . ?"

"Frank. And this conversation is just between us. It is completely off the record. I'm going to talk and I don't expect you to say anything. I just want you to listen."

Orlansky looked amused. "You have intrigued me. So, tell me, what is so important that you have approached me in secret in a garage?"

"Gregor Karpinski."

Orlansky's brow furrowed and Frank got the impression that Orlansky was genuinely puzzled.

"He's a bouncer at one of my clubs," the gangster said.

"He's also in the hospital after coming out on the wrong end of a discussion with a friend of mine."

Santoro assumed that someone like Orlansky, who was used to dealing with the police, would be able to mask his emotions if he wanted to, but Orlansky showed surprise, and it looked genuine. Either he was a terrific actor or Santoro's revelations were new to him.

"Horace Blair has been charged with murder. Barry Lester is the state's key witness against Mr. Blair. Two days ago my friend interviewed Tiffany Starr, Lester's girlfriend. Two things happened that evening: Karpinski threatened to rape my friend if she didn't back off, and Tiffany Starr was stabbed to death in Rock Creek Park. It's too late to help Tiffany Starr but I'm here to tell you to stay away from my friend. If a hair on her head is touched, I promise to make your life hell on earth. Are we clear?"

Orlansky did not look frightened or angry. If anything, he looked confused.

"You say Karpinski is in the hospital. How did that happen?"

"Ask him, if he survives."

Orlansky seemed troubled. "Detective Santoro, thank you for speaking to me in private. I appreciate the courtesy. I had nothing to do with what happened to your friend or Miss Starr. You can tell your friend that she has nothing to fear from me."

"Then our business is done. Have a nice evening."

When Santoro walked to his car he didn't look back. His heart was beating like a trip-hammer and he couldn't relax until he was out of shooting range. While he drove, Frank thought about his meeting with Orlansky. He was pretty certain that the Russian was genuinely surprised by everything he'd been told. If Orlansky didn't send Karpinski to threaten Dana, there was a good chance that Charles Benedict was behind the threat, and that presented a problem. It was one thing to use his position to threaten a gangster like Orlansky. It was quite another thing to try to strong-arm a member of the bar who also happened to be the attorney for a very powerful and well-connected person who was facing a murder charge. This was especially true when you had no evidence whatsoever that the lawyer had committed a crime. Santoro could imagine the fallout if he confronted Benedict the same way he'd confronted Orlansky.

Santoro pulled into a shopping mall and dialed Dana's cell.

"How is Kansas City?" he asked when Dana answered.

"Interesting. Why are you calling?"

"I had a talk with Nikolai Orlansky. He assured me that he didn't send Karpinski after you. I got the impression that he didn't know anything about what happened."

"Then I think I know who did send that ape. Especially after what I learned today."

Dana filled in Frank on Charles Benedict's background.

"This puts everything that's happened in a completely different light," Santoro said when Dana was through.

"I think it's possible that Benedict killed Carrie Blair and set up her husband. Our problem is that we have no proof. If he did kill Carrie Blair, Benedict is one crafty psychopath. We can't talk to his client without his permission, and unless Karpinski confesses, we have nothing."

Chapter Forty-Five

Charles Benedict tried to get in touch with Gregor Karpinski all day. He called Gregor twice and got voice mail. He left a message telling the Russian to call him about his legal bill. When he still had not heard by eight in the evening, Benedict called The Scene and asked for Kenny Ito, one of the bartenders.

"Kenny, Charlie Benedict here. I need to talk to Gregor Karpinski. Something's come up in one of his legal matters but he's not answering his phone."

"You haven't heard?"

"Heard what?"

"Gregor got fucked up last night."

"Fucked up how?"

"I don't know how it happened. I just heard some of the guys talking. All I know is that he's in the hospital, and it's bad."

"Do you know what hospital he's in?"

Ito told him. Benedict thanked him and hung up. He leaned back and thought. All Gregor was supposed to do was threaten some girl. How could a girl "fuck up" Gregor? The guy was a monster.

Benedict fished out the business card Tiffany Starr had showed him shortly before he gutted her. He went on his computer and Googled *Exposed*. Loren Parkhurst was not listed as an employee. Benedict thought about that. Just because she wasn't listed didn't mean she didn't work for the paper. She could freelance.

Benedict typed Parkhurst's name into the search engine. Nothing. Now, *that* was strange. If Parkhurst were a journalist, she should have published something somewhere. He didn't like this. A woman journalist who didn't show up on the Internet and who was capable of "fucking up" a beast like Gregor Karpinski.

Benedict thought some more, and the more he thought, the more concerned he became. Gregor could tell the cops that Charlie had asked him to threaten Parkhurst. Worse still, if Gregor talked, Nikolai could learn that Charlie used Gregor without his permission. He and Nikolai got along pretty well, but Nikolai was unpredictable.

What to do? What to do? After giving that question some serious thought, only one viable solution presented itself.

Chapter Forty-Six

The drugs! Gregor craved the drugs. When they wore off, the pain returned. When he was a child, Gregor had learned the hard way how to deal with pain inflicted by fists, kicks, belts, and sticks wielded by his father and his fellow schoolboys. Then he grew and thickened and became the one who inflicted the pain. He was used to fighting in prisons and bars and back alleys. But that pain wasn't like the pain that bitch had created.

Gregor never suspected that the whore might be armed and would have the guts to stab him like that, in that place. Some women fought back at first. He liked that. It excited him. Most of the women begged and pleaded. Eventually they all became obedient and willing to do anything to avoid a beating. Except this one.

No woman had ever done to him what that bitch had done. And she would pay. He would find her and he would . . . He was about to think "fuck her," but he might never be able to fuck anyone ever again.

The thought brought tears to Gregor's eyes. Suddenly he was so sad. What had she done to him? How could she? What if she had taken his manhood? What if he . . . ? No, he could not let himself think about that. And no matter what he could not do, he could always make her suffer and scream the way she had made him scream. Oh, he looked forward to that. The hate kept him going.

Then something horrible occurred to Gregor. He was starting to think clearly! If he could think clearly it meant the drugs were wearing off. Suddenly the pain touched him ever so lightly; just enough to turn his hands into fists and compel him to suck in a breath. Soon it would sink its claws in him, and that would be very, very bad. But the bad thing would not happen because Gregor had his magic button, his precious button. Press the button and morphine raced through him and swept away the pain. He started to reach for his wonderful, special button, but strong fingers gripped him and pressed his hand against the side of the bed.

The drugs dulled Gregor's reflexes and it took forever to turn his head and focus. When he did he found himself staring into the lifeless eyes of Peter Perkovic.

Gregor was in a private room, lying in a hospital bed. His complexion was the color of dead fish and wires ran from many parts of his body into machines with multicolored lights and electronic readouts. The machines beeped and buzzed. Normally even someone as physically powerful as Gregor Karpinski would feel fear when subjected to Perkovic's cold stare, but Gregor was still floating in a druggy haze.

"Peter?" he said. When he spoke, his mouth felt like it was filled with cotton.

"You don't look so good, Gregor. How are you feeling?"

There was something odd about Perkovic, but Gregor had trouble tracking.

"That bitch fucked me up," he answered, his speech badly slurred and his eyes unfocused. "She stabbed me."

"That's awful," Peter said just as Gregor figured out what was bothering him. Peter was dressed in a green smock and loose green pants. He was dressed like a doctor or an orderly. How strange.

"Are you working in the hospital?" Gregor asked. He sounded loopy.

"No, Gregor. It was just easier to visit dressed like this."

"Oh."

Suddenly the pain struck and Gregor flinched. It was only a pale shadow of the pain that would come if he didn't press the button. He tried to raise his hand, but he didn't have the strength to break Peter's grip.

"Soon, Gregor. Soon I will let you press the button," Peter said. "But first you must tell me what happened."

Gregor started to tear up. "She stabbed me in my prick, Peter, in my balls."

"That's terrible. Why did she do that?"

"I told her what to do but she would not obey. Then she hurt me."

"What did you tell her? What order did she disobey?"

"To back off, to stop asking questions about the Blair case."

"Ah, did Nikolai ask you to speak to this woman?"

"No."

"Why didn't you ask Nikolai if you could threaten her?"

"He told me Nikolai said it was okay."

"Someone said this?"

"Yes. You know I wouldn't do anything unless Nikolai said it was okay. He told me he'd talked to Nikolai and Nikolai said it was okay. Nikolai isn't mad at me, is he?"

"No, no, Gregor. Nikolai wishes you well. He hopes you make a full recovery."

The pain hit and this time Gregor arched his back and grimaced.

"One more answer and you can press the button. Who told you to talk to the woman?"

"Charlie, Charlie Benedict, the lawyer. He said it was okay. Please."

"Thank you, Gregor. Nikolai wanted me to tell you something. This woman who stabbed you . . ."

"He doesn't have to worry. As soon as I'm out, I'll make her scream, I'll rip her up."

"No, no, Gregor. Nikolai does not want you near this woman. She is off-limits to you forever."

"What?"

Gregor spasmed. The pain was becoming unbearable.

"Say you understand. Say you will forget about this woman forever."

"Please," Gregor begged.

"Say it."

"I won't hurt her ever. Ahhh!"

Peter released Gregor's hand and he stabbed at the button until the morphine chased the pain. Within moments, he forgot the woman and Peter and everything else because he was floating high above his troubles on a cloud of good feeling.

Perkovic studied Karpinski for a few seconds more, then shook his head. Gregor was an idiot, a fearsome windup toy. Peter knew he would forget his promise, but Peter would remind Gregor when he was well enough to remember. Now he had to tell Nikolai about Charles Benedict.

Chapter Forty-Seven

Dana was surprised to see Stephanie Robb follow Frank Santoro into Vinny's.

"I told Steph I hired you and what you learned in Kansas City," Santoro said. "She's pissed that I went behind her back but she agrees that it's time for all of us to get on the same page."

"And just so you know," Robb added, "I still think Horace Blair killed his wife, but after what you found out about Benedict, I'm willing to listen."

"I also told her about the chow here," Santoro said as the waitress came over and everyone ordered burgers, fries, and beer.

"I've been giving this case a lot of thought," Santoro said when the waitress left, "and I'm convinced that Charles Benedict killed Carrie Blair and is framing Horace for her murder. I don't know why he killed Carrie, but let's assume that he did. Can we account for the evidence against Horace in a way that implicates Benedict?

"Let's start with the keys. Something about them bothered me when we conducted our experiment at

Blair's mansion. Do you remember what the keys looked like, Steph?"

Robb looked confused. "They looked like keys."

"Right, but there was something odd about one of them. The two keys we found in the grave—the single key and the front-door key on Carrie's key chain—looked old and abused. They were dull, they had scratches on them. The key we took from Blair that wouldn't open the front door resembled the keys from the grave but looked much newer and less worn."

"Why is that important?" Robb asked.

"Remember Ernest Brodsky?"

"Of course."

"Remember how he earned his living?"

As soon as she made the connection Robb looked sick.

"Dana and I went over the surveillance tapes we got from the River View Mall. On Tuesday morning, a Porsche resembling Carrie Blair's Porsche entered the mall's parking lot. I couldn't read the whole license plate but two of the letters match Carrie's license and are in the right place on the plate.

"Around the time I saw the Porsche on the tape, a man entered Brodsky's store and left carrying a small paper bag that was big enough to hold several keys. The man made a real effort to keep his face hidden. He was wearing a sweatshirt with a hood and he kept his head down. I went over Brodsky's receipts for Tuesday. He sold two keys for cash right around the time the man in the hoodie went into his shop.

"Later that night, shortly after Brodsky closed his store, a Mercedes drove out of the mall. Brodsky's car was found in the mall parking lot, so it's a good guess that he was kidnapped from the mall. Benedict drives a Mercedes.

"Here's the way I see it. Benedict kills Carrie and figures out a way to frame Blair for his wife's murder that includes making it look like Blair dropped his front-door key in Carrie's grave while he was burying her. He has Brodsky make a key that looks like Blair's front-door key but isn't. Then he kills Brodsky so he can't be a witness. If I'm right, we also know how the gun, hairs, and blood got in the trunk of the Bentley. The second key Brodsky made was a copy of the Bentley key Carrie had on her key chain."

"This is all guesswork, Frank," Robb said.

Santoro smiled. "Not completely. As soon as I made the connection between this case and Brodsky's murder, I called Wilda Parks at the crime lab and asked her if there was any way to tell if the key on Horace Blair's key chain—the one that wouldn't open the front door—had been made in Ernest Brodsky's store.

"There's a whole branch of forensics that involves tool-mark identification. Wilda explained that keys are made from blanks that don't have any 'cuts.'

'Cuts' are the ridges on the key that interface with the components of a lock. If they are positioned correctly they cause the lock to lock or unlock. These cuts are made in a grinding machine. Different grinding machines will leave different tool marks on a key shaped by that machine.

"I checked with Stuart Lang at the River View Mall. Brodsky's grinding machines are still in his store. Wilda called this morning. The tool marks on the key on Horace's key chain—the newer-looking key—were made by Brodsky's machine."

"But what about the fingerprints, Frank?" Robb asked. "Horace Blair's prints were on the key we found in the grave. Blair didn't have a key to his front door on his key chain, so the key in the grave is probably his front-door key. How did Benedict get Blair's key?"

"I don't know," Santoro said. "But Blair called Benedict as soon as we arrested him. That means they knew each other. I'm sure Blair could tell us if Benedict had an opportunity to get the key. Unfortunately, we can't ask him because Benedict won't let us talk to his client. But let's forget about the key for now. There's one more connection between Brodsky and this case. Why was Barry Lester in isolation, Steph?"

"He had a fight with one of Nikolai Orlansky's goons."

"Gregor Karpinski is a beast. Lester's not. He's a wimp. So why would Lester provoke Karpinski?

I think it was a setup to get Lester into isolation so he could snitch on Blair. If you remember, Benedict really worked us over to get us to put Blair in isolation. Well, Benedict also represented Karpinski in an assault case.

"Now, here is the clincher for me. If Blair didn't confess to Lester, then someone fed Lester the location of the grave and the contents of the prenup. Only two people talked to Lester while he was in jail. Dana interviewed one of those people, Lester's girlfriend, Tiffany Starr. The next day, Starr was stabbed to death. I read the autopsy reports in Starr's and Brodsky's cases, then I talked to Nick Winters. In both cases, the knife wounds were almost identical: one shot to the heart."

"Fuck," Robb said.

"Yeah, Steph, I agree."

"There's something else that links Karpinski and Tiffany Starr," Dana said. "I talked to Starr on the day she was killed. That night, Karpinski lured me to an industrial park and threatened to rape me if I kept asking questions about the Blair case."

"Are you okay?" Robb asked with real concern.

Dana nodded.

"Karpinski isn't so hot, though," Santoro said. "Dana put him in the hospital."

"How could you possibly do that?" Robb asked.

"I'll tell you later," Santoro said.

"I'm certain the fight between Lester and Karpinski was a setup," Dana said, anxious to change the subject. "I'd bet everything I own that Blair never confessed to Lester. And if he didn't, then the odds are that Tiffany Starr told Lester where to find the grave and what was in the prenup. If you need more proof, check Tiffany's bank account. You'll find a recent two-thousand-dollar deposit."

"How do you know that?" Robb asked.

"I'd rather not say," Dana answered.

"Damn," Robb said. "I was so sure Blair offed her. Now I don't know what to think."

"I'm sure that Benedict has been leading us around by the nose, but I don't have any idea how we can prove it," Santoro said.

"If we could talk to Blair, he could tell us if Benedict had an opportunity to get his house key," Dana said, her frustration evident.

"That's something that's not going to happen as long as Benedict is Blair's attorney," Santoro said.

By the time Dana got home she was exhausted. Jake was watching a basketball game. Dana pecked him on the cheek, headed straight for the bedroom, and fell instantly into such a deep sleep that she never noticed when Jake climbed into bed an hour later.

Sometime during the night Dana started dreaming. In her dream she was in a narrow shop with a low ceiling. There was almost no light, and the confined space was making her claustrophobic. Dana wanted to get out of the shop, but the floor was covered with so many keys that she could barely move. She was starting to panic because each step made her sink deeper into the pile of keys, which sucked at her like quicksand. Dana struggled toward the door. She began flailing and she didn't stop until she shot up in bed, damp with perspiration, her heart beating furiously.

Dana cast a quick glance at Jake to see if she'd awakened him but he was sleeping soundly. She went to the kitchen, filled a glass with water, and sat at the table. It was four in the morning and the sky was pitch-black. No moon, no starlight. She could sure use something to illuminate the problem Charles Benedict had posed for her, Dana thought. She was certain he had murdered Carrie Blair, but she hadn't a clue as to how she could prove it.

If only they could ask Horace Blair if Benedict had an opportunity to get Horace's front-door key. But no one could talk to Blair while Charles Benedict was representing him.

Then an idea occurred to Dana. She smiled. She thought about it some more and her smile widened. To the best of her knowledge, she and Charles Benedict had never met, and Benedict definitely did not know about the Ottoman Scepter. Dana looked at the clock on the kitchen stove. It was 4:45 on the East Coast and three hours earlier out west. Dana was fired up, but she knew that she would have to practice patience, because Marty Draper would be too upset to give her a crash course on Asian antiquities if she woke him out of a deep sleep at 1:45 in the morning.

Part III

The Revenge
of the Ottoman Scepter

Chapter Forty-Eight

Santoro and Robb got out of the elevator and spotted the nurses' station. A heavyset brunette was on the phone, reading from a medical chart, when they walked up. The detectives held up their identification and the woman held up her hand as she continued to talk.

"How can I help you?" the nurse asked as soon as she hung up the phone.

"We want to speak to a patient."

"What's the patient's name?"

"Gregor Karpinski."

The nurse had started to look at a white board with room numbers and patient names, but she stopped.

"Mr. Karpinski passed away last night."

"He's dead?" Santoro said.

The nurse nodded.

"How did he die?"

"I don't know. I wasn't on duty."

"Is there someone we can speak to?"

"Dr. Raptis was here. Let me see if he's available."

Santoro and Robb walked far enough away from the nurse's station so they could talk without being overheard.

"What do you think?" Robb asked.

"I don't know. From what I heard, he was in pretty bad shape, stab wounds to the groin, head trauma."

Before Robb could reply a young man in a white coat walked up to the nurses' station. He was short and slender, and his long black hair looked as if it had been finger-combed. Santoro guessed he was in his late twenties. The nurse pointed to the detectives. The doctor's glasses had slipped down his nose and he pushed them up as he walked over.

"Hi, I'm Dave Raptis. Nurse Arlen said you wanted to know about Gregor Karpinski."

"He is—I guess 'was' is more appropriate—a witness in a case we're investigating," Santoro said. "We came up here hoping to talk to him, but the nurse told us he died last night."

"That's right. He passed away about three in the morning."

"Was Mr. Karpinski your patient?" Robb asked.

"Dr. Samuels did the surgery. I'd looked in on him a few times since he was admitted."

"Was his death a surprise?" Robb asked.

"Actually, it was."

"Why is that?" Santoro asked.

"He died of cardiac arrest."

"Why was that surprising? I thought he was in pretty bad shape."

"Oh, he was, but the damage he suffered was to his genitals and head. There was nothing wrong with his heart."

"Was there anything suspicious about the death? Anything that would make you suspect that he was murdered?"

"Murdered?"

"Mr. Karpinski was a witness in a murder case. His death could benefit some people. Can you think of anything that would help us figure out whether he died from natural or unnatural causes?"

The doctor looked concerned. "Gee, I don't know. He had died by the time I got to his room. It never occurred to me that he might have been murdered, so I wasn't looking for anything like that."

The detectives talked with Dr. Raptis a little longer before they headed for the elevator. Santoro got his cell phone out and speed-dialed the medical examiner's office while they waited for the car to come. After he spoke to Nick Winters, Santoro called Dana Cutler and told her that another avenue for proving that Charles Benedict had killed Carrie Blair had been closed.

Chapter Forty-Nine

At 10:30 a.m. The Scene was deserted except for a handful of alcoholics who were nursing drinks at the bar. Peter Perkovic found his boss going over the books in the back office. Orlansky looked up when Perkovic walked in. Perkovic looked upset.

"What happened?" Orlansky asked.

"Gregor is dead."

"How did he die?"

"They're saying cardiac arrest, but I saw his chart when I went to the hospital. There was nothing wrong with his heart."

"So?"

"There are ways. An injection of potassium would be my choice."

"There will be an autopsy?"

Perkovic nodded.

"Can you get the results?"

"Of course, but potassium poisoning is virtually undetectable."

Orlansky stared into space and Perkovic waited patiently. Orlansky came back to Earth.

"Charlie?" he asked.

"A dead Gregor cannot talk to the police. And Charlie would know that it would upset you to learn that he told Gregor you had said it was okay to threaten this woman."

"I agree. Talk to me as soon as you know the results of the autopsy."

Chapter Fifty

One look at his waiting area and a potential client would know that hiring Bobby Schatz was going to be an expensive proposition. The magazines on the end tables focused on life in the Hamptons, Saint Croix, and Biarritz. Elegant sofas stood on either side of a Persian carpet that was laid across a polished hardwood floor, and the lawyer's receptionist, who was so stunning that she could grace the cover of *Vogue* without makeup, was positioned behind a handcrafted mahogany desk.

The first and only time Dana had worked with Schatz, the capital's preeminent criminal attorney had hired her to assist in the defense of an American-born terrorist who had tried to blow up the football stadium where the Washington Redskins play. The relationship had ended under strange and unpleasant circumstances.

"May I help you?" the receptionist asked in a friendly voice that betrayed none of the disdain she may have felt for a woman wearing jeans, shades, and a motorcycle jacket. Schatz had stopped representing biker gangs and other lowlifes long ago. Nowadays, the defendants he escorted to court were disgraced hedge-fund managers and nattily dressed political perverts.

"Tell Bobby that Dana Cutler wants a moment of his valuable time."

"Do you have an appointment?"

"No, and I don't need one. Just tell him who's in the waiting room."

The receptionist hesitated, but something about Dana made her reconsider. She pressed a button and conveyed the message.

"He'll see you," she told Dana. The woman started to get up but Dana motioned her to stay seated.

"Bobby and I are old friends. I know the way to his inner sanctum."

Dana walked down a narrow hall, past offices staffed by the attorney's associates, then stopped in the doorway of a large corner office decorated with expensive art and photographs of Bobby with the rich and famous. Sitting behind a desk the size of an aircraft carrier was a thickset man with slicked-back dyed black hair who was dressed in an elegant gray pinstripe suit. A red polka-dot bow tie was secured under the collar of a white silk shirt, and a silk handkerchief poked out of the pocket beneath the jacket's left lapel.

Schatz remembered his last meeting with Dana. "Do I need to call security?" he asked, only half kidding.

"No, Bobby. I'm not going to shoot you—at least not today."

"That's a relief."

Dana sat in a high-backed armchair and took in the view of the Capitol dome.

"You're still doing well," she remarked.

Schatz shrugged. "I get by."

"You'd do even better if Horace Blair was a client."

"Once was enough, thank you," Bobby answered.

"You two have a history?"

"Ten years ago, I had the displeasure of representing Horace when he was charged with drunk driving."

"That's right! Wasn't that the trial where he met Carrie Blair?"

Schatz nodded.

"What was the problem?"

"My client. Carrie Blair was the prosecutor and she had one witness, the arresting officer. I made mincemeat of him during cross. If we'd rested without putting on any witnesses we would have won, but it was love at first sight for Horace and he insisted on testifying so he could make gooey eyes at Carrie."

Schatz shook his head in disgust. "I did everything I could to talk him out of taking the stand, but he blew me off. Then he confessed during cross-examination, just to impress Carrie. I would have smacked my head against the counsel table but it would have been unseemly."

"I thought defense attorneys were supposed to

put the interest of their clients first," Dana said with the hint of a smile.

Even ten years later, Schatz did not appear to see the humor in the situation.

"I don't like to lose. Ever. In any event, I don't see how I can represent Horace. Charlie Benedict is representing him."

"That's true, but he shouldn't be Blair's lawyer. You should."

"What's your interest in Blair?"

"I think he's being framed and I want you to help me prove it."

Schatz leaned back in his chair, steepled his fingers, and studied Dana.

"Who do you think is framing him?"

"Charlie Benedict."

"Now you've got my attention."

"Bobby, how much do you know about the Ottoman Empire?"

Schatz listened intently as Dana told him about her quest for the scepter and all that had followed.

"That's some story," Schatz said when she was finished.

"That it is. What do you think of it?"

"I think you've convinced me that Horace is innocent and Benedict might be guilty. But how do you intend to prove he's innocent with Benedict as his lawyer?"

"The key to this case is—if you'll pardon the pun—the key with Blair's fingerprints that the police found in Carrie's grave. If Benedict killed Carrie Blair, he had to get hold of it before he buried her, but I don't know if he had an opportunity to do that. What I do have is a plan that will let me find out. And the first step in that plan will be to get Horace Blair to fire Charles Benedict and hire you."

"How are you going to do that?"

"By meeting with Horace Blair and convincing him that his attorney is trying to frame him. To do that, I have to talk to Jack Pratt, his civil attorney, the other lawyer who is allowed to meet with Blair. Do you know him well enough to set up a meeting?"

Chapter Fifty-One

"Thanks for coming over, Charlie," Rick Hamada said.

"It's always a pleasure, Rick," Benedict answered as he took a seat across the desk from the prosecutor. "So, what's the reason for this get-together?"

"The Blair case. You have no idea how much shit has been raining down on me since we arrested your client."

Benedict smiled. "Oh, I think I have a small idea."

Hamada didn't return the smile. "Yeah, you probably do. You probably engineered the calls from the governor, the mayor, and every other politician in Virginia and the District of Columbia who gets money from Blair."

"Not me," Benedict protested. "I don't run in those circles."

"Then it's probably Jack Pratt doing your dirty work for you."

Benedict shrugged. "If he is, he's doing it without my knowledge. And I'm sorry you're getting annoying calls, but you still haven't told me why I'm here."

Hamada's cheeks puffed up. Then he expelled the air he was holding.

"I've been ordered to offer Mr. Blair a deal. This wasn't my idea. I think I've got a pretty good case. If I could get my hands on a copy of the prenuptial agreement I'd have an airtight case, but I can't. Mancuso is worried that we won't be able to prove a motive without the prenup, and our only evidence about the contents comes from Barry Lester. Mancuso is nervous about using a scumbag like Lester to convict a person as prominent as your client. Personally, I think Lester will hold up, but I'm not the big boss. I just work here."

"What's the offer?"

"Blair pleads to manslaughter and we drop the murder charge. I told Mancuso he's making a mistake, but I'm not the only person getting nasty calls."

"Interesting."

"It's better than interesting, Charlie. It's a fucking fire sale as far as I'm concerned."

"I'll take the offer to my client and see what he thinks."

"Get back to me. All I can give you is two days. Then the deal is off the table."

The two lawyers talked a little longer, then Benedict left. As soon as the door closed behind Blair's attorney, Hamada phoned Frank Santoro.

"He just left," Hamada said.

"How do you think it went?" the detective asked.

"I have no idea."

"But you got him thinking about the prenup?"

"Yeah, I played it up big. Now we just have to wait to see if your plan works."

"Absolutely not!" Horace Blair said.

"At least think about the offer. Hamada hasn't decided whether he'll ask for the death penalty. Even if he doesn't, you're still looking at a possible life sentence as opposed to ten years. And, with your connections, you'd probably be out on parole at the first opportunity."

Every muscle in Blair's face tightened. He leaned toward Benedict, his face scarlet with anger.

"Let me make myself perfectly clear. I did not kill my wife. I am innocent and I will not plead guilty to anything, not even if Hamada offers me a jaywalking charge. Do you get that?"

Benedict held up his hands in a conciliatory gesture. "Hey, Horace, ease up. I'm on your side. I believe you're innocent one hundred percent, but I have a duty as your attorney to bring you any offer a prosecutor makes. I'd be disbarred if I didn't."

"Then you've done your duty and we will have no reason to ever discuss a plea again."

"I'll tell Hamada."

Blair was still angry when the guard escorted him back to his cell. Benedict was just disappointed. He had a pretty good fix on Blair's personality and he had not expected the millionaire to take the offer, but he had held out hope that he might. If Horace had pled, Benedict's life would have become much simpler. Oh, well, life was like that. Sometimes it didn't hand you an easy solution to your problems on a silver platter.

Chapter Fifty-Two

Horace Blair looked terrible. His hair was snarled and he was unshaven. There were dark circles under his eyes. The night before, the guards had placed an insane person in isolation and the man had howled like a dog for several hours before running out of steam. To make matters worse, the other inmates had added to the din by screaming at the lunatic and the guards. Horace had pressed his pillow over his ears, but his attempts to block out the manic baying and the angry shouts had failed, and he was exhausted.

Horace was used to being on the go constantly, so he found surviving the empty hours that comprised most of his day in jail very difficult. He could not help spending a lot of his idle time thinking about his case. When he could not sleep he found himself mulling over the evidence that had landed him in jail. Much of it made no sense. There were all these anonymous tips. There was the gun, which he had never seen until Frank Santoro held it up in front of his eyes. There was the other evidence the police had found in the trunk of his car. And Barry Lester!

How had that little weasel learned the terms of his prenuptial agreement and the location of Carrie's grave? But what bothered him the most was that damn key with his prints on it. How had a key to his front door found its way into Carrie's grave?

Horace was trying to solve these seemingly impossible problems when the door to his cell opened.

"You have visitors," the guard said.

Horace was eager for any change in his mind-numbing routine. The guard led him to a contact visiting room. He assumed that his visitor would be Charles Benedict. Instead he found Jack Pratt waiting for him.

"How are you holding up?" Pratt asked with genuine concern.

"How do you think?" Horace answered angrily. "I can't sleep, I get no exercise, the food is inedible, and I'm facing the possibility that I may be executed for a crime I never committed. Not to mention the fact that the businesses I've cultivated all my life are swirling down the toilet."

"Don't worry about business. The people you've put in place are doing a great job."

Suddenly all of the anger drained out of Blair. He looked like a beaten man.

"I don't know how I'm going to get by in here. I'm going crazy."

"You have to stay positive, Horace. You can't let this thing beat you. And right now you've got to focus. We have something very urgent to discuss."

Blair looked up.

"You have to change attorneys. You're making a big mistake by having Benedict as your lawyer."

"Why? What have you learned?"

"Very little that's good and a lot that is very bad," Pratt replied. "Even if I didn't know what I've learned recently I'd be urging you to drop Benedict. He's out of his depth with a case like this. He has handled a few murder cases but only one went to trial. Most of his caseload involves narcotics and prostitution. He's had some success with those cases, but a friend in the commonwealth attorney's office told me that there's something fishy about the way some of his victories were achieved."

"Such as?"

"Nikolai Orlansky is a mobster, Russian Mafia. A lot of Benedict's business comes from him, and a lot of those cases have been dismissed because of missing witnesses or evidence, not because of anything Benedict has done. Basically he's a lightweight, a .250 hitter. You need a big bat in your corner, Horace. You need to get rid of this guy. Especially after the way he fucked up your bail hearing."

"What do you mean?"

"In court a witness can't testify to what another person has told him if the testimony is introduced to prove the truth of the statement. That's the hearsay rule. For example, if you're my witness and I ask you where the sun rises, you can't say, 'I don't know, but Joe told me it rises in the east.'

"But there are exceptions to the hearsay rule. A witness *can* testify about something someone told him if a lawyer 'opens the door' by asking a question that invites the witness to testify to what someone else has told him.

"Benedict killed your chances for bail when he asked Detective Santoro questions that let Santoro testify about everything Barry Lester told him about the prenup and your supposed confession. That was an amateur mistake no decent lawyer would ever make."

Blair looked crushed.

"Don't beat yourself up for hiring Benedict," Pratt said. "You didn't have a lot of time to think after you were arrested and you trusted him because he gave you the DVD and didn't ask for anything in return."

Pratt paused. "Horace, we go back a long way, and you know I'm your friend as well as your attorney. Do you believe you can trust me?"

"Of course."

"I'm going to tell you something that is going to be tough to hear. There's another reason you have to get rid of Benedict. There's a good possibility that he did not make a mistake at the bail hearing. He may have acted intentionally so you wouldn't get bail."

"What are you talking about?"

"There is someone waiting outside I want you to meet. Dana Cutler is a private investigator who knows more about your case than anyone else. She's convinced me that Charles Benedict murdered Carrie and has been framing you for her murder from the start."

Horace listened to Dana's tale of her quest for a mythical golden scepter and the trail of clues that led her to the conclusion that Charles Benedict killed Carrie and framed him for her murder.

"There's one piece of this puzzle I can't solve," Dana concluded. "If Benedict murdered your wife and is behind this frame, he had to get your front-door key. Did he have an opportunity to do that before the body was discovered?"

Horace looked completely defeated. "I've been a fool," he said so softly that Dana had to strain to hear him.

"Benedict is a brilliant criminal," Pratt said. "We'd all have fallen for his tricks."

"I certainly did, and I know exactly how he got the key."

Horace told Dana and Pratt about Benedict's demonstration with the keys at his home on the evening he brought over the DVD.

"Do you remember telling me that you had seen Benedict perform magic at a Bar Association awards dinner, Jack?"

Pratt nodded.

"I know very little about magic but I imagine that

a magician would have little trouble swapping my house key for a look-alike that would not open my front door.

"And the evidence in the trunk of my Bentley. The trunk was locked and there was no sign that it had been forced open, but Carrie had a key to the Bentley. After he murdered Carrie, Benedict could have made a copy and used the key to get into the trunk."

"That must be it," Pratt said. "But, unfortunately, this is all guesswork. However, Dana has a plan."

Horace looked at the investigator. For the first time in a long while Horace Blair thought he might be saved.

"If I've learned one thing about Benedict," Dana said, "it's that he's very, very smart. I have theories about every step he's taken to frame you but I can't prove any of them because Benedict dots every I and crosses every T. And that's what's going to trip him up."

Chapter Fifty-Three

Charles Benedict woke up with a smile on his face. The nubile young blonde who had shared his bed last night had been expertly trained by one of Nikolai's whoremasters, and her performance had left him drained and satisfied, but not as satisfied as he was with the way the case was proceeding.

If there was an afterlife, Tiffany Starr and Gregor Karpinski were residing in very hot accommodations in its low-rent region. He had no idea where Ernest Brodsky was, and he didn't care. What mattered was that none of them could testify against him.

Better still, Horace was falling apart. His arrogance would alienate the jurors and he would make a terrible witness. Meanwhile, Benedict would make enough subtle errors to ensure his client's conviction. With Horace behind bars for Carrie's murder, the case would die and he would be safe.

Benedict stretched and got out of bed. He was on his way to take a shower when his cell phone rang. Caller ID told him that Jack Pratt was on the line. He debated not answering, because he couldn't stand the supercilious prick, but curiosity got the better of him.

"Hey, Jack, what's up?"

"Horace would like to see you at the jail as soon as possible."

"Oh, about what?"

"He'll tell you. When can you be there?"

Pratt's tone was not friendly and alarm bells began to go off.

"I should be able to make it by nine-thirty."

"Good," Pratt said before ending the call abruptly.

Benedict showered and shaved and arrived at the jail an hour and twenty minutes later. When he told the jailer at reception why he was there he was shown to a contact visiting room. When the door opened he saw Horace Blair, Jack Pratt, and Bobby Schatz.

"Hey, Charlie, come on in," said Schatz, who had met Benedict at several Bar Association functions.

Benedict didn't move from the doorway. He looked back and forth between his client and the two attorneys.

"What's going on?" he asked.

"I've decided to hire Mr. Schatz to defend me at my trial," Blair said. His voice was firm and Benedict knew immediately that there would be no way to change his mind, especially with Pratt and Schatz in the room. He faked a smile.

"Bobby is a terrific lawyer. I have no problem being second chair to someone of his caliber."

"I haven't made myself clear," Blair said. "Your services will no longer be required. Mr. Schatz will take over all aspects of my defense."

"What's the story here, Horace? Is this about the plea offer or the bail hearing? I told you I have a duty as an officer of the court to tell you any plea offer the prosecutor makes, and you heard the evidence at the bail hearing. If you think Schatz could have done better, you're mistaken."

"The problem is experience," Pratt said. "You're an expert in certain types of cases. If this were a drug case, we wouldn't be having this conversation. But you're not experienced when it comes to homicides, and Mr. Schatz is."

An image of the three men sprawled in pools of blood flashed through Benedict's brain but he realized very quickly that his best move was to bow out gracefully. He ignored Pratt and addressed Blair, forcing himself to sound magnanimous.

"I'm sorry you feel this way, Horace, but you're in excellent hands. I want you to know that there are no hard feelings on my part. I wish you the best."

"Thank you, I appreciate everything you've done for me," Horace said.

Benedict could tell that he didn't mean a word of what he'd said. What had happened to make Blair decide to fire him?

Benedict rang for the guard and all four men felt uncomfortable in the ensuing silence. As soon as the heavy metal door closed behind Benedict his fists curled into a knot and he had to restrain himself from smashing them into the concrete walls as he walked toward the exit. It was that motherfucker Pratt. Benedict was certain of it. He toyed with the idea of waiting for him in his parking garage or breaking into his house and blowing his brains out but passed on those ideas quickly because there was no benefit to them. What he needed to do was remain calm and assess the situation.

The evidence was still in place and the evidence pointed unerringly toward guilt. Schatz was good, but Benedict didn't think he was good enough to convince a jury that Horace Blair did not kill his wife. So maybe he had no reason to be concerned. Sure, he would lose the money he would have made defending Blair at trial, but he could go on with his life without having to worry about being arrested for Carrie Blair's murder. Even if Schatz got Blair off, the cops and the prosecutors would still think Blair killed his wife. And if Blair was convicted with Schatz handling the trial, no one would think that he'd thrown the case. By the time Benedict parked in the lot behind his office he had concluded that getting fired wasn't such a bad thing after all.

Benedict entered the building through the side door. He settled behind his desk and read through his mail. Then he buzzed his secretary and asked for messages.

"Robert Curry called about the Hernandez case, Martin Schechter wanted you to call about the deposition in *Raines*, and a woman named Myra Blankenship called from Seattle."

"Blankenship? What did she want?"

"An appointment."

"Did she say what it's about?"

"No, and she didn't leave a phone number."

Benedict frowned. The name rang no bells. Oh, well. If Myra Blankenship showed up, he would find out what she wanted.

Chapter Fifty-Four

The day after Horace Blair fired him, Charles Benedict's receptionist surprised him by announcing that Bobby Schatz was calling.

"What's up, Bobby," Benedict said in a cheerful voice.

"I'd like to take you to lunch."

"Oh?"

"Can you meet me at Venezia at one?" Bobby asked, naming the most expensive Italian restaurant in D.C.

"Why do you want to meet?"

"I want to pick your brain about Horace's case."

"Does your client know we're meeting?"

"No, and I don't want him to know because he'll tell Pratt, and Pratt will throw a fit."

Schatz paused. When he spoke again his tone was conciliatory.

"Look, Charlie, I know how it feels to be dumped by a client, and I'm sorry it happened to you. It's Pratt who got you fired. He's got a bug up his ass about that bail hearing and he convinced Blair you weren't competent. When he called me I told him you were perfectly capable of trying Blair's case, but he insisted that you were out."

Benedict paused for effect to make Schatz think that he was hesitant to meet, but meeting Blair's new lawyer was a no-brainer. It would give him a chance to learn some of Bobby's strategy and find out if there were any holes in his plan.

"Okay, Bobby. One it is," Benedict said. He was smiling when he disconnected.

Bobby Schatz was waiting in a booth the restaurant reserved for him whenever he called. The maître d' showed Benedict to the back, where he and Schatz would be hard to see and just as hard to hear. Then he hovered while Bobby asked Benedict if he'd eaten at Venezia before.

"It's my first time," Charlie admitted.

"Do you mind if I order for you?" Schatz asked.

"Go ahead."

Bobby told the maître d' what he wanted in rapid-fire Italian, then asked for a recommendation for the wine. The maître d' thought for a moment before making a suggestion. When Bobby agreed, the maître d' smiled and left them.

"You're in for a treat," Bobby assured Benedict. Then he got down to business.

"I haven't had a chance to read the file yet," Schatz said.

"I'll messenger it over to you tomorrow."

"Thanks. But, from what I've heard, Hamada has a strong case."

"I agree."

"Why don't you give me your take on how to defend Blair."

Over the antipasto and the first glass of wine, Benedict told Schatz how he thought the commonwealth attorney was going to present his case.

"So where's the weakness?" Schatz asked when Benedict finished.

"Quite honestly, I don't see any. I mean, there are the anonymous tips. You can argue they're suspicious. And I made the point at the bail hearing that it's hard to explain how that key got in the grave."

"Yeah, I thought that was very astute," Schatz said.

"But you're still left with the evidence the cops found in the trunk, and the prenup."

Schatz leaned forward and lowered his voice. "But they don't have the prenuptial agreement—the actual document—and that gives me a way to wedge open the case. Hamada's theory about the motive hinges on the idea that Blair killed his wife to keep her from getting twenty million dollars. How are they going to prove that?"

Rick Hamada's boss, Ray Mancuso, was also worried about not having the prenup, but Benedict decided to keep that tidbit to himself.

"Barry Lester will claim Horace confessed the

motive while they were locked up together," Benedict said.

"Charlie, think about it. Everything Lester claims Blair told him about the prenup was in the newspapers, and those stories are inadmissible hearsay. I've had my investigator running down Lester's background, and I'll have a field day with him. I even think I've got a shot at keeping his statements about the prenup out because they mirror the newspaper story."

"Hamada can subpoena Pratt to bring the agreement to court," Benedict said.

Schatz smiled. "He doesn't have it. There are only two copies. They can't make Blair incriminate himself by subpoenaing his copy, and no one knows where Carrie hid hers. So Hamada is fucked if he's counting on producing the document in court."

"That is a lucky break," Benedict said.

"You aren't kidding. If Hamada can prove that Blair was going to have to pay Carrie twenty million dollars during the week she was murdered, Blair can start making plans to furnish his cell on death row."

Chapter Fifty-Five

Charles Benedict was in an excellent mood when he returned to his office. The meal at Venezia had been outstanding, and Bobby Schatz's plan for defending Horace Blair was not. Schatz was one of the best, but even great boxers like Muhammad Ali lost on occasion, and once in a while a great pitcher will get tagged for a home run. If Schatz tried Blair's case the way he said he would, *Commonwealth v. Blair* would be tallied in Schatz's loss column.

A woman with glasses and short, gray-streaked black hair looked up when Benedict entered his waiting room. She was dressed expensively in a severe charcoal-gray pantsuit, a black silk shirt, and a tasteful pearl necklace.

Benedict asked his receptionist about the visitor in a low voice.

"Her name is Myra Blankenship," she whispered back. "She came in an hour ago. I told her that I didn't know when you would return but she insisted on waiting."

"Didn't she call a day or so ago?"

"I believe so."

"Did she tell you what she wants?"

"She said it was confidential and she'll only talk to you."

Normally Benedict would have had his secretary deal with someone who walked in without an appointment, but Blankenship's attire suggested that she had money, and someone with money always deserved an audience. Benedict walked over to his visitor. Blankenship sprang to her feet. The attorney flashed his warmest smile.

"I'm Charles Benedict. I understand you want to see me."

"Myra Blankenship," the woman said as she extended her hand.

Benedict shook it. "How can I help you?"

The woman looked over Benedict's shoulder at the receptionist. "The matter is rather delicate. I'd prefer to discuss it where we can't be overheard."

"Of course."

Benedict led Blankenship to his office.

"I flew here from Seattle as soon as I heard," Blankenship said as soon as Benedict shut the door.

"Heard what?"

"That Carrie Blair had been murdered. I was in Asia on a buying trip. I was supposed to return a few weeks ago but I was delayed. I e-mailed several times and called but Mrs. Blair didn't get back to me. I was very upset. I thought the deal had fallen through. Then I arrived back in the States yesterday and learned that Mrs. Blair had been murdered and her husband was in jail."

Benedict had no idea what Blankenship was talking about.

"Don't get me wrong. Mrs. Blair's violent demise is a terrible thing, but there are millions involved and I'm anxious to know if she left any instructions, or if perhaps Mr. Blair was interested despite his"— Blankenship paused, looking for the right words— "present situation."

The phrase "millions involved" had piqued Benedict's interest.

"What is it you do, exactly?"

"I'm sorry. I'm just wound up, and I'm still a bit jet-lagged. I'm an art dealer. Martin Draper owns a gallery in Seattle. He sells contemporary pieces: a lot of glass, modern art, some local artists, and a few with national reputations. Every once in a while he is approached about acquiring Asian art. My specialty is Oriental antiquities. I lived in Asia for several years and made contacts there. When a customer wants something in this area, Martin calls me."

Blankenship paused, and her eyes lost focus as if she were looking at something far away that only she could see.

"The scepter is special, Mr. Benedict. Martin could sense it. He called me immediately but I must admit I've never handled anything like it before."

"What is your connection to the Blairs?"

"They have a home on Isla de Muerta, an island off the coast of Washington State. They came to the gallery looking for pieces to decorate their home. Some of the art they wanted was from Japan and China. That's how I met them, through Martin.

"I only met Mr. Blair one time. Mrs. Blair was usually the person who came to the gallery. It wasn't unusual for her to visit the gallery when she was in Seattle. I was consulted because the piece she was interested in was within my area of expertise."

Blankenship paused. Benedict thought that she looked anxious.

"The papers said you're representing Mr. Blair," the woman said.

Benedict nodded. He had been fired but no substitution of counsel had been filed yet, so technically he was still Horace's lawyer.

"Has he mentioned the scepter?"

"Not specifically. Perhaps you can tell me a little about it so I'll be knowledgeable when we discuss it."

"When Sultan Mehmet II conquered Constantinople in 1453 he was concerned that there would be an appeal to Rome for liberation that would set off a new round of Crusades."

Benedict nodded knowingly, although he had no idea what Blankenship was talking about. He'd had one history course in college, and that was many years ago and he couldn't remember if Constantinople had been mentioned. All he knew for certain was that Constantinople was now Istanbul and Turks lived there.

"The Eastern Orthodox Church commanded the loyalty of the masses," Blankenship continued, "so Mehmet asked Gennadius, who was hostile to the West, to become the first Patriarch of Constantinople under Islamic rule. When Gennadius accepted, the sultan gave him a gold, bejeweled scepter as a symbol of authority. This scepter disappeared until it was rediscovered by Antoine Girard, a French soldier of fortune, in a bazaar in Cairo in 1922. Girard spent many years authenticating the scepter. Then he was murdered and the scepter was stolen.

"Recently, we were contacted by a person who purported to own the scepter. He was in financial straits as a result of some very bad investments and had to sell it. I thought of the Blairs immediately."

"Why the Blairs? Why not a museum?"

"May I be frank?"

"Please."

"And can I count on you keeping a confidence?"

"Of course."

"My seller insisted that I only deal with a private buyer. I don't know this for a fact but I suspect that he didn't want me to approach a museum because the scepter may be stolen goods."

"But why the Blairs?"

"There are no longer any jewels in the scepter,

but the scepter is solid gold. However, the value of the gold is secondary. The historical importance of the scepter makes it incredibly valuable."

"What does that mean in dollars?" Benedict asked.

"I can't say exactly, but as I said, we're talking millions. That's why I contacted Mrs. Blair."

"You mean Mr. Blair," Benedict said.

"No, Mr. Blair never seemed terribly interested in art or collecting. But Mrs. Blair had a true appreciation of the value of the scepter."

"From what I've learned, Carrie Blair didn't have the kind of money you're talking about."

"But she was going to. That's why I had to get back to the States. The week Mrs. Blair died was the week she would have met the terms of a prenuptial agreement she had entered into when she married Mr. Blair. Under the terms of that agreement, she stood to receive twenty million dollars, part of which she planned to use to buy the scepter."

Benedict's heart thudded in his chest but he kept his voice calm.

"There's been a lot of speculation about this prenup but no one seems to have seen it," he said.

"I have. Mrs. Blair showed it to me."

"Why did she do that?"

"I called her about the scepter, assuming that she would talk to her husband about purchasing it, but she told me she didn't want Mr. Blair involved. I was dubious about Mrs. Blair's ability to pay, so she gave me a copy of the agreement."

"You have it?" Benedict asked casually, giving the impression that the prenuptial agreement was of little interest to him.

"Not with me."

"In Seattle?"

"No, I brought it here. It's at my hotel, in my file. Mr. Benedict, can you tell me what Mr. Blair said about the scepter? Did Mrs. Blair tell him about it? Does he have any interest in obtaining it?"

Benedict pretended to be in conflict while his visitor fidgeted.

"Ms. Blankenship, I've sworn to keep your confidences, and an attorney also has a duty to keep secret those matters his client discusses with him."

"Of course," the woman answered as she leaned forward expectantly.

"Will you promise not to divulge what I'm going to tell you?"

"Yes."

"Mr. Blair has mentioned the scepter."

"Then he's interested?"

"I'm not certain. During one of our conferences—when we were discussing Mrs. Blair—he told me that she had mentioned purchasing an expensive historical relic. Presumably that was the scepter."

"What else did he say?"

"Nothing. You can understand that his present predicament has dominated his thoughts, but we have high hopes that we'll win his case. And then he can turn his thoughts elsewhere."

Benedict's features displayed an expression of the utmost seriousness.

"I can assure you that Mr. Blair is innocent. He loved his wife very much. If Mrs. Blair wanted this scepter, Mr. Blair might want to honor her wishes. But I'll have to convince him that she was sincere in her desire to possess it."

"I can give him that assurance."

Benedict shook his head. "No offense, but your word would not carry a lot of weight."

Blankenship straightened up. She looked insulted.

"Mr. Blair knows me. We've had business dealings."

"I didn't mean to disparage you, but let me ask a question. Will you profit if you broker this deal?"

"Of course."

"And I assume we're talking about a very hefty commission."

Blankenship hesitated before nodding.

Benedict spread his hands. "Surely you see the problem. If Mr. Blair was unaware that Mrs. Blair wanted to pay several million dollars for the scepter, your statement won't convince him if you are going to make a large profit from the deal."

"What do you suggest?"

Benedict thought for a moment. Then he brightened.

"If I had a copy of the prenuptial agreement to show Mr. Blair, it would convince him that Carrie trusted you and was deadly serious about buying the scepter. Do you think you can get me a copy of the agreement to show to Mr. Blair?"

The woman's head bobbed up and down. "Definitely."

"I assume that you have to act quickly if this sale is to go through?"

"Very quickly."

Benedict looked at his watch. "Where are you staying?"

Blankenship named a hotel near Dulles Airport and gave Benedict her room number.

"I have a few matters I must attend to," Benedict said. "Go back to your hotel and I'll call you when I'm done. We can meet and you can give me a copy of the agreement. I'll take the document to Mr. Blair today and tell him about the urgency of making a decision about buying the scepter."

"Thank you," the woman said.

Benedict smiled. "I hope this works out for you. And it might take Horace's mind off of his troubles. Of course, you understand that the utmost secrecy is required. Don't tell anyone, even Mr. Draper, we've met, and do not, under any circumstances, discuss the scepter or the prenuptial agreement with anyone. From here on in, we must keep this matter strictly between us until I have an opportunity to discuss it with Mr. Blair."

Benedict saw out Blankenship. As soon as the door closed, the lawyer went online and typed in Martin Draper's name. His search turned up the existence of a Martin Draper Gallery in Seattle. A description of the art the gallery handled jibed with what Myra Blankenship had told him.

A search for Myra Blankenship turned up a small website that gave her academic credentials and a brief statement about her specialty, Asian antiquities.

Benedict called the gallery. Draper answered the phone. Benedict gave a false name, then said he wanted to contact Myra Blankenship. Draper said she was in Washington, D.C., on business, and hoped to be back in Seattle soon. He also confirmed that she had just returned from Asia.

Benedict told his secretary to hold his calls. Then he leaned back in his chair and closed his eyes. Blankenship was a gift from the gods. The problem was time. Benedict would have to act fast, because it would soon become public knowledge that he was no longer Blair's attorney.

Benedict made a decision. He would meet Blankenship and get a copy of the prenuptial agreement. Then he would kill Blankenship and dispose of the body. After that, he would go to Blair's estate. There was a good chance he could get into the mansion unseen. Horace had told him that the houseman lived in a cottage on the estate and that there was only a skeleton staff now that Carrie was dead and he was locked up. He had gotten the codes for Blair's front gate and house alarm so he could get suits, ties, and shirts for Blair's court appearances. When he was inside the mansion, he would hide the copy of the prenup. Then he would tip off Rick Hamada to its hiding place with enough specificity to establish probable cause for a search warrant.

Chapter Fifty-Six

Dana took off her wig and glasses as soon as she shut the door to her room in the hotel near the airport that Santoro and Robb had chosen for the sting. There was a desk, a couch, and a bed. Across from the bed was an armoire that concealed a television. A suitcase was on a stand next to the armoire.

Dana turned on the TV and channel-surfed to kill time while she waited for Benedict to call. Rick Hamada and Bobby Schatz had primed the pump by building up the importance the prenuptial agreement held for the commonwealth's case, and Dana could tell that Benedict had been excited by the bait she had dangled in front of him. Now they had to hope that the cover that had been provided by Marty Draper and the hastily constructed website for "Myra Blankenship's" fictitious business would hold up.

Nothing on TV held Dana's interest and she switched off the set. Her room had been rigged with surveillance cameras and microphones in case Benedict attacked her in the room. One of the microphones crackled when Stephanie Robb tested it.

"Can you hear me?" Robb asked.

"Yeah, you're fine."

"Benedict is still at his office. I'm guessing he'll wait until it's dark to make his move."

"I hope he does it soon. That damn wig makes my head itch."

"Hey, no one ever said police work was easy," Santoro quipped. "We'll tell you when he leaves."

"Benedict is definitely a man of many talents," Robb said shortly after sunset. "He just boosted a car from a shopping mall and he's headed your way. We're going to get him, Dana."

"Just make sure you've got me covered. I don't want to end up as his next victim."

"Don't worry. We've got undercover cops all over the hotel. Just sit tight until he shows up."

Twenty minutes later, the phone rang.

"Yes?" Dana said.

"Hi, it's Charlie Benedict. I took care of my other business and I'm going to go to the jail to talk to Horace. Do you have the prenup?"

"Yes."

"Great! I'm in the parking lot. Can you bring it down? It will save time, and I know you're in a rush to find out what Horace is going to do."

"I really appreciate this, Mr. Benedict."

"Charlie."

"Where are you parked?"

"Come out the back. I didn't want anyone to see us, so I'm in the next-to-the-last row. I'll blink my lights when you come out the rear door."

"I'll be right down."

"Did you get that?" Dana asked Robb after she ended Benedict's call.

"We're repositioning everyone now. Give us five minutes."

Dana put on her wig. When five minutes were up, she threw a trench coat over her jacket and shirt. Then she grabbed a copy of the prenuptial agreement that Jack Pratt had worked up and took the elevator to the ground floor.

Dana took her time walking to the back of the hotel. Few people were in the back lobby and fewer still were in the parking lot. A set of headlights flashed at her as soon as she stepped out of the hotel. They were in a section of the lot toward the back that was completely dark. Every other section was lit by well-spaced lamp poles.

Charlie had stolen a beat-up Honda that was all alone in the next-to-last row of the hotel lot. Dana noticed shards of glass from a shattered streetlight littering the asphalt. Benedict got out of the car as soon as Dana reached it. He was wearing a hooded sweatshirt, jeans, and scuffed trainers. Dana knew how he had dressed when he went to Ernest Brodsky's shop, so she wasn't surprised, but she frowned as if his getup puzzled her.

"Hi," Benedict said with a disarming smile. He

pointed at the manila envelope Dana was holding. "Is that the prenup?"

"Yes. Why are you dressed like that?"

"Before I tell you, would you like to see a magic trick?"

"What?" Dana answered, feigning confusion.

Benedict pulled back his sleeves. "Nothing in my hands or up my sleeves, right?"

"Uh, yes," Blankenship answered.

Benedict made a pass and a large hunting knife suddenly appeared in his hand. Dana's mouth opened and her eyes went wide with surprise. Benedict had practiced the move he'd used to kill Ernest Brodsky, Tiffany Starr, and his other victims so often that it was automatic. As soon as Dana was distracted by his trick, his hand snaked out and he stabbed her, anticipating the thrill when the knife sliced through her flesh and invaded her heart. Instead, the knife recoiled and it was Benedict who looked as if he'd just witnessed magic.

Before he could move again, Dana grabbed Benedict's wrist and twisted. The lawyer felt a bone snap, his eyes widened with pain, and he dropped the knife. Dana sidestepped and smashed an elbow into Benedict's temple. Then she swept his feet from under him. Benedict fell hard. His head bounced off the asphalt and he was momentarily dazed. Before he could react, Dana broke his arm, then rolled the lawyer on his stomach and cuffed his hands behind his back. The pain in his broken wrist and arm was excruciating and he screamed. Dana knelt down and whispered in Benedict's ear.

"The wrist was for setting Gregor Karpinski on me, and the arm was for Tiffany Starr. I can think of a lot of other things I'd like to do to you but cops are here to take you into custody, so you're lucky."

Moments later, Frank Santoro, Stephanie Robb, and four uniformed police officers ran up.

"Good work," Robb said.

"It was my pleasure," Dana said as she took off the wig and glasses she'd worn to play the role of Myra Blankenship. Then she spread back her overcoat and looked at her torso. A tear in her shirt revealed a vest designed not only to stop a bullet but also to deflect a knife thrust.

"You were right, Frank," Dana said. "Benedict used his knife in the same way he used it on Brodsky and Starr."

"I was pretty certain he wouldn't change a successful MO."

"My wrist!" Benedict gasped. "Take off the cuffs. It's broken."

"You should have thought of that when you tried to kill Ms. Cutler," Santoro said.

"Who is Cutler?" Benedict asked.

"Tiffany Starr knew her as Loren Parkhurst and you thought she was Myra Blankenship, but she's the person who figured out how to nail you, Charlie."

Dana drove to police headquarters and gave a statement. She was finishing up when Robb and Santoro walked in.

"Really good work, Dana," Santoro said. "If you ever want back on the force, you'll get a letter of recommendation from me."

Dana smiled. "Right now, all I want is a good night's sleep."

Santoro laughed. "I hear you."

Dana grew somber. "It dawned on me as I was driving here that everything I've done in this case has been for Carrie Blair, but I only met her when she was pretending to be Margo Laurent. What was she like?"

"She was tough," Robb said. "Dedicated."

"She loved putting bad guys away and she hated to lose," Santoro added.

"What was she like off the job?"

"I didn't know her in that way," Robb said. "When she married Horace Blair she became 'The Society Prosecutor.' It put a lot of people off and made a lot more uncomfortable. Most of us make a decent living, but none of us can even dream of being in her tax bracket."

"I think she buried herself in her work because she was unhappy," Santoro said. "From what I hear, the marriage hadn't worked in a long time. Of course, I got that from the gossip columns and wagging tongues in the prosecutor's office and the cop shop."

"I feel sorry for her," Robb said. "She got what most of us can only dream of getting—the money, the mansion, the fancy cars—but it didn't seem to make her happy."

Dana wondered if she and Carrie would have gotten along. She guessed they might have, but she'd never know now.

"I'm really beat," Dana said. "Do you need me anymore?"

"Go home and get some sleep," Robb said. "And thanks again. We'd never have gotten Benedict if it wasn't for you."

"Remember, you don't have him yet," Dana said. "He is one tricky bastard. Don't let your guard down for a minute."

Chapter Fifty-Seven

Frank Santoro had tried to question Benedict when they drove out of the hotel parking lot. Before the first word was out of the detective's mouth, Benedict asked for a lawyer and demanded that he not be questioned. The detectives drove in silence to the closest hospital, where his broken wrist and arm could be treated. The last thing they wanted was a motion to dismiss for police brutality.

Charles Benedict had never taken an IQ test but anyone with near perfect SAT scores had to have a hefty amount of brain power. He began tapping into every bit of it during the drive to the hospital. By the time he arrived, Benedict had devised two plans.

For Plan A to work, Benedict had to get out of custody. Magicians were experts at disappearing. Benedict had disappeared from Kansas City with half a million in drug money and had never been found by the Mexicans or the Kung Fu Dragons. He had planned for another escape years ago. If he could get out of jail, he would vanish into thin air. Stashed in safe places were disguises, documents that would establish false identities, and offshore accounts that would let him live in luxury.

Plan B was his backup. It involved asking for witness protection and spilling his guts about Nikolai Orlansky's operations. That plan could pose serious problems for his health, and he did not want to go there unless all else failed.

At the hospital, Santoro cuffed Benedict's good hand to the bed and the detectives watched him closely. As soon as he had doctors and nurses for witnesses, Benedict demanded that he be allowed to phone an attorney, leaving the detectives no alternative but to honor the request. Benedict called Marcus Foster and told him to meet him at the jail. He also whispered the number of his secretary, who could let Foster into Benedict's office so that Foster could get several checks from the register in Benedict's desk.

Foster was waiting at police headquarters and asked to confer with Benedict as soon as the prisoner was booked in. The first thing Benedict did when the door to the interview room closed was sign one check for Foster's retainer and a blank check to cover his bail.

Benedict was asleep in his cell when the noise of the bars opening awakened him at 3:30 a.m. Benedict blinked at the guard.

"You've been bailed out," he said.

Benedict's spirits soared. In minutes, he would be out the door and into the night. Before dawn, he would be gone.

Marcus Foster was waiting in reception. Benedict thanked him for acting so quickly. The two attorneys walked out of the jail into the crisp night air and Benedict looked up at the stars. He smiled and took a deep breath. Freedom was great!

"Can you give me a lift?" Benedict asked his lawyer. "They took my car."

"Sure. I parked down the street."

Benedict followed Foster. Before they reached his car, a black SUV with tinted windows pulled to the curb. A very large man got out. Charlie recognized him as someone who frequented The Scene.

"Glad to see you're out, Charlie," the man said as he flashed a wide smile.

"It looks like you've got a ride," Foster said. "Let's meet at my office at noon. That will give you time to get some sleep."

Warning lights were flashing.

Charlie was about to ask Foster to wait when Peter Perkovic got out of the car and pulled his jacket aside so Charlie could see his gun. When Benedict turned toward Peter, the first man slipped a needle into his neck.

Chapter Fifty-Eight

"Benedict is free on bail!" Christopher Rauh screamed.

"I have people out looking for him," Stephanie Robb said.

"How did he make bail so fast?" Rauh asked.

"We took him to the hospital because his wrist and arm were broken," Frank Santoro said. "He lawyered up while he was there. We couldn't listen to the conversation because of the attorney-client privilege. I'm guessing he told Marcus Foster to spring him right away. Foster was at the jail in record time."

Rauh swore again.

"Calm down, Chris," Hamada said. "We'll find him. Santoro, Robb, and I are working on the presentation to the grand jury. I'll get a murder indictment so we can hold him without bail."

"Has Benedict shown up at his condo?" Rauh asked.

"Not so far."

"So where is he?"

Nikolai Orlansky knew that part of Charles Benedict's training as a magician involved escape from restraints, so Orlansky made sure that the lawyer was gagged and confined in a straitjacket, with his ankles securely manacled to a ring embedded in the cement floor of the warehouse to which Peter Perkovic had transported him.

Shortly after Benedict regained consciousness he realized that he had little chance of escaping. Even if he could get out of the straitjacket and the manacles, two of Nikolai's goons were watching him.

Benedict had no idea how long he'd been unconscious, so he had no idea how long he'd been a prisoner. He was starving, so it could have been days. He was still disoriented from the drugs that had been injected into him, so maybe that meant he'd only been out a short time, unless they'd given him more drugs. The lawyer tried calling to the men, but they ignored his muffled cries. He tried to remain calm and think of ways to escape, but nothing came to mind.

After what seemed like hours, a door opened. The guards looked behind Benedict, who could not turn his head far enough to see what was happening. Footsteps echoing off the concrete told him that someone was drawing near. Then Nikolai was standing in front of him, with Peter Perkovic at his side.

"Charlie, Charlie, Charlie," Nikolai said with a sad shake of his head. "What a mess you are in."

Benedict tried to speak. Nikolai nodded to Perkovic, and Peter removed his gag.

"What the fuck, Nikolai?" Benedict said as soon as he could generate enough saliva.

"I am sorry, believe me," Orlansky answered. "But you see my problem."

"No, I do not. I have no idea why I'm tied up in this fucking warehouse. And I've got to pee, so can you let me out of this S&M getup?"

"I am also sorry for your discomfort, but it won't last for long."

"What have I ever done to deserve this?"

"It is not what you have done, although I do have a bone to pick with you about the way you treated Gregor. No, Charlie, it is what you might do that troubles me.

"Peter has been keeping me apprised of the police investigation into several murders. You are in trouble, Charlie. The authorities have an open-and-shut case against you for trying to murder a woman in that hotel parking lot last night, and there is considerable evidence that you framed Horace Blair for the murder of his wife, which suggests that you were the person who murdered her."

"They can't prove I killed anyone."

Nikolai nodded. "You are very skilled at covering your tracks, but there may be too many tracks this time. If I were in your shoes I would cut a deal. I would tell all you know about my activities in exchange for freedom."

"I'd never rat you out," Benedict stated emphatically. "Look, Nikolai, I've got an escape plan. If your men hadn't kidnapped me I'd be gone by now and no one would ever find me."

"The world has changed, Charlie. If they can find bin Laden, they can find you. *When* they find you, the authorities will be pissed off that you gave them such a hard time. They will want to make you pay for wasting taxpayer money on the manhunt that could have financed education, or higher pay for politicians, so they will want to see you on death row. They will want blood, Charlie."

"Jesus, Nikolai, we're friends. I'd never sell you out."

"I don't doubt that you are sincere now, but will you still feel this way when you are facing a death sentence? I like to think the best of people, but I cannot take the chance that I might be wrong, because I do not want to pay for my crimes. So I must hope for the best but plan for the worst."

"Don't do this."

"I have to, but I really do like you, so I will make sure your end will be painless. So long, Charlie."

"Wait!" Charlie said, but Nikolai gave terse orders to the two guards and walked away.

Chapter Fifty-Nine

Horace Blair sat in his breakfast nook and looked out at his garden. He had been out of jail for a week and today would be his first day in the office. Everything had happened very quickly after Benedict was fired. Soon after, Jack Pratt and Bobby Schatz had come to his cell with Rick Hamada to tell him that Charles Benedict was under arrest, and that he was a free man. He had left the jail in a daze, not really believing that his ordeal was finally over.

Horace wanted to thank Dana Cutler, but he had not seen her since Pratt brought the private investigator to the jail. She had made it clear during her visit that she was acting for Carrie and did not want to be paid. But he would figure out a way to let her know how much he appreciated what she had done for him.

Blair's ordeal had taken a lot out of him. Anger had kept him going much of the time while he'd been locked up, but he felt as if he had only a limited supply of energy, and fighting for his freedom had drained most of the tank. When he took a bite out of his croissant it tasted like cardboard. He set it down half-eaten. He had no appetite. When he woke up at five he had thought about swimming, but he didn't have the energy for it so he'd stayed in bed for another hour. He'd given his newspapers a cursory read, but he couldn't concentrate. The garden, which usually gave him joy, now left him cold.

An image of Carrie invaded his thoughts and suddenly he was choking up. He had not loved Carrie for some time, but he had always cared for her. It made him sad to think that she had died young and in such a terrible way. He could not imagine how she felt when Charles Benedict snuffed out the vibrant flame that animated her, and he prayed that her death had been mercifully swift and free of suffering.

Horace's eyes filled with tears. He could not remember the last time he had cried. Was he crying for Carrie or himself? Maybe he was crying for both. He was one of the most powerful men in America but he did not feel powerful. He felt old, empty, and alone, and he had no one with whom he could share these feelings.

"Your car is ready," Walter said.

Horace took a deep breath and nodded, too sad to speak. Walter left and Horace pressed a napkin to his eyes to dry his tears. He had an important meeting in one hour and he could not afford to show weakness, but he did feel weak, and he had no enthusiasm for battle.

Horace levered himself to his feet. He closed his eyes and regrouped emotionally. He was free. He had won. But he didn't feel like a victor. He felt like a tired old man.

Chapter Sixty

Dana Cutler was in a terrific mood when she left the office of the attorney who had hired her to help clear the Baltimore Ravens running back. The charges were being dismissed, thanks to the testimony of witnesses she had found, and the client had given her season tickets to show his appreciation.

Dana had a big smile on her face when she slid behind the wheel of her car. She was about to start the ignition when her phone rang.

"Dana Cutler," she answered.

"Miss Cutler, my name is Earl Chan and I am in need of your services."

"What would you like me to do for you, Mr. Chan?"

"I feel uncomfortable discussing the matter over the phone. It's quite complicated. Would you join me for dinner at Venezia at eight tonight?"

Dana was intrigued. Venezia was way out of her price range, so she had never dined there; and she didn't have any plans for the evening because Jake was in New York, talking to the owner of another gallery that was interested in showing his pictures from the Arctic expedition.

"I'll be there," she said. Mr. Chan thanked her and hung up.

Michelangelo's was the fanciest Italian restaurant Dana had ever eaten in; for Dana, the words "Italian food" usually brought to mind pizza and meatballs and spaghetti. As the maître d' at Venezia led her to Mr. Chan's table, she didn't spot a single pizza or meatball, and she didn't recognize a single dish. The only familiar sight was the red wine she saw on many of the tables.

Mr. Chan stood up as soon as Dana arrived. He was a dapper, middle-aged Chinese man with straight black hair and almond eyes. Dana guessed that his suit was hand tailored, and he sported several bejeweled rings and a Rolex watch.

"Thank you so much for coming," Chan said. His accent was British and she wondered where he'd been educated.

Dana sat down and was presented with a menu. As soon as they ordered, Dana asked, "How can I help you?"

"I am a curator of the Asian Art Museum in Seattle, and the museum would like to enlist your services."

"Oh?"

"How much do you know about the Han dynasty?"

Warning bells went off, but Dana remained calm. "All I know is that it's Chinese."

Chan nodded. "Correct. The Han dynasty was the second imperial dynasty of China, and it was founded in 206 B.C. by the rebel leader Liu Bang, who was known posthumously as Emperor Gaozu of Han. To the north of China proper, the nomadic Xiognu chieftain Modu Chanyu conquered various tribes inhabiting the eastern portion of the European steppe. By the end of his reign, he controlled Manchuria, Mongolia, and the Tarim Basin, subjugating over twenty states east of Samarkand.

"Emperor Gaozu was troubled by the Han-manufactured iron weapons that were traded to the Xiognu, and he placed an embargo on the sale or trade of these weapons. The Xiognu was still able to find traders willing to supply the weapons. In 121 B.C. the emperor ordered the execution of five hundred of these merchants, and Chinese forces attacked representatives of the Xiognu who traded for the weapons. In retaliation, the Xiognu invaded Shanxi province and defeated the Han forces. After negotiations, the matter was settled with a royal marriage alliance, but the Han were forced to send large amounts of tribute items such as silk clothes, food, and wine to the Xiognu. The rarest item was a jade dragon of incalculable wealth.

"The Xiognu kept meticulous records and the jade dragon is prominent in them until 14 B.C., when all mention of it ended. Over the years there have been repeated sightings of the treasure but they've all been debunked, until now.

"Early this month we were approached by an Indonesian businessman who has fallen on hard times . . ."

Dana started to laugh. Chan looked puzzled.

"Don't tell me you want me to fly to Indonesia to see if the treasure is real."

"Why, yes."

Dana smiled and shook her head. "Who put you up to this, Mr. Chan—if that is your name?"

"Well, I . . ."

"Its okay, Larry."

Dana turned around and saw Jake Teeny walking toward her. A big smile was pasted on his face.

"Ten minutes. Not bad. I thought he'd keep you going for a little more. Dana, meet Larry Winston, a reporter for the *Washington Post*. Larry, this is the very clever Dana Cutler."

Winston broke into a grin. "My pleasure."

"You are such an ass," Dana told Jake.

"Now, hold on. I'm not the only one you should be cursing. Horace Blair is paying for our meal, and Bobby Schatz got us the reservation. I'm just responsible for the entertainment."

"You're still a jackass," Dana said, but she was smiling.

Winston stood up. "Jake is a jackass, but I agreed to help him for the chance to meet the woman who earned that rag *Exposed* two Pulitzers. I'll leave you lovebirds. It's been a pleasure, Dana."

Jake took the seat Winston had vacated.

"Were you really in New York today?" she asked.

"That was another subterfuge. But the meal you are about to eat is the real deal, and it has been specially prepared at Bobby's direction by the chef. So enjoy. You deserve it."

Acknowledgments

I always need the advice of experts to make my books seem real. Once again, Medical Examiner Karen Gunson and forensic expert Brian Ostrom rode to the rescue by advising me on how to kill people and commit crimes. I also want to thank Dr. Mary Meyer, Commonwealth Attorney Brandon Shapiro, fellow writer Bob Dugoni, Peter Jarvis, Ami and Andy Rome, Jay Margulies, Robin Haggard, and Carolyn Lindsey for their help in researching and writing *Sleight of Hand*.

Readers see a polished final draft. My editors help whip my raw and inadequate first drafts into shape. If you like this book, a lot of the credit has to go to my intrepid editors, Claire Wachtel and Caroline Upcher, and copy editor Ed Cohen. Thanks also to Elizabeth Perrella, my super publicist, Heather Drucker, Jonathan Burnham, Michael Morrison, and the art department and sales force at HarperCollins.

Thanks also to Jean Naggar, Jennifer Weltz, and everyone else at the Jean V. Naggar Literary Agency. You are the best.

This book is dedicated to the people who have made Chess for Success one of the most effective educational programs in the country. If you want to learn more about Chess for Success, go to www.chessforsuccess.org.

And last, but never least, thank you, Doreen. You continue to inspire me to do my best.